CHASING THE MINOTAUR

A NOVEL

TERRY HAYMAN

Chasing the Minotaur. Copyright © 2010 by Terry Hayman

Chasing the Minotaur: a novel / Terry Hayman

Published 2010 by Fiero Publishing
www.fieropublishing.com
Cover art: Dance à Bougival (modified) by Pierre-Auguste Renoir (1841–1919); bull head by paulasierra/depositphotos
Spine bull head by kubera/depositphotos
Back cover art: La Montagne Saint Victoire Barnes, Paul Cézanne (1839–1906)
Book and cover design copyright © 2020 by Fiero Publishing

ISBN-13: 978-1-927920-25-1

First Print Edition: January 2011

To my wife, Faith, for too many reasons to mention except this - without you, there would have been no trip to Provence and all the magic we found there.

A GIRL FROM THE STREET

The young woman slipped from the snowy honking and bustle of Manhattan's evening rush hour, into the Hebbler Gallery on Wooster Street. As the thick door closed behind her, all the clatter from the street outside *hushed*.

It so startled the teen that Max Hebbler, watching from softly-mumbling crowd in the south atrium, thought she might drop to her knees in a primitive reflex.

She did not, thank goodness. But she did reach back one black-gloved hand to steady herself on the door frame. With her other hand, she pulled off her purple ski hat and stuffed it into the pocket of her dirty red bomber jacket. For another moment she stood very still, eyes fixed, long died-black hair half-covering her face. Max wondered if she worried about her boots tracking in the dirty slush from the sidewalk outside. Or if she looked at the other patrons and art lovers standing in small groups before the carefully-arranged paintings of artist Emery Lake and saw how out of place she was. The clothes, the excessive black eyeliner, the attitude.

Yet even as Max allowed himself the uncharitable hope the girl would turn and leave, the girl shook back her hair. Max took an involuntary breath and his old heart jumped.

Mein Gott. The hair. The little chip nose.

It was Lyssa.

No. Of course it was not Lyssa because Lyssa had been dead what? Eighteen years? Yes. Eighteen years, forty-three days, a handful of hours. The hours, Max could not know because he had not been there when his daughter died. He had only the coroner's estimate.

But...*mein Gott.*

Max ran his hand over his face. It was the light, of course. The winter light outside had been strange all day, shifting from silver gray to boiling pitch. And even though the gallery had its own carefully controlled lighting, especially for the showing of these paintings, the narrow windows to the street let in just enough of the outside strangeness that the front room felt infused with spirits.

Perfect for an Emery Lake showing.

The girl, still hesitating, had let some of her nonchalance crumble and now seemed clenched in fear. Following the direction of her gaze, Max saw she was staring at the signs pointing to the north atrium where, in just under an hour, Max would be sliding the front off a specially-constructed crate containing the most recent, and possibly last ever, painting that Max's star artist had completed.

Did the girl know Emery? Was that it? Was there a final piece of the story Emery had not told him?

Or was there...something else?

Even as Max decided impulsively that he must find out, the girl's courage faltered. She turned back to the door as if about to leave.

Max detached himself from the art journalist who'd been babbling *sotto voce* this whole time, writing his feature out loud to get Max's editorial comments. Max reached the door just as the girl slipped out. He caught her by the sleeve. She jerked around in fright as he stepped out after her onto the sidewalk, letting the gallery door close behind him. It had grown bitterly cold. The cars rumbling past drove icy wind against him and the girl.

"I didn't mean to frighten you," he said in his friendliest voice.

"What? What do you want?"

It was starting to sleet with a fine mist that stung his forehead and cheeks. "I want you to come inside."

"Why?" Her eyes were wide as they looked at him, the pupils small, and Max wondered if she was high on something.

"We have food, you know. Near the back. And some wine if you're of age."

"I'm twenty," she said, sticking out her chin. She sounded maybe seventeen.

"Ah. There you are, then. We do have some non-alcoholic punch. It's very good."

"I..." She hesitated and he saw her eyes welling up, her chest start to jerk. She turned away from him.

"Do you have some personal connection with Mr. Lake or his paintings?"

The girl brought herself under control, turned her sleet-misted face to him again, and Max felt his heart tighten. If only he had had such a chance with his daughter, this last effort to pull her back from wherever it was she'd run off to...

"Is he...?" the girl said. "Mr. Lake. Is he here?"

Max cocked his head at her, recognizing that she hadn't answered his question. He decided not to push it. "No, he's not. He's said he might make if for the unveiling tonight, but with Emery, it's all, well, speculative."

To his surprise, she smiled. It made her look radiant. The sleet had accumulated to a fine sheen on her hair that seemed to sparkle in the streetlights. Had Lyssa been so perfect near the end? So vulnerable and open? In his dreams Max thought she was. The most painful thing, of course, was that Max had spent so long erasing the ugly last time he'd spent with her, all their quarreling, that his memories of Lyssa's face were blurry.

"That fits," the girl said quietly and laughed, a pained sound.

"What? That Mr. Lake is not here? Or that we don't know if he will be?"

"Both."

The wind gusted suddenly, blowing Max's own carefully-coiffed silver hair and he realized that he would look like a drenched rat soon if they didn't move this inside. He could feel the accumulating sleet on his face start to run.

"Won't you come in?" he said. "The food is really good. Think of it as dinner. Enjoy the paintings. We're going to unveil his latest at eight p.m., whether Emery is here or not."

"I know," the girl said quietly and the fear was suddenly back in her eyes.

"Is there a problem with that?"

"No. Of course not. Maybe. I just... I love Mr. Lake's work. I'm... I guess you could say I'm a fan, even though I've never had the money to actually *buy* his stuff. But his last series, the stuff he did, it scared me. It made me... I don't know if I want to see any more."

The words seemed to slip directly into Max's head somehow, to rattle around in his brain, and unsettle him. Which made no sense, because not only was he getting cold and impatient, but Max *knew* all of Emery Lake's paintings, the whys and wherefores, at least as much as Emery had been able to explain them to him. So Max understood. And yes, there was tragedy, but that wasn't all there was. Not by half.

Without thinking, he found himself grabbing the girl's hands and holding them tightly. "You *must* come inside," he said, struggling to sound friendly, rather than desperate. "Let me give you some food, then let me take you from painting to painting, even the scary ones, and tell you what I know of them. The real story. I think that you need to know."

He saw her take a deep breath and felt the shudder that ran through her. But she didn't pull her hands back. And just holding her gloved hands in his, Max felt so warmed that for a moment he didn't care that he was getting drenched on this most important of nights.

"Alight," she said.

"Good. Good!" He pulled her after him into the warmth, into the smell of people and of bouchées of curried chicken with diced mango, tartlets of sundried tomato with olive tapanade, proscuitto-wrapped asparagus spears, avocado slivers on crackers, crostinis of chimichurri beef with spicy Argentinian parsley sauce and roasted red peppers and Queso Fresco, roasted pumpkin and coconut soup in the back for the truly hungry. The clink of glasses. The hum of people discussing art, Emery's art, in Max's gallery.

With a sigh of relief, Max released her and shook himself off, careful not to touch his hair. He began to brush off the girl's shoulders too before he caught himself and stopped.

"First let's get you comfortable," he said.

He walked her to the coat check where he helped her out of her jacket and gloves, the ski hat still stuffed in the bomber jacket's pocket. Underneath, above the jeans and black army boots, she actually wore a very chic, black chiffon number that made her look older than he'd thought. Maybe twenty after all. Yet it also highlighted the white luminescence of her skin and the dark mascara she wore around those watchful eyes. The frightened animal. As desperate as Lyssa had been.

Steady, Max.

"My name, by the way, is Max Hebbler," he said and extended his wet hand again.

She took it lightly. "Like Hebbler of The Hebbler Gallery?"

"The same. And you are?" He held his breath, half-expecting her to say, *Lyssa, of course. Don't you recognize me, father?*

"Amy."

"Amy with a last name?"

She gave a half smile. "Just Amy."

"Alright, Just Amy. Do you want some food first, or shall we start with the paintings?"

"Food later. Paintings now. With stories about why he painted them like he did, right? Especially the scary ones."

"'The Death Cycle.'"

She shivered. "Is that what he called it?"

Max shook his head and glanced at his watch, wiped off beads of water. "It's what I call it. And you know what? I think if it's really those that bother you, we should start there. So you'll actually have a chance to understand before the unveiling."

He saw her swallow and nod. "Can I get a drink first?"

Max looked hard at her. Something in the way she said that reminded him of Emery's bad times. And Lyssa's. But he nonetheless nodded and led her over to the punch and waited for her to fill her glass.

Then, reflecting on all that he had to tell her and how impossible it was that she would ever believe him, much less understand as Max did, more with his heart than his head, he asked the wine steward to pour him a tall glass of the fine Beaujolais he'd ordered for this event.

When he had it in his hand and Amy had refilled her punch glass, he led her towards the back of the gallery and the disturbing series of paintings showing various scenes of apocalypse. There was one of dogs ravaging a child. One where townspeople had gone mad and were burning their own houses. Each still had Emery's usual transcendent human figure in them, but in each, that figure was being buried under the larger masses of dark imagery. Overwhelmed.

Small wonder that these were the only paintings Max hadn't had to beg and borrow for tonight's retrospective. Only two of the death cycle paintings had actually been sold. People admired them, usually in a hand-to-the-throat sort of way, but no one wanted one of them hanging in their home.

Now Amy stood before them and he could see her own hands shaking as she brought them together to clasp in front of her. Maybe, Max mused uncomfortably, he should post a warning sign before this rear part of the gallery: *Warning! Emotionally-secure patrons only! Extended viewing may cause despair!*

"What...what caused him to do this?" Amy said now, her voice barely a whisper. She was focused on the Sally Anne painting. The glowing nurse tending the sick and dying. A nuclear winter rose in the background.

Max stood before her, smiling tightly. "You know who his usual transcendent figure is, don't you?"

"His wife."

"Mathilde Guillaume. That's right. They married when he was only twenty-two and still painting science fiction and fantasy covers. She was a flautist with the New York Philharmonic, but also a figure model. At least she was for Emery."

Amy had moved closer to him, unable to take her eyes off the existential anguish of the painting yet apparently needing Max's damp warmth or presence to reassure her. It made Max feel young again. Strong and sure. He wanted to put an arm around the girl's shoulders but he restrained himself as she seemed to shrink even further before the painting, her voice coming out as barely a whisper.

"She died, didn't she? The papers didn't say how."

"Lung cancer," Max said, just as quietly. "Like a nuclear winter. These were all painted before she died. And then—"

"Oh my god." She finally looked up at him and the fear was so intense her eyes had welled up. "And then he finished just one more work? The one you're unveiling tonight?"

She backed away from him, heading left into the north atrium where they'd had to specially raise the roof to accommodate the huge, crated work that not even Max had seen, on his promise to Emery. The crate stood on a knee-high plaster pedestal that stretched side-to-side just shy of the work's twenty-seven foot span, and was spotlit right now in soft blue and amber lights.

Amy began circling it, looking up at its imposing height with her mouth open.

And for the first time that evening, Max hesitated. Because the power of Emery's works to move people, while it made for good business and publicity for the gallery, might be too much on this night. For this young art lover, at least.

Max thought he knew what the newest painting would express. What it *had* to express after the bizarre narrative Emery had delivered with it. But what if he was wrong? Could he really risk showing Amy something that might be the last little shove she needed to destroy what was obviously a rather precarious emotional stability? It would perhaps be better to just send her home.

He should forget telling a story she wouldn't believe anyway. Forget the foolish desire to be her surrogate father, to have a second chance to save Max's own daughter by proxy.

Just *send her home.*

Yet even as he stepped to intercept her where she was now backing away from the display, she spun around on him with eyes so wide and panicky he found himself reflexively holding out his arms to her.

She didn't fold herself into him, but she did grab his hands with her own and shook them. "Tell me!" she demanded. "Tell me what happened to him!"

So he did.

TOO MANY THINGS END

At the end of August, Mathilde "Mattie" Lake had gotten so bad the doctors said they could do nothing for her but ease her pain. And that much could be done at home. So Emery brought her back there, to their lakeside home in the Catskill Mountains where all the fall colors were out and the first bite of winter was in the air, and he transformed the large study on the first floor into a cozy "healing" room for her. He refused to use the term hospice.

There, with the help of a nurse who attended three times a week to help with treatment, Emery cared for Mattie all day long. The healing room, you see, had the primary advantage of being immediately joined to Emery's studio. So he could continue working, alternating desperate painting with the warmly reassuring mask he wore whenever he went in to see his wife.

Not that Mattie ever believed the mask.

And she kept getting worse.

Finally in November, Thanksgiving Thursday, Emery made his first-ever stab at bargaining with God in his own unique way.

He quietly rolled his H-frame easel and brushes from his studio into the room where Mattie lay sleeping, studied her gaunt pallor for a moment, then crept out again to retrieve his canvas, his colors table, and his custom-made palette that came out from his colors table on an adjustable arm. His stealth wasn't smooth, for Emery was not a delicate man. He was tall and blunt-faced, with shaggy brown hair that came down around his shoulders. And because he had been contemplating for some time what he was about to do, he wore five days of beard on his face and had deep rings under his eyes.

Nor was he in the best of physical or emotional states. When he brought in the rest of his painting supplies, his hands shook more than he could ever remember them doing before. His stomach was in hard knots.

It wasn't fear of the planned portrait *per se*—he'd never been afraid of painting anything in his life—but of it not being good enough.

He repositioned the H-frame to a stop near the foot of Mattie's bed, stepped back from it, and tried to slow his heart by just looking at her.

It was almost eleven a.m. and Mattie still slept, but for a moment that seemed part of her beauty. For as large and blunt as Emery was, so perfect and delicate was his wife. Even now, with her lower face covered by a rubber oxygen mask, her ivory-pale arms sprouting tubes to a pole and bags that kept her hydrated, sedated, medicated, she was improbably beautiful. An angel trapped under a white cotton bedspread.

Yet he couldn't miss how she was wasting away more each day. It made him chew his lips and turn to face the window scene that Mattie would see from her bed when she woke up. The north end of Long Lake, stretched ominously beyond the pines and birch trees missing half their leaves. Everything was gunmetal gray, waiting for a storm. Mattie insisted he keep her window partially open always. He could hear the hush out there, taste the storm coming.

"Fine," he whispered at God. "You do your bit, I'll do mine. But this painting, if I make it complete enough, if I capture all the glory you've created in her, and if I let it show how you can take it away any *fucking* time you please..."

He stopped and fought for control.

"If I can do that, then you spare her, okay? That's the deal."

He jerked back as a gust of wind seemed to come out of nowhere and shudder the window. He realized he was panting his mouth dry and he shook himself angrily. When Mattie woke up he had to be collected, confident, the way he always was. He took a series of long, deep breaths. He set his jaw and stretched out his strong, rough fingers like a cat does its claws to reassert his dominion over them.

Okay. Now begin..

Quietly, methodically he adjusted his large canvas horizontally on the H-frame so its bottom would sit just below his knees when he sat. He'd have to stand to reach its upper portions. He detached the table of charcoal pencils, oil paints, acrylics, brushes, rags, turpentine, cardboard pieces and precision knives—he planned to use his signature combination of traditional oils, acrylics, and airbrush—from the rear of the H-frame, rolled it around to the front of the canvas, and locked the wheels. Where to position his chair was not a question. He had contemplated the optimal connection point for days and finally chosen a place neither starkly head-on, nor geometrically beside, but just back from where he'd normally sit near Mattie's wasted hips. There he would paint as comforter, protector, and fierce advocate.

Painting so that she'll live, damn it.

Almost without thinking, his drafting charcoal was in his hand and he was sketching the proportions of the portrait – the bed, the walls, Mattie's head...

A shuddering breath told him she was awake and he stopped to look into her eyes. They stared at him from above the hissing plastic of the oxygen mask that covered the bottom half of her face, what her nurse who was in the downstairs suite most days called non-invasive ventilation. Mattie reached a wasted hand to the mask and pulled it up and off.

Emery forced himself to only watch, making no effort to help.

His stillness made her smile as he'd known it would. As pixie to his giant, she'd always pushed to assert herself. It was part of who she was even now.

"You're going to paint me?"

He forced a casual shrug. "Something to do. Don't worry. I'm bringing in the ventilator before the turpentine comes out."

He should have tried to give her his own smile then, he knew, but couldn't. Despite all his anxiety, he'd begun slipping into creation mode, the first continuing stage of which was intense scrutiny. He saw how the corner of her eyes tightened as she laughed at him. Then tightened again in pain, this time squeezing her full expressive lips together like she'd sucked a lemon.

She stifled the cough that would sometimes bring up ugly phlegm or blood and waved the air with an emaciated hand, ending the wave with a casual raised middle finger at the ceiling.

Exactly, Emery grimaced.

When her chest spasm passed, she caught his eyes. Her own pale green ones sparkled more than they had in days. "How will I be? Naked?"

It cut through his intensity enough to make him smile and he shook his head. "Only if you pose for it that way."

That made her chest lift as if to laugh and her face pinched together again to stop a spasm. "*Tabernac,*" she swore. It was her child side, full French.

"Sorry," he said. "But this one is strictly naturalistic."

Her eyes were still closed. "I thought you said 'full of glory.'"

"You heard?"

Still closed. "Don't make deals about your art, my love. Not with him. He's too harsh a critic. Nothing's ever good enough."

"Shhh."

For a second her fear almost restarted Emery's own. But having actually begun his drafting of the picture, his fear was gone. Because unlike Mattie and the performance anxiety that had ridden with her always, fear was not a part of Emery's process. Once he was into it, he was simply into it. It became. He was the midwife. And every baby was beautiful. Even the dark and sickly ones, like all his paintings of the past year had been.

But Mattie's eyes were pressing him, so he changed the topic. "Did Violet come up to see you last night?"

Mattie's eyes opened and her head came up. "She's home?"

"Her car's in the driveway. I was working and didn't hear her come in."

"Did she bring Ben?"

"I...don't think so. I looked in on her this morning. Just her there."

Mattie's head fell back on the pillow. "I was afraid of that."

Emery went back to his canvas, sketching in long, quick strokes – the bed; the ventilator equipment; the IV drip; the patterns made by the dull light from the white lace curtains behind him, opposite the bed; finally Mattie, with the thin remains of what had once been the most glorious mane of chestnut hair he'd ever seen.

"She's losing Ben because of me, you know," Mattie said. "Because of all the time she spends out here with me."

"She's losing Ben because he's a gutless wonder," Emery said, not pausing his sketching.

"You're hard on him."

"Violet's a ball of fire like her mother. If he can't juggle fire, he should stay out of the furnace."

"That's what you think of yourself, hunh? A fire juggler?"

"Damn straight. And the furnace is life incarnate, of which you and Violet are the prime spirits. You are the heat that shapes the universe. You are the— Oh, damn."

"Broken charcoal?"

"It can't take the heat either." He threw it over his shoulder and reached for another from his box of colors and inks.

"Is that what you're going to capture here, Emery? Me as a fireball?"

"Newsflash, my darling. That's all I've been capturing of you from the first time you walked into my studio."

It made her grin and start to laugh, cough in pain, then laugh angrily, teeth bared at the ceiling as her chest and small body convulsed and writhed under the thin sheet.

"Like I said," Emery murmured and continued sketching.

* * *

"Mr. Lake has a daughter?"

Max nodded. "Violet Lake. Attractive but not stunning like her mother. She inherited her father's sturdy frame and his bluntness of attitude. Used to play the piano and she got into Julliard on a scholarship, but left shortly after her mother grew ill. She decided to study business and marketing at NYU instead."

"Which is why her boyfriend left her."

"Perhaps. Or maybe she was still discovering who she was. Needing to connect with her parents..."

* * *

"God, Mattie, no. Come on."

Emery had finally dropped his roughing pencil when Mattie showed no sign of recovering. He leapt to her bed, grabbed his wife's wasted body and held it to him. But her coughing, the way it clenched her body forward against him like steel bands close to snapping, still didn't stop.

He pressed her oxygen mask back on her face with one hand, stabbing the emergency button over and over with his elbow. Of course it had to be a holiday morning. Mattie's nurse was with her family and the fall-back hospital connection wouldn't get anyone here from Breakabeen for at least twenty to forty minutes.

They were going to be too late.

Half releasing Mattie, Emery fumbled with one hand to load a syringe of morphine into her IV line, but Mattie's hand grabbed his wrist and held it, her head shaking back and forth.

Oh, shit.

And it was his painting that had done it, wasn't it. Or his deal with God. Or his making her laugh. Something, damn it. If he'd just come in as usual and sat quietly with her, held her hand, she'd have been okay. She'd have kept going. The chemo would have miraculously reversed the fucking Stage Four proliferation of cancer cells and her healthy tissues would have come back. They would have.

"What do I do, Mattie?" he said, squeezing and rocking her as she jerked and shook, unable to get her breath.

Her eyes locked on his and were filled with such terror that he wanted to look around her head or into his own skull to see what she was seeing. "What? What is it? Can I kill it for you? Drive it back?"

Then her body took a long, tortured pull of air from the oxygen mask and simply stopped.

Nothing.

Her eyes were still wide, staring at him in horror. Only with no spark. Nothing in them.

Nothing.

Her body, which had become so light over the last few weeks, suddenly felt like a sack of lead and Emery's arms, holding her, began to slip...

The door banged open behind him and his head turned in a small jerk, the arrival hidden for a moment by his barely-begun canvas.

Then he saw it was Violet. Of course it was Violet. Violet, looking almost like a plus-sized version of the woman her mother had been when Emery first met her, except that Violet had none of the real worldly knowledge yet. For Violet was innocent. Unscarred by life. Untried. Untested. Beautiful and pure.

For a second Emery wanted to tuck Mattie's dead body down and into himself to shield his daughter from the sight. Or to keep it for himself, maybe.

But of course he couldn't, and Violet saw.

"Mom?" It came out brittle, half-hoping. Pleading.

Emery shook his head, unable to speak. He'd believed he lost most of his ability to speak with Violet around the time she'd grown breasts and become aware of them, but now he wondered if he'd *ever* been able to speak to her. Or to Mattie. His tongue felt like a huge, swollen log in his mouth.

"When?" Violet said, her eyes welling up angrily. "Now? Just now?"

Emery nodded.

"And you didn't call me?" Her voice rose in an uncontrolled hysteria. "My mom's dying and you didn't even call me? I'm right upstairs! I'm right *here*! And you didn't call me? What are you? What kind of freaking father are you?"

He opened his mouth and waited for whatever he had there to come spilling out for her.

Absolutely nothing did.

RESCUE MISSION

"The portrait," Amy said. "Did he finish it? Is that what's in the crate?"

Max paused, then shook his head. "I don't think so. When his wife died, Emery stopped painting completely. He stopped coming into the city. He eventually stopped even taking my phone calls. When I drove all the way up to his lake house to see him, he refused to let me in. A year passed. Two. Three..."

"But he came out eventually, didn't he?"

There was a desperate need in her voice as she asked, which Max took as a good sign. She wanted *to be saved. She wanted somehow for things to work out. Which was more than Max had been able to say for Emery during this time.*

"If it had been only up to him, I do not think Emery Lake would have ever come out of his house. He would have died there or gone slowly mad."

"But...?"

"But he had a daughter, you remember. One who loved him, in spite of his difficult nature. He also had me."

* * *

Mattie's dead.

That, as always, was the first thing that came into Emery's head when he opened his eyes this afternoon. But this time there were smells with that. The Castle Despair, as Violet liked to call his little lake house property, smelled...musty. Sour.

He unclenched his fingers from his sheets and blinked in surprise that he'd noticed.

And the light... Afternoon light filtered in through the dusty air between the closed curtains of his bedroom like Heaven trying to check up on him. Like it wanted to know if he was still angry at God, at the world, at Life in general.

Well he was. In between his anger at himself, and his unrelenting grief that seemed to rage and rage within him and refused to quit even in his quiet walks by the shore. Such was his emotional stamina that it raged even when his body had completely fallen apart on him. His hair was a matted mass down his back. His beard lay coarse and tangled on his chest. His back, even lying down, was always sore and often in spasm.

But the grief and anger seemed to pause for just a moment this afternoon as he lay there newly woken and he smelled himself in the sheets, and he saw the light.

And sensed a presence.

"Mattie?"

It came out cracked and dry since he spoke so little these days, allowing only Violet to visit him and ensure he was eating and bathing.

There was no answer, but something crunched somewhere. The sound of voices?

Emery slapped a hand against his chest, grabbed his beard, and held his breath. He'd dreamt of Mattie so often, pursuing her over and over into the abyss where he *lost* her over and over, that for a moment he believed it was her. She'd followed him back to the land of the living. She was here.

The sound came again and the eeriness faded. Not Mattie. Stupid. Someone was in his driveway. They'd either walked or driven up and stopped before he'd woken up.

What day was it? Thursday? Wednesday? Violet only came up on Fridays so it wasn't her. Max swore he'd never come without calling first. So who? Some art fan? Reporter? Real estate agent?

Damn them all! Why couldn't they all just leave him alone!

Roused to a sudden territorial fury, Emery leapt from bed and cried out at the sharp pain that shot through his back. He grunted over to the en-suite bathroom fumbled through the fly of his boxer shorts. He peed, then splashed water on his face to fully wake up.

Move. *Move.*

He grunted back into his bedroom, pulled on some jeans and a ripped red tee-shirt, and stumbled downstairs in his bare feet. If he just had a shotgun, he could shoot it in the air over the head of whoever it was and make them go away. Shout at them to read the goddamn signs! Look at the unmowed weeds out front and the filthy windows for fuck's sake! You think I want *company?* What did he have to goddamn—

"Daddy!"

He tripped on the last step and went sprawling onto the downstairs landing, hitting his chin hard on the floor when he fell, thankful for the cushion of both his belly and his beard. He scrabbled up painfully to his knees to see two people silhouetted in the doorway. One was Violet, holding the house key he'd given her. The other was Max Hebbler, the gallery owner who had first dibs on showing all his new work. Max Hebbler, the silver-haired financial fox who'd supported him before he was famous so that he could scoop his fame and fortune *after* Emery had made it. Max Hebbler, one-time friend, confidante, father figure...

"What the fuck are you doing here, Max?" he said.

"Daddy!"

"Hello, Emery."

Emery swiped at his eyes, watering hard from the pain of his fall. Maybe at something more? He pushed back his straggly hair from his head and staggered up to his feet. There! Taller than Hebbler. Taller than Violet. Taller than the whole goddamned world! And Jesus did his back hurt.

It must have shown in his face because Violet rushed forward and put one of his arms over her shoulders, trying to support his weight. He allowed it but refused to slump, keeping his watery eyes fixed on Hebbler.

"Why're you here, Max?"

Hebbler smiled unctuously. Emery could almost see him flicking an imaginary piece of lint off his tailored white linen suit. How he'd impressed Emery when he'd first shown him his gallery and introduced him to his coterie of serious collectors who'd lay down sixty or a hundred thousand on a painting without blinking an eye. Such a step up from the gawking, pimple-faced fanboys and girls of the annual San Diego Comic-Con. Even from the movie producers who'd courted him like they'd courted Frank Frazetta and Frank Miller in their days.

No, Hebbler represented *real* artists. The elite of the New York scene. Of the world.

What a load of crap.

"It's good to see you, Emery," Hebbler said, not moving from his place in the doorway as if not trusting the crazy artist to not attack him should he step inside. Or maybe Hebbler was more like a fucking vampire. Couldn't enter the home unless the resident invited him in.

Well this resident was not going to fucking do that.

"Daddy," said Violet, "Max is here because I asked him to come. He and I have arranged something which I want you to listen very closely to before you say anything. Can you do that?"

The firm reproof in her voice was something she'd gotten from her mother and Emery felt himself unconsciously drawing back his scowl, feeling guilty. Then his suspicion slid forward again as he looked down at his only child holding herself under his right arm. His one-time painting arm. The arm he wiped his ass with. Ate with. Picked his nose with. Flipped the bird at God with.

He drew back his arm and shambled back away from Violet so he could keep both her and Hebbler in his sight.

"You talk. I'll listen," he said.

Violet flushed where she'd been left standing like a supplicant, but Emery couldn't tell if it was embarrassment, fear, or rage at the way he was treating her. He'd stopped being able to read her when her mother died. Of course, if Violet bled or cried, he'd go to her aid. Fathers did that. But from the time when she'd come in and found him with Mattie dead in his arms, and screamed that he wasn't much of a father or a human being... Well, Violet might still come around to make sure he had food and other basics, but she'd spoken her true heart and it didn't contain him.

So his would not contain her.

She stared at him now with her lips pressed together. Then she looked about his entryway, into his kitchen, what little you could see of it from here. Though he had no doubt that even from here it was a mess. Emery had also long ago stopped putting things in their proper place. Because, when you thought about it, nothing had a proper place in the world anymore. With Mattie gone, there was this big sucking vortex that moved everything off center, that skewed alignments, messed with horizontals and perspectives. Nothing *fit*. Anywhere.

"Have you had lunch today?" Violet said. "Or breakfast?"

He opened his mouth but couldn't think for a moment what to say.

"You just got up, didn't you. And you haven't had a shower yet today."

That tone of voice again. It flipped his power position neatly on its head and he felt like a rebellious child who had no words. So he lifted the bottom of his tee-shirt and jiggled his belly flesh at her.

Hebbler discretely turned his face.

Violet shook her head and walked up to him. She grabbed his flabby arms and turned him towards the stairs. "You go upstairs right now and shower and try to find some *clean* clothes to put on. I will clean up the kitchen and make you some scrambled eggs and fruit."

"Don't have any—"

"Fruit? Eggs? Of course not. Max and I picked up groceries on the way over. Now go."

Max and I? Emery blinked back at the doorway with the ugly thought that this silver-haired art dealer, who was married to a second wife, with whom he had three children, was also diddling Emery's twenty-two-year-old daughter.

Then Violet had physically pushed him to the stairs and he found himself going up, no more able to resist her commanding will than he'd been able to resist her mother's.

* * *

"IT'S LIKE THIS, DADDY," Violet finally said.

She sat across from him at the kitchen table as he finished the eggs, toast, and cut watermelon, cantaloupe, and green seedless grapes she'd prepared for him. And though her head was a third again as large as Mattie's, her nose stronger and more bulbous like Emery's, it easily could have been Mattie sitting there. Same voice. Same insistent posture. The intensity. The determination.

"If you stay in this house like this, never going out, never trying anything new, you're going to die."

She said it and held his eyes so gravely he almost rediscovered his long-dead sense of humor. "We all die," he said.

Okay, not so funny. But come *on*. Violet had drawn back like she'd been slapped and her eyes filled with tears. Was this how she negotiated in this music booking company she was now working with? She'll kick her father while he's holding his dead wife, she'll reject the gift of music her mother gave her and everything Mattie and Emery dreamed for her, but if he makes one little joke *at his own expense*, she takes it like a personal attack.

Even as he sank his chin into his beard, though, she pulled out of her hurt, looked around his kitchen, and said, "Are you drinking again?"

"What? No. I promised Mattie..."

"And that's *all* you promised? You think you're doing Mom any honor by moping around here day in and day out? You think that's what she'd want? It's so selfish!"

"You don't know," he muttered at her.

"I do know!" Violet shot back. "I know that Mom always attacked life, even when she was scared. And so did you! I don't think she would have married you if you hadn't."

"Um...Violet?" Hebbler said quietly from where he stood near the fridge, behind her. "Perhaps you could tell him what—"

"Be quiet, Max," said Violet. "Daddy, I know that, regardless of what I think of you, or Mom thought of you, or what either of us might have wanted from you, there is a certain sense of manifest destiny to your painting. Just like there was with the painters you considered your heroes. Who were they? Picasso? Renoir? Van Gogh? Their gift *had* to be expressed. Isn't that what you told me once? The world *demanded* it of them. If they hadn't painted, all those secrets, those particular visions of the world, those keys to the truth of things, would have been lost forever. Well your gift is like that and you're not allowed to just let it die!"

Emery stared at her, struck completely dumb by her outburst.

"Of course," Hebbler mused from behind her, "Van Gogh did kill himself. Shot himself in the side of his chest with a revolver, then suffered, Christ-like, for two days before dying."

Both Emery and Violet turned to stare now at Hebbler, who shrugged. "Just saying."

"You...want me to shoot myself," Emery said dully.

Again Hebbler shrugged. "Or stay here and waste away. Of course Van Gogh's family had a history of psychiatric illness, or organic illness – acute intermittent porphyria, I believe it was. It gave him seizures, acute pain, sensory distortions. But at least you can relate to his last words, yes? 'La tristesse durera toujours.' The sadness will last forever. Might as well just snip it off then. End your life. Give up." He casually pointed a long finger at the side of his chest. "Bang."

"Max?" snarled Emery. "Fuck you."

"Please do not talk to me. You're dead."

"Shut up."

"Dead. Killed yourself. Just like Mattie. Oh, no, wait. She did not get that choice, did she. In fact I do remember the three of us talking once about life, just living, was probably the greatest gift that God ever—"

"*SHUT! UP!*"

Emery found himself on his feet, his chair tumbled behind him, his body shaking with a fury so powerful it burned out even the emptiness of *no-Mattie* as he stepped around the table.

Then Violet was up too, standing between him and Hebbler. And he wanted to strike Violet as well. Swat them both like flies, goads. Why the hell had they come out here like this? "You want another *painting* out of me this badly, Max? You want to squeeze my bones until something drips out on the canvas for you? Hunh?"

"We just want *you*, Daddy," Violet said. She'd grabbed him so her thumbs dug into his biceps. "Yes, we'd like you to paint because we both believe that's your destiny, but mostly we just want you to *live* again. That's why Max and I have arranged a trip for you. Actually a trip for two – me and you. We're going to France. First to Paris, then down to Aix-en-Provence where Mom was born.

We're going there so you can find some closure, maybe. Or just some beauty. You paint or don't paint, I don't care. But you have to get out of here. You have to *try!*"

Her eyes filled with tears on that and Emery's rage got dragged into confusion. What the—? Violet had never cried more than a few times growing up, never even shed a tear at her mother's funeral. Now she was a maudlin mess who cried at the drop of a hat, over a father she barely acknowledged?

"Mattie's parents...," he said. "They're dead. I...don't get it."

Hebbler cleared his throat. "The south of France also played host to many of your favorite painters. Paul Cézanne. Henri Matisse."

Emery shot him a harsh look.

"Pierre-Auguste?" Hebbler tried.

"Renoir."

"He spent the last part of his life in Cagnes-sur-Mere. Died there."

"Death again," Emery said.

"He died an old man. After a full life. He was painting on the day he died with his paintbrushes strapped to his arthritic hands."

Emery shook his head but felt his beard sway as he did and suddenly had the vivid picture of himself as a large, angry bear. Maybe a bear who'd been hibernating. Who was smelling things again. Seeing the light in its cave. Responding to invaders prodding at him. Maybe even...ready to leave the cave?

Violet was still gripping his arms, her thumbs still digging into his biceps.

He looked down at her, then at her hands. "That hurts."

She released her grip immediately.

"Where would we stay?" he said.

Her face flushed a bright pink and she blinked so hard and fast that the earlier tears now spilled down over her cheeks and into the furrows of her smile. Renoir would have painted that. *Pierre-Auguste.* What pretentious familiarity.

He spun his gaze back to Hebbler. "You know what, Max?"

"What?" the dealer sniffed.

"You're blind. You think you know people. You think you can manipulate them. Prod at them with a stick until you get the response you want. Make them dance. But you're absolutely blind to how that just drives us away."

He saw it strike home as the silver-haired art dealer went pale and his chin dropped. Then Hebbler closed his mouth again. Tightly.

Emery looked back down to Violet. "Alright. You and I. When?"

"This Saturday."

"Hunh?" He literally rocked back on his heels and Violet had to catch him again by the arms to steady him.

"Max and I... *I* thought it would be a good idea to make sure you didn't have time to change your mind or back out. I've already booked time off from my work. I've arranged for your house to be looked after. I'm staying over here tonight and tomorrow to help you pack and get ready."

"My passport..."

"Is up to date. I checked. You renewed it for that Japan exhibit just before..."

Yeah. Before.

Emery was mentally staggering. The bear half asleep. But waking? Time to come out of the cave into a world without Mattie? *Was* there anything worthwhile out there for him anymore?

And it was that last niggling little question that finally made him squinch his eyes closed, rub at his face, and say, "Alright. We staying in a hotel? Bed and breakfast? What?"

"That," said Violet with something hidden and dark in her eyes, "is going to be a surprise."

THE CITY OF OLD THINGS

Falling into the night.

That's what the plane right over the Atlantic felt like to Emery. One long, endless fall from where he had been to where he was going.

It came from the abdication of control, he guessed. From letting Violet pack his clothes and toilet kit, to letting her insist he shave and cut his hair before they left. Which meant yesterday. Scissors and razor on his beard. Scissors and more scissors on his hair, wielded by Violet who possessed a surprisingly experienced touch. Where had she learned that? From whom? That he couldn't even guess only heightened his sense of vertigo and helplessness. He was being shaved naked and hurtled across the Atlantic by a young woman he didn't know. A stranger to him. He should probably change that.

"Daddy? I've got to pee."

"Hm?" He looked over at her, startled back to the reality of the packed 747 they were on. He had an aisle seat, necessary when you were over six-foot-two and your knees screamed in agony if you could not occasionally stretch out your legs.

This also meant, though, that he had to get up to let his daughter, in the middle seat, get out. So he did, sat back down, went to tug on his beard, and found only his bare chin.

Naked.

He gulped a breath and pressed his fingers into his closed eyes, fighting a sudden panic that he knew had been hiding just under his dazed calm ever since he'd boarded this flight. Ever since he'd agreed to this trip.

Breathe.

"You'll be just fine, you know."

He laughed at the familiar voice. Hallucinations now. Wonderful.

"Emery, let it go, my love."

Let what go?

"All your reservations. Recriminations. Constipations." Mattie's voice laughed at him. "You've got things to find."

That much, at least, was vintage Mattie. She loved silly rhymes. Something about learning English as a second language. So his hallucinatory abilities were obviously sharper than he'd have thought.

The voice laughed again. "And you called Max blind."

"Don't you—" He flung his fingers off his eyes as he turned to reproach her, but of course there was no one there. Just an empty middle seat. The passenger who had the window seat, an older woman whom Violet had been talking with earlier, lowered her book and looked over her glasses at him skeptically. He gave her a pained grin and rested his head back on the too-short head rest, staring at the drop-down video screens two rows up. Some stupid comedy he'd chosen not to watch. Without sound, it was almost bearable.

By the time Violet came back from the bathroom at the rear of the plane, he'd almost wiped the hallucinated Mattie completely from his mind and was having savage fun figuring out the plot silent movie. Very Hollywood. Predictable.

"You look almost happy," Violet said as she waited for him to move and let her back to her seat.

"Just trying to let it go," Emery said.

"What?"

"Hunh?"

"You said…"

"Nothing. Here."

He got up and stepped into the aisle so she could slide back in.

* * *

They'd started their descent into Charles de Gaulle before it occurred to Emery that he and Violet had hardly spoken the entire flight.

To some extent it seemed natural. He'd spent so much time alone in the lake house since Mattie died that he wasn't really used to communicating. But somewhere along the line, obviously, Violet must have just accepted that was how he was and had stopped trying to talk with him.

Hence his lack of knowledge about her and her life.

Had she ever talked to him? When she was a little girl? Emery racked his brain and came up with a chirrupy little girl running in and out of his studio when they still lived in Brooklyn. She'd talked. He'd ignored her.

And later? Violet in junior high school, beaming after winning some award for her piano playing. But Emery had just been given a commission to do two pieces for the lobby of the Trump Tower. He'd been both flush with the money and furious at the restrictions "The Donald" had put on him for the pieces. Violet had babbled at him. Emery had snapped at her. Then Mattie had stepped in and privately scolded him about it until his ears had

29

burned so hot he'd thought they would catch fire or melt. She'd been so *angry...*

He turned and looked at Violet now. A beautiful young woman who'd lost her mother and might as well have lost her father at the same time. Except that she'd obviously felt responsible for him, so had kept visiting, doing the minimum, going through the motions of filial responsibility, shouldering the burden.

"Do you hate me?" he asked her suddenly.

She jerked a little and looked from the window to him. "What?"

"Do you hate me?"

"No. Of course not."

"Do you resent me?"

"Dad, what's this all coming from? Are you feeling airsick? Have your ears not popped?"

Emery closed his mouth and looked forwards again. Mattie had always been able to understand exactly what he meant, where he was coming from, like she could read his mind. Maybe that had made him lazy about explaining himself because he realized now that he was not good at it. Not even good at understanding it.

"Dad?"

"When I was painting I had a way," he mumbled.

"What?" She reached out a hand and felt his forehead. "Are you catching a cold or something? You feel okay."

"I'm fine," he said and tried to smile at her. It sounded just as hollow in his ears as it had all the times he'd heard Mattie say it in her last year of life.

* * *

You've got *things to find.*

Where? Here?

Violet had booked them into a small hotel just off the Boule-vard Saint Germaine, a little west of Boulevard Saint Michel. The area was characterized mostly by chi-chi little shops that sported names like Louis Vuitton, Arthus-Bertrand, Chanel, Hugo Boss, and Cartier, on winding side streets so narrow it seemed impossible the delivery trucks could ever make it through.

Yet make it through they did each morning, shortly after the procession of garbage and recycling trucks, in a two hour dance of rumbling machinery outside their windows. Enough to wake the dead, which Emery figured he pretty well was by that point.

"But Nortre-Dame's just a short walk," Violet gushed. "So's the Louvre, the Musée d'Orsay, the Champs d'Elysée. Do you remember when we came here when I was ten? We took that boat ride down the Seine?"

He stared at her from the middle of the queen-sized bed he'd basically camped out in since arriving the afternoon before. Violet had dragged him out to *Les Deux Magots* last night for crêpes, then brought him a meal to eat like a picnic this morning here on his acetate bedspread – a strong goat cheese on hard bread, under-ripe nectarines, peach yoghurt, a cherry pastry, orange juice. Everything was spread out before him on a towel.

Things to find...

Violet had an adjoining room and had obviously been out exploring the neighborhood this morning. And she'd eaten already, since she wasn't having any of this.

"You don't remember any of it, do you," she said now, deciding to cut herself a round of goat cheese and bread after all.

He shrugged and readjusted the pillows between his back and the headboard, the sheets and covers that covered his bare, hairy legs. The truth was that the trip to the famous *brasserie* last night had indeed sparked memories. He remembered how much Mattie had loved places like that when they'd come here for his two shows. They'd probably even eaten in that particular one, though Emery didn't usually recall names unless he'd painted them.

But the small tables, the precise and tasty portions, the relaxed service that only came when you called and otherwise was happy to let you sit there all night sipping your wine and watching the tourists and Parisians stream by – those things he remembered.

And Violet was probably in some of those memories too, if he examined them closely enough. But they hurt too much to do that so he reflexively shut them down. In fact his shut-down reflex was so strong that everything, even the room here around him, was a little foggy now, lost in a haze. Emery was floating. Maybe what he was supposed to find was *himself*?

"Dad!" Violet said. "I asked you a question."

"Hunh?"

"The Seine boat cruise. Do you remember it?"

He looked deep into her eyes, brown, where her mother's had been green, and shook his head.

"Figured." She said it lightly and popped the remainder of the bread and cheese into her mouth, but he could hear the hurt in her voice and see the lines around her mouth go tighter.

Emery felt guilty. It pushed him out of his intense lethargy enough to ask, "Did you want to do that boat cruise again?"

Her eyes snapped back at him as if checking to see if he was being deliberately cruel. Then they softened. "That's for kids and tourists." She laughed. "I mean real tourists, who can't speak French and don't know the difference between a *bidet* and a toilet."

"There's a difference?" Emery said lamely.

Violet gave him the laugh, then began cleaning up the food. "So do you want to hit the Louvre today or the Orangerie? See Monet's *Water Lilies*?"

He cocked his head at her. She was a puzzle, he saw. He just wasn't sure what kind. "You've been reading up on Monet?"

She grinned as she finished putting the remainder of the hard baguette, the cheese, and the nectarines in the plastic bag she'd come in with. "And Manet. And Frédérik Bazille, and Degas,

Pissaro, Berthe Morisot, and all the other *impressionistes* you said you were so inspired by when you started out."

Emery frowned. "I never said that."

"You did."

"Show me the interview when I said that."

Now she was by the door, a big, solid girl, yet with the same gamine, teasing expression her mother used to wear. "Oh, you'd never have said it in an interview. It was too private. Too 'pedestrian' an inspiration. But you told Mom once. On one of your first real dates with her. Walking—"

"—along Mission Beach down in San Diego," he finished for her. "After dusk. The water lapping at our feet. So quiet it was like we were in a different world."

He let it hang like that in the air, remembering the cool wind after a long day of Comic Con, and the way his heart was beating so fast he still could not cool down. All because of the diminutive sex bomb beside him. She'd seemed to understand him so intensely. When he'd spoken of the short leap between how the impressionists tried to capture the moment and how he too was always reaching for that split second...

He blinked and realized Violet was looking at him with her face contorted into something he couldn't read.

"When did she tell you that?" he asked.

She shrugged. "I don't remember. We talked a lot. She talked a lot about you, about the two of you."

Emery dropped his head and stared at the bedspread covering his lap, feeling the spread of his belly now too. "Got pretty boring, I bet."

"Never."

Then she was out the door and he was left wondering whether he was supposed to get dressed. Had he actually agreed to go out somewhere?

* * *

THE LOUVRE WAS PRETTY MUCH as he'd remembered it – a huge, stuffy, cantankerous place whose sense of order and space owed too much to a higgledy-piggledy preservation of art history, whose stone floors taxed the feet while the too-high paintings and sculptures taxed the neck and made Emery feel like he was going to collapse after an hour of wandering. Violet couldn't honestly think he'd find anything he needed in here.

And yet...

He kept thinking he saw flashes of faces he recognized in the wide hallways of art, standing in front of some painting or other. The faces never stayed, and the familiarity slipped from the niggling sense of knowing the persons to knowing *of* them, as if he'd seen their faces somewhere.

Following one such twinge of familiarity, Emery found himself drawn back to the medieval paintings of the fifteenth century, to the flashes of brilliance that stood out amidst such primitive, religion-riddled dogma, when Leonardo and Botticelli caught the ineffable that was always there, had always been, in every age, every culture.

And when a bearded man who could have been Leonardo himself led Emery onwards to Antonio Canova's sculpture of the winged Eros awakening Psyche, cupping her breast, raising her out of her turgid slumber into her full sexuality, Emery felt a tug just above his navel. There *was* something all around them, always there, that had to be brought forward again and again for people to study and grasp.

Why? What was the point? What did it get you?

Yet the *struggle*... That he understood. He'd been a part of it for so many years. Thrown his whole self into it. So to be here, amidst so much evidence of how wide that struggle was through the centuries, all these geniuses and lesser lights searching and panting and pouring their lifeblood into their works... Was it any wonder he was catching some of that madness as he wandered?

But it *was* madness, Emery thought as he walked on. Incomprehensible madness.

"Daddy? Are you okay?" said Violet when she finally caught up to him in a blank space of the Salle de la Joconde. This was the huge side room off the Grand Galerie that was specially designed with wooden floors, natural and artificial lighting from above, lots of room for endless herds of mooing viewers who knew without understanding why that they had to gawk at the picture hanging there – *La Joconde*, in Italian *La Gioconda*, the cheerful. In the English world it was called the Mona Lisa.

"Daddy, what's wrong?"

Which was when he realized he'd been crying, tears streaming down his face like he had a fruitful inner well.

He raised his bare forearm to his face and wiped away the tears. "I don't know," he said. "This isn't what I'm supposed to find."

"What? Too old-fashioned for you?" said Violet. Then, in her mother's voice, "You need to go to the *Musée d'Orsay*."

"Fine!" he capitulated. "Let's go there now."

"What? Go where?"

Emery looked down at the confusion on his daughter's face and smiled. It hadn't been Violet suggesting the Musée d'Orsay; it was just more of the madness.

He took Violet's elbow and steered her out of the room, saying, "I'll explain outside."

* * *

OUTSIDE, walking through the Tuillerie Gardens, then across the Seine to reach the Musée d'Orsay, Emery took deep breaths and looked about himself for the mysterious faces which would beckon to him then vanish. There were none here. Only back in the Louvre.

And aboard the airplane getting here? Mattie's voice?

File that for another time.

Because here now, walking through the hot sun, Emery's mind seemed right enough. Not happy? No. Of course not. Because sanity in this world *demanded* a permanent low level base of pain that came from human stupidity and cruelty and mortality. And Emery felt that. *Ergo* he was sane.

"Are you going to explain what you meant back in the Louvre?" said Violet as they climbed the steps to the d'Orsay's entrance.

He started. He'd almost forgotten she was beside him. "What did I say?"

"You spoke to me like I'd been demanding we come here. Or somewhere. I'm assuming it was here, since this is where we are."

He looked at her, remembering her mother's voice issuing from her lips, and raised a hand to his hot forehead, wiping away the sweat along his hairline. "I'm...hearing things, I guess," he said. When she said nothing, he added, "And seeing things. Things that aren't there. Voices of your mother. Faces of...other artists? I'm not sure."

Violet studied him intently as if waiting for him to laugh. When he didn't, she nodded gravely and said, "Okay. I'm thinking it's just you finally getting out of that damn lake house. Maybe the hot sun too. Maybe jet lag."

"Maybe insanity."

"All painters are crazy."

"I never was before."

"Says you."

"I never heard voices that weren't there before."

Violet looked down at the concrete. They'd stopped just outside the front doors of the museum. "You never heard voices that *were* there before."

"Hunh. Okay."

She raised her face to look at him. Serious but not crying. Good, because Emery didn't think he was able to deal with any more of her crying. He felt crappy and out of his element enough as it was already.

"I'm just trying to say, Dad, that maybe when you came out of seclusion, you came out farther than you thought."

"Whatever that means."

"It means we're almost having a real conversation here, the second one today. When was the last time, before we came here to France, that we did that?"

He had no answer to her so he just huffed and pushed through the doors of the museum, walking quickly to the cashier to get their tickets. The plane ride, the hotel, their food this morning, the Louvre – Violet had been picking up the entire tab for these things, Emery realized. On a junior helper's salary, helping book musical acts. Wasn't that what she did? How much was she paid? He knew she was better off than many young people because her schooling had been paid for and she lived rent-free in the loft Emery owned on the lower east side of Manhattan. So Violet had started work without huge student debts and had a decent place to live. But still, if there was one thing Emery's commercial success had given him to date, it was the fact he'd never have to work again for the rest of his life if he so chose. The least he should be doing is paying for this vacation with his daughter.

She caught up to him now and he turned to her with her ticket. She took it with a thank you, gasped a little in delight as she looked past him into the grand central atrium that stretched down a flight to an expansive white-and-black marble floor covered with sculptures to walk amongst. There were roomed exhibits on either side of it and up its walls, up and up to a great glass arch of a ceiling letting in a wash of natural light. You could feel how this had once been a train station. Yet now it was the most elegant and spacious of art galleries, housing everything after the ages of the Louvre but before the modern craziness of the George-Pompidou Center. Basically the d'Orsay was mid-19th century to the early twentieth. Emery's time period. The golden time of painters.

At least that was what he *used* to believe.

Perhaps Violet caught some of his unconscious excitement because her eyes were sparkling when she turned back from it all and asked him if he wanted her to get them both headsets so they could have an audio commentary on all the works.

"Not for me," he said. "I want to get see if I can understand what the artist was saying without being told." *And if they were truly saying anything at all.*

She laughed. "Okay. You want me to walk around with you or... Never mind. I can see from your face. Meet back here at...four o'clock?"

He nodded. "Thank you."

She shrugged. "Always eager to please." She turned and walked off.

Which left Emery on his own to take in the entire grand *Musée*, but there was really no question where he was going to go, was there. He checked his museum guide, then headed left for the claustrophobic side columns of space that held the escalators and stairs. His blood thrummed in his limbs and he found himself eagerly climbing the escalators as they rose.

The paintings of *les impressionistes* were on the top floor. They called to him.

FAMILIAR FACES

Henri de Toulouse-Lautrec. The unmistakable style and subject manner of the paintings greeting the visitor to the floor would have let Emery pick them out as Lautrecs even if he hadn't known these particular pieces well already. He lumped them in his mind with Edgar Degas, Lautrec's precursor, both of them drawing dancers and common people at their most basic. Emery couldn't view too much of either of them before he'd smell the sweat of unwashed clothing and bodies, feel the stickiness of the sex, whether on prostitutes, lesbians, ballet dancers, or nudes washing themselves in wide steel tubs.

And it wasn't just knowing what they must have smelled and felt like. Emery could actually feel them. Smell them. Right now. Real magic. It made a vague panic of emotion threaten to push its way up through his throat, but he swallowed it down and looked further into the hall.

Because it wasn't Toulouse-Lautrec or Degas whom Emery had come up here to see. No, he thought and walked into the very middle of the first room of this upstairs wing. No. It was these. Oh, God. It was these.

The whitewashed rooms, lit from above by natural light and virtually empty of other tourists right up to the next archway, held the actual paintings of Claude Monet, Berthe Morisot, Alfred Sisley, and of course Auguste Renoir, the impressionist who saw only good in people, who found life and laughter in the poorest—

"*Oh, mon Dieu!*"

Emery jerked back into himself as he saw who'd spoken. It was a strikingly patrician man with a receding hairline but flowing, beautiful chestnut hair, who'd entered this room from the next and spoken the word over the shoulder of his suit jacket. He caught Emery's eye and smirked as the woman he'd apparently addressed, followed him through the archway. She was dressed in a ridiculously formal blue dress that actually seemed to have a bustle and a decolletage that went right up to her throat. As Emery looked, he was shocked by the intensity of the woman's dark hair and gaze boring into his, uncomfortably familiar.

Then she strode into the room, skirts rustling, up to the man with the beautiful hair, and took his arm. He pulled his arm out and instead wrapped it around her waist, moving in a way that Emery was pretty sure meant he was stroking the hidden side of her bust.

"Édouard! Your brother!" she snapped in French. *Ton frère!*

"Is not here," he responded in the same elegant tongue. "I am. I'd like to paint you naked again."

The woman blushed and "Édouard" winked at Emery like he knew him. It seemed a clear invitation to approach, to engage the two in conversation, use his rusty French to enquire what brought them to the museum today, to this section of it specifically. What had they found here?

Yet Emery felt paralyzed, his heart beating fast. For to take that step forward and speak to them would be to either destroy the illusion of who he believed them to be, or to confirm it and his own insanity.

Which the man seemed to understand. He smiled directly at Emery, projecting considerable charm, and slowed his French speech as if he saw in Emery's face something that pegged him as foreign. "All these men..." He waved his hand around to indicate a wall of Pissarro nature scenes and another that featured Monet's breathtaking *Rue Montorgueuil, Paris 30 Juin 1878* with its French red-white-and-blue flags filling the walls of the street.

"And women!" said his companion.

"These 'impressionists.' Do you know where it all took them?"

Emery found himself gagging on his dry throat but forced himself to clear it and said, "Wh-where?"

"Go down the hall a few rooms. Look at Van Gogh's work. Lunacy! Or Cézanne's. The man was an infant who couldn't paint. You can't help but laugh at him. Everyone laughed at him all the time. He had no social skills."

"*Édouard!*" his companion said. Though she then looked at Emery from under her dark brows and admitted, "Paul really did seem to make a profession out of struggling at his painting."

"Never quite getting it right," said Édouard.

"But always thinking he was almost there."

"Kind of like Vincent," said the man.

"Yes," said the woman.

"And Claude Monet..." said the man.

"Sad."

"Reduced at last to endless scenes of water lilies."

"Though at least he sold those."

"He did quite well, actually."

"Wh-what do you think of the others?" Emery interrupted. *Qu'est-ce que vous pensez des autres?* He hated the hesitation in his French. It had been so long.

"The others?" said the woman.

"Manet?" Emery said and swallowed, looked at her. "Or Berthe Morrisot?"

The man smiled slyly. "Manet was *not* an impressionist. He was himself." While the woman shook her head in disgust and looked past Emery with her smoky eyes as if he were not truly there. "We need to go!" she whispered at the man.

He shrugged at Emery, and led her out of the room.

Emery fought the urge in his chest to tear after them, grab them and *demand* that they tell him who they were and what they were doing here. Didn't they understand how he had once *worshiped* these painters? Even if he no longer aspired to be one of them, you couldn't just brush them aside, any of them. They were the building blocks, the firm foundations of *everything* in art.

He swallowed once, twice, stopped the shaking chill in his limbs, and strode after them.

But by the time he'd passed around the blocking partition in the next room that had a mid-room display of Sisley's works, the couple was gone.

And there, on the north wall was *Le Balcon*, "The Balcony", painted by Édouard Manet in 1868-1869, featuring a trio in formal nineteenth century garb just behind a balcony rail in what looked like French manor house, the foremost model being an attractive woman seated and staring out into the viewer's world with intense, oversized black eyes and thick black eyebrows. She had been both a talented painter and Manet's favorite model/sexual companion who was pressured to finally marry Manet's brother, Eugène. Her name – Berthe Morisot.

"Not an impressionist?" Emery muttered in English. "He and Berthe just made an impression on *me*."

Or some couple had.

They'd grabbed him, laughed at his needs, then vanished.

Feeling suddenly sick to his stomach, his arms and hands shaking, Emery strode through the Van Gogh room, not slowing for fear of running into further visions. He passed the Cézannes and Cailebottes and Boudins and Bazilles, striding faster and faster until he was almost running, knocking his way past people idling in the doorways, out into the stairwells. Down. To the last flight of stairs descending to the main atrium of the museum.

And it was like it was still a train station, but the trains were the statues and paintings, the artists were the passengers and conductors. There were too many of them. Didn't they understand that? Everywhere. Hundreds of artists from hundreds of years. Sweating and thinking, plotting, agonizing, arguing, committing, *creating*. All aboard! Don't get left behind! Look where we're going! And they all screeched and screamed at him now until even the air seemed to be moving and filled with the steamy heat of them.

Not enough air.

He had to find Violet.

He was choking. Suffocating.

Had to get out of here.

He ran for the stone stairs and leapt down them three at a time until he tripped over a young boy coming up and went somersaulting through the air like a man leaping to his death.

GAPS IN HIS MEMORY

In Emery's mind, the next thing that happened was boarding the TGV, *Train de Grande Vitesse*, at the *Gare de Lyon*.

Monet had done a painting of this train station, Emery remembered, looking from the trains and crowds and ubiquitous *patisserie* food shops up to the high, steel-girder-and-windows roof like a child. But it was older then.

No, Monet's station was the *Gare Sainte-Lazare*. But same thing. He'd tried to catch a train station filled with hissing steam and smoke. Impressions. Nothing clear. The truth was in the obscurity. All life was obscurity.

"That's how my mind feels right now," Emery said to no one in particular as he hoisted his heavy suitcase from the concrete to the steps of passenger car number three, then up the narrow steps inside to the top level of the train.

Behind him, his daughter, Violet, answered. "Like what, Daddy?"

He stopped and looked back. Of course she was there with him. She'd been with him all the time, hadn't she. It was the only way to explain how he'd gotten from tumbling down the steps of the

Musée d'Orsay to here. How he'd somehow bought tickets for this trip. Or had she bought them?

"I...am having a bit of a blank spot," he said. "Missing time."

She looked up at him sharply from where he'd trapped her on the stairs. "Keep going," she said quietly. Store your luggage on the racks up there and go to seat 329. I'll be right behind you."

Emery did, feeling foolish. Feeling old. Was this what Alzheimer's felt like? Not knowing where you were or where you'd been? Or had he hurt himself more than he'd thought in that tumble?

As he walked to his seat, he reached his hands up to his head and thought he felt a lumpy part around the back, but couldn't be sure. He wasn't in the habit of feeling the shape of his skull. He found his assigned seat and sat. Violet joined him a moment later.

"Now," she said after she'd stowed her smaller knapsack on the racks over the seats, "tell me what you don't remember. What time period?"

He frowned and thought hard. Realized he actually had wisps of post-fall memories. Someone carrying him to the front of the museum? Violet and a doctor, *un médecin.* A meal in a café. The computer-screen-lit darkness of an internet café with people playing video games, Violet...doing something. Booking tickets?

"Mostly...continuity," he said now. "I've got flashes of things, but no solid connections from the time I fell in the *Musée d'Orsay.*"

The train started up. They hadn't gotten here any too soon.

"The doctor said most of it should come back," Violet said. "You sustained a pretty bad concussion. You were knocked unconscious for a good ten to fifteen minutes. The doctor didn't do an MRI or anything, but he didn't think you'd suffer permanent damage."

She said it like a recitation.

"You've told me this before," Emery guessed.

"A few times. You seem to be getting increasingly with it, though. You want me to go over what's happened since you fell?"

"How about I tell *you* what I remember. Then you fill in the blanks."

She drew back her chin with a surprised smile. "Definitely an improvement. Okay. Shoot."

* * *

THE BACK and forth took most of two hours. By the end of it, Emery could almost feel his thoughts coming back together in his head like plops of wet sand or pudding splatting into place in his skull, creating a recognizable trail between the fall and here.

Even more, though, was this vague feeling that they were finally getting somewhere. Which was something, given he had no idea where that was.

"Where exactly are we going, Violet?" he finally asked directly.

"Aix-en-Provence."

"And staying where?"

She grinned like her mother used to grin when she had something particularly devilish up her sleeve. "I told you that was going to be a surprise."

"Which I don't get until I actually walk into the place?"

"Pretty much."

He tried to frown at her but it hurt too much, whether because of the mental or muscular effort he wasn't sure. Rather than push it, though, he took to staring out the window at the countryside rushing past. It could have been upstate New York, but without the mountains and streams. More pine. More stunted and twisted trees. More spread out and broken up by farmers' fields. And the houses were different, obviously. Endless little villages of square white stucco like the French only knew how to build one way. Always a church spire in there too. And it might have been his imagination, but the sky seemed to be getting bluer and brighter as they headed south.

Which was saying something. It had been over eighty degrees the whole time they'd been in Paris, and mostly sunny. But here there were no clouds or haze. Just sharp blue. Searing light. Trees etched against it like colored cutouts.

It was why, obviously, so many Parisian painters had headed to the south of France at one time or another in their lives. For the "different light", as Van Gogh had termed it. The dry, more consistent warmth too. Renoir, Picasso, Matisse, and Cézanne, among others, had chosen to spend their last days there.

"We could stay outside Cannes," he mumbled. "Lots of topless beaches down in Cannes."

"They have topless beaches everywhere, Dad. It's the French Mediterranean."

He turned his head, frowning. "Are you going to go topless at them?"

"Not with you there."

"Thank God."

He turned back to the window.

Later he said, "You mother used to make me eat ratatouille, heavy on the eggplant. She said it was a native dish of Provence."

"You don't have to eat *ratatouille*. Or *bouillabaisse*. Or *salade niçoise*. Or eel stew. Or *anchoïade*. I'm not my mother."

"What's *anchoïade*?"

"Crushed anchovies in olive oil. You serve it with vegetables. Very *provençal*."

Emery screwed up his face. "Now ratatouille doesn't sound so bad."

"Hey, if a Disney rat can cook it..."

"What?"

"Never mind."

Back to staring out the window.

Yet somehow, over the next hour and a half, with a short stop to drop some passengers in Marseille, Emery found himself talking more with Violet than he could remember doing the entire time he'd been in Paris with her. Hell, maybe more than the last three years...ten or fifteen years...of his life.

He found her to be whimsical but hard-headed, much like her mother had been. But both more idealistic and more cynical too. Which was a puzzle he brooded over during the last stretch between Marseille and Aix-en-Provence. He decided, with some pain, it was because Violet was simply more intelligent than Mattie had been.

Because Mattie, for all her musical sensitivity, hadn't read much. Nor had she paid much attention to politics. *"The French smoke and are depressed; Americans eat too much and think they deserve to run the world,"* had been pretty much the extent of her analysis..

Whereas Violet...

"The only thing," Violet had looked up from her French magazine to explode, "that's saving America from exploding like France is exploding—all these riots – the alienated youth and Muslims—is its size and diversity. No single group back home is big enough to band together and really shit disturb."

"African Americans?" Emery said.

"Sure. Except we've also got Mexicans, Natives, Chinese, the Japanese who were sent to internment camps in World War Two. And women, don't forget. Half the population. More. Still stuck battering at the omnipresent glass ceiling, eighteen million cracks in it or not. Oh, and Mormons and Catholics, Jews, our own Muslims, Christians. We've got so many damn disenfranchised, discriminated against, beaten down, mistreated groups that the idea any one of them can take over the national stage to complain for long is ludicrous."

"So America's happier than France because we have more unhappy groups of people."

"More stable," Violet said. "I never mentioned happy."

"Are you happy?"

She turned her head to look at him in surprise, but with something guarded in her eyes. "I'm...working at it."

"Good."

There was a long pause, then Violet asked, "When Mom was alive, before she got sick, were you happy?"

Emery was about to shoot back an automatic yes, but checked it, remembering his self-destructive period, times of struggle. He finally nodded. "Mostly."

"When you were doing your art?"

He looked into his lap and frowned. "Art's not about happiness." Then he jerked as he felt Violet's hand on his bare forearm. The touch sent such a crackling longing for Mattie through him that he had to turn his face away from her and stare out the window.

"What's it about then?" said Violet quietly behind him.

"I don't know."

"What did you *used* to think it was about?"

And Emery was thrown viscerally back in time to his struggles with darkness and light, heavy washes and smeared oils and turpentine, with transcendent heroes and heroines he felt forever compelled to insert, as if his time illustrating superhero comics in his late teens and early twenties had squeezed an unlimited supply of hero ink into his heart that leaked out into everything else he created.

But he didn't think it was the heroism he'd been after. Not really. It was something that heroes just happened to usually be part of. It was the essential struggle of life. It was good vs. bad. Creation vs. destruction. Healthy growth vs. the perversions of cancer and war. Hell, big vs. small.

"Struggle," he said at last.

He felt Violet turn away from him as if she believed. Or maybe in disappointment. Well fuck it. He was disappointed to. By himself. By life. By art.

"This sky is very blue," said Violet in Mattie's voice.

He didn't have the courage to turn and see whether it was his daughter speaking or his own madness.

Find it.

* * *

"THE TGV STATION'S actually a bit east of Aix-en-Provence," Violet explained when they debarked, slinging down one large suitcase and one smaller carry-on apiece. "So we won't see Aix today."

"We just grab a taxi to...where?"

She grinned and got him walking in through the high steel-and-glass station. "A little farm a bit east of Aix. Shouldn't take us more than about fifteen minutes."

"We're renting a house? Staying in a bed and breakfast?"

She pointed to the taxi signs and led him out the other side of the station to the line of them that were picking up people in the order that they came out. "We're *using* a house," she said. "The entire farm, in fact. It belongs to an artist named Claude Avrochet. He does mostly expressionist stuff, plus some of that weird *ordures accumulées* with—"

"I know. I've seen his work. He's obsessed with nature versus society. He's a favorite of Greenpeace."

"Oh. Okay. Have you met him?"

He held off answering for a moment as the family of three in front of them pulled away in a taxi, making the next one that pulled up theirs. They managed to squeeze their two big suit-cases and one carry-on in the trunk of what turned out to be a BMW. Their second carry-on went in the front seat beside the drive while Violet and Emery slid onto the leather seats in the back.

Violet pulled out a set of folded papers from her purse and read off the address to the driver, who punched it into his GPS. As they pulled away, Emery reached out and snatched the papers from his daughter's hand.

"These are from a house exchange site," he said.

She looked at him sideways, smiling but wary. "That's right."

"This is a house exchange."

"Yes."

"Meaning that we're taking over Avrochet's house..."

"And car, and cat, and garden plants, computer, phone. Everything."

"And he...?"

Violet looked at her watch. "Probably arrived at your lake house about two hours ago. Max would have been there to welcome him and make sure that the maid I hired put everything in good shape first. All your private stuff I made sure was locked in your downstairs den. The kitchen computer only works on a Guest account. All your files are protected but he can still use the internet."

"And my paints," Emery said slowly. "My studio. He's a painter."

"That's what sold him on the idea because his family—he has two school-aged children—had only done exchanges within France before. But he'd heard of you, knew your work, said he needed something drastic to shake up his own process. He needed a change of scene."

She'd blurted it out and now caught her upper lip with her teeth, holding her breath and watching him

And this time when Emery heard Mattie's voice in his head it was clearly a remembered one, no strangeness or insanity, but just as strong as if she'd been right there in the car with him, goosing him with her thumb as she liked to do.

You know it's always better to beg for forgiveness than ask permission.

To which he would always say, *What have you done now?* and cringe.

Then she would tell him. Once it was signing an agreement to purchase the lake house before he'd even had a chance to see it. Once it was committing them to host her extended French family there for a whole week. (They'd needed tents on the lawn, negotiations with the neighbors on the lake, a redone sceptic system beforehand.) Once, much further back, when they were still living in Brooklyn, she'd whispered in his ear in the middle of sex that she'd gone off her birth control two months before and she thought she was pregnant.

Pregnant.

That had made him more scared than anything in his life. And angry. Betrayed. He never thought he completely forgave her, in fact, until almost a year after Violet was born. By which time he was so in love with his little daughter that he could not recognize the man he'd once been, the one so set against ever fathering a child.

This child. The one right here, whom he'd virtually abandoned as she'd gotten older, then completely after Mattie's death, and who'd just paid him back by engineering the forcible ejection of him from his last safe place. *Better to ask forgiveness...*

"Okay," he said at last because there really wasn't anything else *to* say..

Violet burst out in a nervous laugh, hugged herself, grabbed his arm, and kissed him on the cheek so happily that the driver, Emery saw, smiled hugely in his rearview mirror, obviously listening along.

"Oh, Daddy!" Violet said. "I'm so glad. I so wanted to involve you in the planning but I didn't think you'd... The thing is I could never afford to swing this otherwise and Max agreed you had to get *out*, get somewhere else if you were ever going to paint again."

Ice shot through his veins and he peeled her fingers off his arm. "I'm not going to paint again."

Violet's hands shot to her mouth. "But... But... Avrochet's house, his studio..."

Emery shrugged but he turned from her to look out the car window. The highway they were on, the *Autoroute*, was in good shape, with signs whizzing by everywhere. They all said where you were going—*Bump. Swerve.*—but not where you were. And Every already knew where he was going. Nowhere. Age and death.

"I'll be curious to see his studio," Emery said. "I can still appreciate art. Some of it. I just don't create it anymore."

"But—"

"That part of my life is over." It came out so harsh that it almost scared *him.* He couldn't bear to see how it hit Violet. His daughter. Like her mother, always pushing at him, trying to get him to be something more than what he was.

All of a sudden Emery felt such a huge heaviness in his limbs that he was sure he was going to sink through the seat of the car, or at least pass out.

"Don't you see?" he whined softly at the window. "Mattie's gone. The struggle's done."

Only silence and the hum of the car's wheels answered him.

AVROCHET'S FARM

The "farm" was only that in the loosest of definitions. For however great a painter Claude Avrochet was—Emery's recollection of his work was, truth be told, pretty fuzzy, which didn't speak well of its quality—he was clearly not a ruler of the earth.

As the taxi jounced along the winding, poorly paved driveway overhung with what looked like endless scrubby pine trees, what Emery saw around him was gentle wilderness. The drive opened to a large gravel circle in front of the modest two-story, with a garden taking up a twenty-by-forty yard spread directly on the far side of it. A swath of sunflowers and shorter green plants – vegetable garden, not floral. Beyond it, trees and unmowed, uncultivated fields dipped and rose to a fence line maybe half a mile off. And flashes of blue where other houses or "farms" out here had swimming pools to cope with the heat.

When the taxi slowed to a stop, Emery handed Violet a sheaf of twenty-Euro bills with which to pay the driver, then he climbed out and walked up to the house proper.

More tangled trees and colorful, weedy underbrush, as well as a few beaten paths, wrapped around the far side of it, snugging in far too tightly for Emery's taste. The house itself followed the national blueprint he'd seen all the way here on the TGV. It was made of cinder block, wood, and white stucco. Anywhere from forty years old to a hundred and forty. Two stories, with small windows, all with blue-painted wooden shutters now shut against the sun. A chimney rose up the right-hand wall.

All in all a great place to play as a kid. A bucolic setting for an artist. But a farm? Hardly.

Then he stopped and shook his head, frowning hard to bring back what he'd seen but hadn't registered. It must have been something he'd glimpsed when he'd climbed out of the taxi?

Retracing his steps back to the taxi, he passed it and walked to the edge of the vegetable garden, the patch of sunflowers directly behind him. He looked at his watch. Six-thirty p.m. The sun was behind him. He felt it over his right shoulder. He was therefore looking east, maybe northeast. And there in the distance, with the late afternoon light giving it the same pale white-and-grey-under-blue he was so familiar with, lay perhaps the single most riveting symbol of artistic struggle ever.

It thrummed through him. It filled his lungs, his blood.

"Dad?" Violet calling him from somewhere. "Dad? I've got the key. *Monsieur* Avrochet mailed it to me two week ago. And I've paid the driver."

There was the thunk of a trunk lid closing, then a car door, and the sound of the taxi leaving. Still he didn't want to look away. Until Violet was standing right beside him, wrapping herself around his arm and looking in the direction he was looking.

And even then, it wasn't until he heard her deep sigh of appreciation that he made himself crack his neck to look down at her face.

"It's beautiful," she said. "Isn't it."

"The *Mont Sainte-Victoire*," he breathed, turning back to the singular humped vee in the distance, its long ridge-line spread out away from them like they were looking at the side of a giant rock wave that had rushed across the south French countryside towards the sea until it ground to a halt here. Permanently. "It's not just beautiful. It's what it represents."

"Which is?"

"It's Cézanne's. Paul Cézanne!"

"I know who Cézanne is, Daddy. He lived in Aix-en-Provence, right? That's what the place is known for."

Emery shook it away, shook her away so he could wave his hands as he spoke. "What *Cézanne* is known for is mostly two things – his apple still-lifes and this." He stabbed a finger through the air at the mountain as if he could touch it. "He traveled to the town of Le Tholonet, which must be out there in those hills, to paint the mountain over sixty times. In every light. Every style. It was his touchstone, the place he studied and recorded to see how his experiments with color and perspective were evolving. Like driving over and over and over again into a single place..." Emery found himself corkscrewing a shaking fist through the air ahead of him and stopped. "As if that would let him finally get to where he needed to be. To find or share what he sought after so long. Do you see?"

Violet was studying him with an expression somewhere between fear and awe, and Emery realized he was suddenly drenched in sweat. His forehead, his neck. His underarms were drenched and he knew he must smell awful and look crazy. All after he'd sworn he was *done* with painting.

But Cézanne's mountain! How could Violet have known to find them a place with a view of Cézanne's mountain? How could she know that the one thing she could do that might actually, in time, somehow penetrate the crusty webbing of sorrow and self-disgust that was wrapped around his heart, was this thing?

"Do you see?" he repeated.

"Maybe?" she said.

But she didn't. How could she? Even Emery didn't understand it. He just recognized in his gut suddenly how Cézanne's mountain had always been one of his own artistic touchstones. It represented truth, discovery, touching the divine. And the fact that they'd come here without him choosing, suggested a *calling*. Like the mountain needed him as much as he needed it.

Was this what he had felt in Paris? Had it been calling him even then?

He swiped a hand feverishly across his forehead and laughed, and Violet laughed with him.

"It's hot," he said.

"Shall we check out the house?"

"God, yes!"

And he stumbled, with her hands around his arm, up to the quaint little house of Claude Avrochet and family.

* * *

IT HURTS, goddamn it!

The mantra pounded over and over in his chest as he followed Violet around the house. Still sweaty and excited from the revelation of Cézanne's mountain, Emery had thought he'd fall in love with this house. It was all meant to be.

Instead, from the moment Violet had to struggle with the front door lock, jiggling and pulling on it until they were both afraid the front door handle would break off, Emery's conviction of destiny was sucked away and fear rushed in to fill its place.

Understanding joined it when he stepped inside. Because it was like he'd seen this house before. It was all the pictures of Mattie's childhood house. It was the house her parents had moved to after she'd left home, that she and Emery had visited on their honeymoon, both dead broke and seeing Europe like a couple of college kids, staying in dorms, taking the train, sleeping on beaches and in hostels.

The tile floors everywhere. Cool underfoot. With heavy wooden shutters on everything the sun hit, because there is no central air, just a big fireplace in the living room for the middle of winter when things get cool. And the beds—there were three bedrooms each with their own bed in the tiny house—were solid wood with lumpy mattresses and huge quilt covers over the sheets.

Emery remembered what it was like to snuggle under those, get burning hot, throw them off and freeze in the night air...and snuggle into Mattie's neck until she too woke up and they made love, holding in their grunts and sighs.

It hurts to be here. It hurts.

"They left a welcome basket!" Violet said, drawing his attention to the dining room table just off the kitchen. A large basket of fruit and a bottle of champagne sat on the middle of the rickety-looking table, on a red napkin with frayed edges that had been spread out like a doily. Beside it were a pile of fanned-out books and magazines.

Emery and Violet walked over together and, when Emery couldn't bring himself to shake off his tension, Violet picked up the card from the top of the fruit basket and read it aloud.

In an almost calligraphic French hand, it read:

WELCOME, Lakes!

We are so charmed to be having you in our home. We hope your stay will be one of relaxing and discovery also. The books and maps are of the Provence area and further around it. To explore it, our car, a Renault car, is in the garage beside the house. The key is in one of the kitchen drawers.

We have left a plastic covered sheet beside each appliance, like the dishwasher, to help you in its operation.

The big garbage can is in the garage. You must take it to the end of the long driveway for it to be collected. This is on Wednesday morning before 0700.

A family friend, Charlotte Boulain, can answer any questions about the house and area. She is very south of France style, full of ideas. You can call her from the black phone in the kitchen (no charge when calling inside France) at 06 22 03 13 99.

Violet, may your dreams come true.

Emery, may you find comfort in the beauty of our land.

A+

Claude, Aimee, Jolie, and Luc

"A-PLUS?" Emery said when she'd finished.

Violet smiled and laid the letter down again beside the fruit. "Claude said it's a French expression like 'Talk to you later.'"

"Your mother never used that."

"Mom left home when she was, what? Seventeen? Maybe she just never learned it."

"Right. Because it's the sort of thing only older French people would know."

He turned from her sourly, still fighting waves of sorrow that were washing over him so unrelentingly he thought he'd choke. Coming here was supposed to have gotten him *away* from those feelings, but instead everything, even the quaint French note, seemed to laugh at him and twist another knife into the gaping wound in his heart where Mattie had once lived.

"Okay," muttered Violet behind him. "Okay." He heard her turn and open wide the double French doors that led, with little floor transition, from the tiled dining room to the tiled back patio, as if those doors were usually open and the inside and outside were one.

The outside air drifted in around him and he caught flashes of color in her wake. Bunches of purple hyacinths? Jasmine? Scents of dry grasses and pine trees. A cluster of wild pink orchids.

The trees cocooning the back of the house, he also noted, weren't quite as close in as he'd thought. Those twisty-limb ones had to be olive trees. The taller ones were oak. But mostly it looked like pine everywhere. The wild bushes and flowers were thick amidst them.

The patio, meanwhile, ran as a ten yard strip of flagstones across the back of the house, half shaded by a dark green awning that was held up by metal poles planted into permanent holes drilled through the tile-and-concrete slab of the patio.

More chairs and smaller tables out there, along with an above-ground round swimming pool just beyond the patio. Twelve foot diameter? More for kids than adults. The pine trees had to be constantly dropping needles and cones into it.

"Dad, come and look at this!"

Violet. Emery followed her voice out the back doors and to the right, to a second large building that had not been visible from the front of the house.

The simple wooden door stood open and Emery stopped in front of it, feeling the musty heat of the enclosed space pouring out at him. Then he held his breath in fear and walked in.

Justified fear.

For beyond the simple vestibule, defined by an ancient armoire for winter coats and boots and hats, maybe gloves and scarves in the winter, was a single large room about twenty feet high. Also about twenty-five by twenty-five feet square, with a large bank of windows on both the east and west walls, half of them open just a crack to allow some air to circulate. Even shaded as it was by the trees surrounding it, the studio's heat was stifling, thick with the smell of dust and turpentine

Avrochet's studio where he would paint, sculpt, whatever. His *atelier*.

An artist's studio.

A workplace. Place of creation. So alike, in some ways, to where Emery used to paint in the lake house.

Used to.

How did that make him feel?

He expected his throat to close up in panic, for the pain he'd felt in the house to somehow redouble and prove out his fears. But strangely, none of that happened. Instead, a kind of nerve-dead lassitude fell upon him like the cocoon around his heart had spread. Maybe from the heat? From what Violet was doing?

She'd extended her hands down and out from her side and was turning in a slow circle, looking up at the ceiling, sweat beginning to bead around her hairline. Emery looked up too and saw that the high ceiling had been painted with remarkably life-like branches and needles and leaves that crawled all the way down to the tops of the high east and west windows and seemed to blend seamlessly with the trees and bushes outside. Translucent light effects. Avrochet had probably used acrylic paint thinned to watercolor consistency. A broad ceiling fan and light fixture hung lost in the center, virtually invisible against the backdrop of the painted canopy.

"Hunh," Emery grunted.

"I love it!" said Violet.

But Emery was more interested in what the man put on his canvases than on his ceiling. He'd noted automatically when he'd entered that on the north wall through which they'd entered, beside the sink and small closed room which Emery assumed contained a toilet, a high set of covered racks had been installed to hold finished works. Or those plus works-in-progress, depending on Avrochet's work habits.

Shaking his head over how Avrochet risked his works in this hot weather, Emery first returned to the door and hunted until he found the switch that turned on the ceiling fan. Then, as the air began to circulate and cool, he returned to the racks of paintings. With a long-trained habit of respect, Emery lifted out one, then another of Avrochet's paintings and lined them up against the west wall. He slanted them so that the remaining bright sun of the day, already filtered through the trees surrounding the studio, would hit the paintings only indirectly, from above.

All oils. And they apparently formed a series. Or a singular preoccupation at least, an idea Avrochet needed to explore over and over.

The subjects were a nude woman—it was probably his wife, Aimee, given her resemblance to a number of other paintings Emery had subconsciously noted on the interiors walls of the house proper; she was an attractive, small-breasted woman with short-cropped, auburn hair—and electronic bits and pieces, that looked ripped from the innards of a very old computer, or maybe a CD player. The nude woman fondled and clutched at the circuit boards, the wires dangling everywhere. Here they looked like stray umbilical cords, as if the woman had just given birth. There they looked like intestines, like she was holding a murdered child or lover or just *parts* of her lover.

The pieces of junked technology were strewn about the broad table by the east wall. There, a large, modeled figure of the woman in the paintings clutched smaller pieces of circuits and wires. As did a wooden carving and some kind of wire-frame figure that ironically clutched a fuzzy teddy bear.

Violet laughed nervously as her eyes swept from the table items back to the paintings. She wiped the sweat from her forehead.

"And I thought the stuff *you* painted when Mom was dying was creepy."

"He's very thorough," Emery said.

"But not good?"

Emery cocked his head, unable to decide. Once upon a time, he believed he knew good from bad, just as he knew right from wrong, truth from lie, reality from hallucination. But now, even here, in the nexus of the world's artistic consciousness, the shadow of the Mont Sainte-Victoire, everything seemed blended together for him and judgements loosened. Once you showed a certain basic artistic competence – an understanding of proportion, color, light, perspective, form – who was to judge whether your creation, your judgement and interpretation of reality was objectively better or worse than any other competent artist's?

Was there a way to judge?

"What do you think?" he said finally. "Does it make you feel?"

Violet laughed and wrapped her hands around herself, clutching her bare arms as if suddenly chilled. "Yeah. Uncomfortable. Like I'm not eager to sit down at a computer any time soon. Mind you that's probably partly because I tried turning on their computer—it was in one of the kids' rooms—and it's pretty ancient. But it's worse here. It's like he wants to graft his wife to something ugly *and* obsolete."

Emery grimaced. "Maybe good, then. I don't know."

"How would *you* do it?"

He looked at her, feeling the clank in his gut that he knew was the anger he was supposed to feel. He'd *told* her he wasn't going to paint again.

But it was a distant clank, dulled by this dreamy feeling that he was somehow caught up in this artistic vortex that didn't allow him to feel yet, just to see, smell, hear, feel, appreciate. Accept?

"It's not something I would ever have painted."

"But if you did?"

He tilted his head and felt the distant clank in his gut again. Vortex or no, fellow artist or no, this artist was no soul mate of Emery. He casually spat on the floor of the studio. "I would have gone blind first."

He turned and walked out of the studio.

Violet burst into sobs behind him.

SEEKING THE MOUNTAIN

The next morning, Emery woke to the sound of church bells and his head spun with confusion.

The smells were wrong, like patchouli or incense. The walls, all ragged-on yellow and orange. The window, small, peeling white paint, open wide to the cool morning. The sound of someone downstairs clanking metal. Metal in his gut. Anger. The vortex.

He kicked off the light quilt and almost fell out of bed onto the tiled terra cotta floor as everything came rushing back. Everything.

Violet.

His heart sped up like a flywheel as he staggered to his feet and remembered how he'd spat and walked away from her yesterday only to hear her burst into tears behind him. He'd stopped just outside the studio door, listened to her sob, and knew then he should go back in and apologize, when all he wanted to do was run away, out through the trees, to the road, back to Paris, to the airport, onto a plane. To home. Home. God, take him back to Mattie.

But he'd just stood and listened to his daughter's heart breaking. Five minutes. Ten. Until she'd finally pulled herself together with sniffs and the sounds of rustling through the studio washroom for toilet paper to blow her nose in.

Emery had walked away before she came out and pretended to be unpacking his things in his room when she came into the house. She'd nodded at him dully and he suddenly intuited what she'd felt in the studio. Pain. Despair. Things ended that could never be put right again. Her hope had finally been crushed as flat as his, drained away so she was only a husk as he was only a husk. Enduring this time with him. That's what dinner had been. She'd gone out shopping and brought back food. Cooked up some hamburgers and they'd eaten in silence. Watched some French t.v., poor reception. Gone to bed, each to their own room.

That was all they had now. Enduring.

It was unbearable.

The flywheel of his heart pounded so hard against his ribs he thought they might crack. The muscles of his chest wall strained in pain. His face flushed. His mouth went dry. He wondered if he was having a heart attack.

Yet he didn't collapse. He could still suck in breath. So he stood there, sucking air hard in and out with his too-flabby belly. And he thought about what to do.

Go to Violet, obviously. Apologize.

And tell her what? He was sorry her mother was dead and her father had given up?

No. She knew that. It was what was killing her.

Too young. She was too young to die like that. He could hear Mattie now, screaming at him to save their daughter that fate.

Easy for her to say. She was dead. And she'd always been closer to Violet. She would have known what to do.

"Dad! Eggs!" Violet. Calling from downstairs. The clanking metal. She'd made breakfast.

Which meant she was probably fine, right? She'd bounced

right back like Mattie had always bounced back after one of their fights or a difficult performance, a difficult week. Violet took after her mother that way. None of the brooding that Emery was prone to.

Emery nodded to himself, scooted around the bed to the set of open shelves Avrochet or someone had built into the wall between what was probably the chimney duct and the window wall. There Emery had unpacked all his clothes, since there wasn't a chest of drawers in the room.

He chose a baggy blue polo shirt and pulled on some fresh underwear and his khaki traveling shorts from yesterday.

He went downstairs in his bare feet, the tile cool and a bit gritty underfoot.

"Smells good," he said with forced energy.

"Orange juice too." She wasn't buying his fakery. Or simply couldn't. Her own voice sounded flat and tired and she wasn't looking at him.

"Just let me pee and wash my hands."

He used the small bathroom they had downstairs, just off the kitchen, and when he came back, Violet already had everything on the table. One setting.

"You ate already?" he said.

"Wasn't hungry."

"Hunh."

He ate his eggs and tried to show he was enjoying them by grunting and sighing with each bite and sip of juice. But he could think of nothing to actually say. What little conversational fluency he and his daughter had discovered on the train yesterday morning had vanished again.

When he was done, she took his plate, glass, and utensils and loaded them in the tiny dishwasher beside the sink. Then she wiped the table and tiled kitchen countertops.

"So...uh...what were you going to do today?" Emery said.

"I signed up for a cooking class in Aix," she said, still not looking at him.

"Starting today? Sunday?"

"No. On Tuesday. I figured I'd take the car in today and find out how to get there. Maybe look around."

She didn't ask him to come, he noticed.

"Did you want to come along?" she mumbled. "If you wear a nicer shirt."

"Um..." Strangely, he did want to come. To see the studio where Cézanne had spent his final days, if nothing else. He remembered reading that some rich American had rescued it and it had been preserved just as it had been in his last days of painting. That would have been interesting, to step back into the era of that great man. To try to imagine what it would have been like to have visited the taciturn old artist when he was alive. He would even change into a slimmer, more fashionable shirt to do that.

But seeing a studio was not what Violet was talking about doing in Aix-en-Provence, was it. And the small part of him that remembered exactly what had happened in the Musée d'Orsay had the niggling fear that if he stepped inside Paul Cézanne's studio today, he just might see the man himself, dead over a century and none the worse for it.

No, better to answer the call of the vortex by going to the mountain itself, not some obvious shrine to its painter.

"I...think I'll just hang out here for the day," he said. "I might go for a walk out across the fields."

Violet said nothing. She just stared at the tiled counter for a minute. Then she draped her wet washcloth over the tap, nodded, and scraped open a drawer that was part of where the kitchen counter jutted out to define its space from the rest of the dining and living area. "There's an extra house key in here. Also one for the studio. If you go out for any length of time, you should probably lock up."

"Okay."

Her face squinched up like she'd just identified something ugly on the countertop. "Right." She walked out of the kitchen to the front door and picked up her purse that she'd left sitting on a folding chair there. "See ya," she said, and left.

She hadn't looked at him once.

* * *

IT WAS BETTER with her gone, Emery thought guiltily as he left the house, locked it behind him, and shoved the key into a front pocket of his blue jeans.

He'd changed from shorts to jeans because he'd remembered the grass beyond the vegetable garden looked long and spiky. Ideally he'd have his hiking boots too, but the idea of wearing hiking boots to the south of France had just never occurred to him.

Running shoes would have to do.

Better with Violet gone because he could now just wear his comfortable clothes and focus his senses on the calling he felt from the mountain. The artistic *vortex*.

What did that mean? Sheer curiosity? Yesterday he'd been sure it was destiny, something supernatural calling to him. Today that seemed foolish, but there was still an urgency that drove him.

He strode out through the loamy smell of the vegetable garden, noting in passing the tomatoes, lettuce, something that looked like it might become string beans, and of course the unbearably cheerful rectangle of half-grown sunflowers taking up the south-eastern-most corner, all their heads pointed vaguely south like they'd figured this was the best position for a suntan.

The last thing he almost tripped over as he passed the sunflowers was a set of pipes and hoses. Automatic irrigation. Of course. Good. Good. One less thing to worry about.

Then he was plunging through the long grass, eyes fixed on Sainte-Victoire's glorious crest of rock ahead.

It made him stumble again, a number of times, as he missed stones and hidden dips, but the ground was surprisingly flat over-all. And his legs, aided by an excitedly thumping heart, kept powering him on like nothing could stop him.

He climbed a couple wood fences.

He crossed a road bordered by telephone poles. Another without.

He circumnavigated two large private properties with swimming pools and impressive grounds.

He hit a stream and wandered south along it until it became narrow enough and filled with rocks that he could cross over.

He walked through a long stretch of pine forest that seemed to bend the light as it filtered through the branches and came out to cross ploughed fields of red earth, then some planted with vines whose grapes were just starting to bud. He startled up a murder of screeching crows who'd obviously not been frightened by what-ever scarecrow or other device the farmer here used to keep them off.

Finally, as his stomach told him he'd wandered well past his lunch hour, he came upon a mortar-free stone wall that ran left and right a fair way and rose over six feet, broken every twenty yards or so by a wooden gate. Pulling himself half up it, Emery saw a small town spilling out from the other side. Could this be Le Tholonet, where Cézanne spent so much time painting the Saint-Victoire? His recollection of the area and his eyeballing of the route before he started walking put the town roughly between the Avrochet farm and the mountain. But it had also been circled with paved roads, part of the big deification of Cézanne the whole are had done in preparation of the hundredth anniversary of the man's death a few years back.

The town directly in front of Emery wasn't that. On this side of the wall, for instance, was just a beaten dirt path that probably served as a rear driveway for the houses in front of him. It wound down to the right and climbed a gradual slope to the left.

The downslope, he guessed, would lead him into the town proper where he could find food.

And other people.

Tourists.

Emery turned left and began climbing as his stomach rumbled. Soon there were no more gates, just the ever-climbing walled path which looked like it kept climbing for at least another couple hundred yards or so.

Emery's stomach rumbled again and he was about to turn back when he realized he was no longer alone.

Strolling down the stony red dust from higher up the path was a short, burly youth of seventeen or eighteen. He was deeply tanned and deeply Mediterranean, with coal-black hair and eyes and a sly grin as he approached, puffing a small, hand-rolled cigarette. Over worn brown boots and pants, his cotton shirt was unbuttoned nearly to his navel. He'd rolled his shirtsleeves up above his elbows. Clutched under his right arm, he carried a folder filled with loose papers. Over that arm's shoulder he also wore a small black sack on a long string that hung just below his hand and swung as he walked like a sexual statement.

Not exactly a thug or physically imposing, Emery thought, but he still looked dangerous. It was in the calculated swagger of his walk and the way he sucked at his cigarette and studied Emery from head to toe, like the boy had a switchblade hidden on him and was figuring out how to use it. And here they were, far from any other human being who could hear Emery if he cried out. So Emery smiled back cautiously, made sure his house key was deep in his front jeans pocket, and slowed as the youth approached.

Then Emery felt his heartbeat increase exponentially for another reason entirely. The thick, coal-black hair that was still parted in the middle so it fell down around the youth's jug-like ears had thrown Emery off. But now, seeing the broad nose and broad face up close, feeling the power of that basilisk stare that would one day be famous throughout the art world, Emery swallowed dryly.

He recognized this boy.

It was a young Pablo Picasso.

THE GYPSY

"Beunos días!" said the youth. Then, seeing Emery's reaction, took out his cigarette with two fingers and tried a rather mangled, *"Bonjour!"*

Emery answered in French, trying not to stare. It could not, of course, be Pablo Ruiz Picasso. The great man had been dead almost forty years. And this was just a cocky boy. Young man? *Boy.* Why would Emery's insanity bring him Picasso as a boy? And why, for God's sake, if such a breach in reality were permitted, would his mind not at least have let Picasso speak English?

The simple answer? Emery wasn't crazy. This was real. And this was not Picasso, just a Spanish tourist who resembled the man.

So Emery spoke French slowly, interspersing English and the little Spanish he knew when the two of them reached an impasse.

"It is a beautiful day," he said.

"Yes. You are going where?" demanded the young man.

Emery waved a hand vaguely towards the Sainte-Victoire. "Just walking. You?"

"Just walking also."

"And sketching?" Emery pointed at the boy's folder of paper.

The boy smiled slyly and inclined his head so his heavy mop of black hair fell down over his eyes. He flicked it back like a bullfighter adjusting his cloak.

"May I see?" Emery could hardly slow the beating of his heart enough to breathe as he asked.

Again the sly look, but a proud one too, as if he'd have been offended *not* to have been asked. With a swaggering turn that puffed up his chest, the boy flicked away his nearly-spent cigarette, swung his black sack off his shoulder, and flipped out his folder of sketching papers from under his arm. With supreme self-confidence he proffered the folder to Emery.

Hands shaking, Emery took it, noting its real heft, the feel of the cracked leather under his fingers, the substance of it, stronger than he recalled from any dream.

He opened the cover and, prepared to gasp, instead issued a sigh of relief. For the sketches inside, of trees, houses, a working man, an automobile in a driveway, were nothing but well-crafted. The youth clearly had talent and had studied his craft, but there was certainly nothing here that jumped out and said "genius." Nothing that proved him to be whom he certainly could not be.

Reassured, Emery closed the folder and passed it back to the boy. "They're very good. Well executed."

Turning up his nose like he'd been mortally insulted, the boy sniffed and stared at Emery with his coal black eyes. "You think to judge my work?"

"It is only my reaction."

"And you are?"

"An artist," Emery blurted. "And you?"

"An artist."

"Who does not yet sign his name to his work."

"Perhaps I am still searching for my name."

Emery studied him closely, wondering again despite himself. "What do people call you?"

The youth narrowed his own eyes at Emery, then looked off at the Sainte-Victoire and back over his shoulder at the direction from which he'd come. "Gypsy!" he said with sudden decision, showing a flash of yellow teeth. "That is who I am. A gypsy who wanders with no attachment. A man who can seek the truth and find it in the smallest of things."

"Gypsy." Emery smiled. Hadn't Picasso spent some time living in a cave with a gypsy boy when he was a teen? In Spain. He later called it the turning point in his life. This boy must have heard the same story.

"Do you laugh at me?" said the boy, suddenly flushing red and bunching his free hand into a fist.

Emery held up both hands in a placating gesture. "No. I don't laugh anymore. At anyone."

The boy strained in place, still red faced, unsure what to do with that. Finally he unclenched his fist and sniffed, looked over at the Sainte-Victoire, and nodded. "You are looking for him too, are you not?"

"Who?"

"The master of Aix – Mr. Cézanne."

"Paul Cézanne." It was such a weird echo of the conversation he'd had just yesterday with his daughter that Emery blinked and rubbed at his head.

"He is the key to the future, yes?" said the gypsy boy and made a corkscrew motion with his free hand not unlike the fevered one Emery had made for Violet yesterday.

"The key," Emery said stupidly.

"The...how do you say?...turning point for all painters. For me. For you, yes? I have heard he comes out here to paint sometimes. Also sometimes his friends..."

"His friends?" Emery felt swooning sick suddenly, like the heat that had been prickling his scalp and underarms had suddenly hit his brain.

"The romantic, Renoir. The crazy man, Van Gogh. And soon, me, the gypsy!"

"And you, Pablo Ruiz," Emery said, surrendering to it and stumbling a bit. Someplace to sit. There had to be a rock, a fallen tree...

"I am the Gypsy! That is all I am!"

Emery stepped off the path to lean against the crooked trunk of a pine tree so that the shade of its branches shielded his big body from the sun. "I doubt that being a gypsy is what your mother, Doña Maria, or your father, Don José, wanted for you."

The boy bared his teeth and said nothing.

"Why did you really come here?" Emery pressed. "Why are you in France now. You are too young. You are supposed to still be in...where? Madrid? Malaga? Barcelona? The art school there."

"They taught me *nothing* there. All of them – usless!"

"Except...except..." Emery racked his brains. It had been too long since he'd read about the man. Too long and too far away to... "Casamegas."

"Carles?"

"Yes. Another painter. The two of you...you studied Nietzsche together. *The Will to Power.*" Details came flooding back to Emery from somewhere. "Yes. Then Casamegas's lover left him and he shot himself in the head. And your painting of his corpse was so powerful, just his head, with the candle behind, all the early influences of the impressionists making it pop with color..."

He finally stopped as he saw the boy's pallor.

"I'm...I'm sorry," Emery said. "I don't know what I'm saying. Just an old book I read somewhere."

"When?" said the boy, his outthrust lower lip trembling. "Where?"

"Where what?"

"You are a prophet? A seer? Or are you death itself? Why have you come to meet me here?"

He was backing away from Emery now, up the slope he'd just walked down. All his earlier bravado had fled and he quivered like the youth he was. With great effort, Emery pushed himself away from the tree and staggered back to the main path.

"Wait!" he called. "Don't go! I have questions to ask you! I need to understand why you changed your art from that"—he jabbed a finger at the art folder the boy carried—"to...all the other things it becomes! I need to understand!"

"You talk like a demon!" shouted the boy who called himself gypsy as he retreated faster.

"I'm just a man!"

"Then you shall not catch me!"

"Just wait, son! Calm down! Please! Just—"

But even as the dizziness Emery had felt finally left him, the boy turned and ran, up the hill, angling right, out of sight around a corner.

Emery stood in the middle of the path, a stone wall to his right, scrub, trees and bramble to his left. Then, against his better judgement, he jogged up the path after the boy.

He reached the turn and stopped, panting, because the hill had topped out. Here the stone wall disappeared and all of the valley over to the Sainte Victoire was spread out in the midday glare before him. The path leading down the hill and every house and road and tree seemed etched in its own colors, amazingly distinct.

There was no boy in sight.

"Damn it."

Emery stood, shaking with sweat, belly sick and still light-headed from the sun. He could feel the skin of his nose starting to burn.

"Damn it," he repeated.

A breeze stirred around him and he felt something on his leg.

He looked down to see a paper wrapped around it and he snatched it up before it fell off again to be blown away.

It was one of the boy's drawings, done in various grades of pencil, which had no doubt been the contents in the swinging sack he'd carried. The picture was of a hiking man wearing jeans, runners, and a baggy blue polo shirt. He walked beside a stone wall and looked hemmed in by it. Defeated.

Emery jerked his eyes up from the drawing to look back down the path to the exact stretch of wall the boy had captured. It had to have been from about here that the boy had seen him hiking and understood instinctively how pathetic it was.

And sketched him so fast?

And left *this* sketch for him to find?

"No, please, God," he whispered without knowing exactly why. He swiped at the moisture leaking from his eyes. "Where do I go?"

Carefully rolling the sketch by the gypsy boy who *could* not have been who he was, Emery finally turned and began trudging back down the path the way he had come. He passed the point where the gypsy had sketched him and walked faster, then faster still until he had to break into a jog, then a pell-mell run down the hill, almost missing where he had come onto the path, the dusty red field he'd walked through to get here.

Emery turned off on it, stumbling as he tromped over uneven clumps of dirt and stones, back through the dusty vineyard, the needle-and-twig-floored forest, on and on. By the time he hit the gurgling river and where he'd crossed, he felt weak from walking and sun and hunger. He slipped on the rocks as he crossed and fell face-down into what turned out to be a stream bottom with mud, banging a knee and scraping up his hands. Too tired even to curse, he sloshed his way out, flicked his wet hair from his eyes, and kept going.

The country mansions with their swimming pools. The roads and the telephone poles. Another field.

He almost thought himself lost, feeling like he was so disconnected from the world that he couldn't possibly have found his way back, when he saw the cluster of sunflowers that marked the edge of the Avrochet garden.

But even as his heart swelled with an overwhelming sense of relief that threatened to bring tears again, he lurched to a stop.

Listened.

No. Not possible.

The sound, faint on the afternoon breeze, was unmistakably a flute, played with great purity and sensitivity. It was coming from the Avrochet home, around back.

Mattie.

It had to be Mattie.

His heart welling up yet again, and full knowing that he must certainly be crazy or have died somewhere back in the stream, Emery began to run through the garden and around to the rear of the house.

CHARLOTTE

The French doors were wide open to the patio and Emery ran to
them, then into the main living space.

He stopped, eyes wide, breathing hard.

Two women sat in the room. One was Violet, sitting on a chair
facing his direction, and her face was so enraptured by the flute
playing of the woman who had her back to Emery that Violet
barely looked up when he ran in.

Which means Violet sees *her*, Emery thought wildly. *She* sees *her!*

Then the flute playing stopped mid-phrase. The flautist
lowered her instrument and turned her body in the chair to
see him.

And for just a second it was Mattie, back from the dead, never
dead, never sick. It was Mattie, the love of his life and everything
was going to be alright. The whole business about her becoming
sick and dying and him losing it, seeing dead painters – that had
never happened.

For just a second.

Then Emery blinked his still stream-dirty eyelids and saw that
he didn't know this woman at all. She was taller than Mattie and

less buxom, at least proportionally. She had finer, lighter-colored hair, almost dirty blond, and she wore it pulled back in a ponytail behind her, something that Mattie had sworn she would never do and never make Violet do. And her skin was the color of the south of France, dark tanned, with full lips and big teeth and many wrinkles around the eyes as she smiled at him now.

"*Monsieur Lake!*" French of course. She turned back to Violet just enough to hand her the flute, which Violet began hastily disassembling and cleaning. Putting away.

It was Mattie's flute.

Violet had brought Mattie's flute to France.

And just now she'd loaned it to a total stranger.

The stranger stood smoothly, with a Grace Kelly turn. She smoothed down her business-gray skirt and straightened her white blouse and collar with no self-consciousness at all before she offered her hand.

"*Je vous en prie,*" she began and continued in French. "I am Charlotte Boulain. I was the nanny for Jolie and Luc when they were young. Claude and Aimee asked me to come by and welcome you to their home. I would have come yesterday, but Saturdays are a very busy day for me."

Emery just stared, then at Violet, still trying to process everything.

"Is there a problem?" the woman named Charlotte said. Her hand was still extended towards Emery.

"You were playing my late wife's flute," he said.

"Oh. I didn't know that."

She dropped her hand and turned towards Violet, who cringed back in her seat and shrugged with a half-hearted smile. "I'm sorry, Daddy," Violet said.

"Why did you bring it?"

"I thought...if I had a lot of time here...I might..."

"You don't even play piano anymore." He said it accusingly, he realized. Bitter. Like her giving up music was a betrayal of her mother. Did he really believe that?

"I know," Violet said. "I *know*. You know she left *me* the flute, though, right? In her will?"

"I was there."

"So...I should be able to bring it with me...here. If I want. Or let someone else play it."

Emery swiveled back towards the new woman. Charlotte. That was her name, right? She was entirely too composed, standing between him and Violet, watching them both with interest. "Are you a professional flautist?" he demanded.

She smiled and showed her overfull mouth of white teeth again. "How kind of you to suggest so. No. I play for pleasure. Though my own flute is an alto, not a concert flute. Your *daughter's* flute is a very fine instrument."

He heard the gentle rebuke in the tone and narrowed his eyes at her. "I guess."

"And I think perhaps this is not the best time for me to be visiting."

"Oh, *now* you're getting squeamish?"

She smiled again, genuinely amused, apparently, because her eyes crinkled up and she looked ready to laugh. "Not about you and the flute, Monsieur Lake. Not at all. It is a beautiful instrument your daughter offered me a chance to play. I'm glad I was able to play it well. No, I'm sorry but I need to leave because you stink."

"What?"

"Sorry. Perhaps that's my southern French. I mean that you smell bad. I don't know what happened to you. I suppose it might have been awful. But whatever you fell in, it has left you smelling like a farmer's field. You need a bath."

Emery's jaw dropped and he looked down at himself, still damp from his fall in the stream and streaked with dried mud. His running shoes had gone from a multi-colored white to something grey and black. Maybe coated with cow dung. He'd been out tramping through or near the stuff quite a few hours.

"I guess...a shower...," he mumbled.

Another laugh from the Charlotte woman. "A hand shower, of course. Claude has never built a standing shower. He is old French."

Then she turned from him, apparently finding the whole situation very amusing. "Violet, it was so charming to meet you. You must play your mother's flute for me sometime. Perhaps we could do a duet. You know if you have any questions at all, or would just like some company traveling about Aix, you just need to call."

Violet had risen and taken both of Charlotte's hands with her own. The mother-daughter-style tableau sent a sharp pain lancing through Emery's chest and he stomped past them, heading for the stairs and the bathroom on the second floor.

Yet even as he stripped off his filthy clothes and climbed into the cold steel of the large, claw-foot tub, he found himself thinking about Charlotte, contrasting her almost unwillingly, with Mattie.

Mattie would never have picked up a stranger's flute in a stranger's house and played it like that. Without rehearsal. Without knowing the instrument. Because while Mattie had been strong in so many ways – always standing up to Emery's bluster, sure of her sex appeal, able from the time she was little to demand her own way – it had always been with a fiery bravado closer to the gypsy youth's than Charlotte's centered calm. And it had always fled completely when it came to her art, her music. That was her sweet brilliance, her vulnerability. Emery believed, in fact, that it was this exceptional vulnerability, her letting down of all defenses to the world, that had made her the musical genius she was.

And Charlotte?

Emery had settled down in the steel surrounds of the tub that, even now in the mid-afternoon heat, was cold and hard under his bum. He turned the spout control to the handheld shower attachment, turned the water taps on full, and adjusted the spray of water to lukewarm.

Charlotte...

He was grimly amused to see himself half-erect and began vigorously spraying himself down. It probably meant nothing other than that Charlotte Boulain had triggered visceral memories of Mattie. Still a surprise, though. His near-clinical depression since Mattie's death had killed his libido. The flirtations of the occasional women he'd met when he'd gone into town these last three years—they recognized him, he supposed from the various photo articles that had been done about him—had mostly angered him.

He slammed off the water and soaped himself down, slowing not at all for the collection of scratches and purpling bruises he'd picked up on his hike. He shampooed his hair with the fruity stuff Violet always bought for him. Lathered. Finally turned the hand shower back on and sprayed all the soap and shampoo away.

Charlotte...

There was a pounding on the bathroom door. *"Dad?"*

He shut off the shower and called through the door. "What?"

"I persuaded Charlotte to change her mind and stay. She's offered to drive us around the area, show us the small towns near here, all northeast of Aix."

Emery almost dropped the hand shower. It was too much like his experiences with the dead artists. He wanted something to happen and it did. He wanted to see someone and they appeared. It was like his whole illustration and painting career. He imagined something and it would come into being.

A picture.

A comic book adventure.

A painting.

His wife.

His fortune.

Now...dead artists and sexual tour guides.

But only the artists maybe had something to work with. Or not, since he'd told Violet he would never draw or paint again. Either way, he'd definitely decided he would never touch another woman, never kiss one or hold one in his arms again.

"Dad?" His daughter's voice through the door dropped low and quiet so he could barely hear. "Please come."

With an oddly shaky hand, he smoothed his wet hair from his eyes and nodded to the room. "Give me five minutes," he said.

WHEN HE FINALLY JOINED THE two women downstairs, he was back in his khaki shorts and wearing a loose, powder-blue linen button-down shirt that he forced himself not to tuck in. He'd shaved quickly, put on his sandals, and combed his still-damp hair—where had all those little streaks of gray come from?—with just a dab of gel to help keep it in place.

He was prepared to be ridiculed for his vanity, but instead felt an odd rush of pleasure at the approving quick up and down both Charlotte and Violet gave him.

"Do I smell better?" he asked Charlotte in English.

"*Excusez-moi?*"

"She doesn't speak much English, Dad," Violet said.

"Maybe just a little," Charlotte added, holding up her thumb and forefinger almost pinched together. *Joost a leetle.*

"Then we speak French," Emery said in French and shrugged as if it were nothing.

But Charlotte lowered her chin and looked at him suspiciously. "You were raised speaking French?"

He shook his head. "Violet was. I took courses and did a massive immersion in it after I met my wife."

"And you learned well."

"I have a good ear."

"Very." She held up her car key and began leading him and Violet to the front door.

"But you, *Madame* Boulain, you work down in Aix, don't you?" said Emery as he caught up to her.

"Call me Charlotte, please. And no, I do not. But I live there."

"Do you work in retail? Do you sell things to the public? To tourists?"

"Daddy!" Violet scolded from just behind him.

"It is alright, Violet," Charlotte said calmly. "Did you close the back doors? You should still lock things up when you both leave the house, yes?" She waited for Violet to rush back inside, then turned to look Emery in the eye. "You wonder why I don't speak English when there are so many English tourists here. The simple answer is that I do speak English. Also German, Italian, and *Switzer-Deutsch*. But my former husband was a British banker. He believed the whole world should speak English, and only the Queen's English. I disagreed. Now I deal with our perfume stores in France, Germany, Italy, and Switzerland, but I refuse to service our stores in England. Do you understand?"

"I guess," Emery said and was stupidly about to add that now that he was clean and standing this close to her, he could tell that *she* smelled very nice, a jasmine-based scent. But Violet reappeared and locked the front door behind them.

"Then let's go," Charlotte said, smiling at both of them. "Why don't we take Claude's car. It is bigger, a Laguna, and one of you can drive it."

* * *

A HALF HOUR LATER, after taking in the south end of Aix-en-Provence, where Charlotte showed them a good *InterMarché* supermarket and everything they'd need for food and supplies, Emery was following her directions as they drove back north and east along the Avenue de Générale Préaude.

"It becomes," she explained, "the Route Cézanne. It goes through Le Tholonet and up to the dam that Émile Zola's father built way back when to supply Aix with its drinking water. No longer, you understand. Now it is the Bimont Dam where we get— Oh, keep to the right here."

Emery did, thankful, as she talked, that the turn wasn't one of the blasted roundabouts the Europeans loved so much. It was hard enough driving this cramped Renault with Charlotte Boulain sitting in the bucket seat to his right. Her jasmine scent, which he'd found faint outside, was overwhelming in the close confines of the car, even with the windows rolled down much of the time. Or perhaps it was only his reaction to it that was over-whelming.

He'd been stupid in his attack of her earlier, his anger, then his condescension. He felt awkward now saying anything. Worse, every time she strained forward or twisted so her breasts pressed against the thin white cotton of her blouse, he found himself getting turned on. *Her bra is white and lacy*, ran in his head like a mantra. He was missing half her commentary.

Then he frowned. His directional sense told him they were now almost directly east of the Avrochet farm. Roughly where he'd gone walking this morning.

"Wait," he interrupted Charlotte. "This takes us through Le Tholonet? This is Le Tholonet ahead?"

"All of this, I think. The main town just ahead on our right. You see?"

She pointed and Emery looked, saw, and couldn't place them. It was as if it had been an entirely different countryside he'd walked through that morning. Or perhaps it was just the light? He'd gone a different direction than he'd thought?

"Charlotte?" said Violet from the back seat of the car. "These trees that have been planted to line so many of the roads here..."

"The tall, smooth ones, with greyish bark and big leaves, yes?" Charlotte answered. "They are plane trees. In America, how do you say, they are 'sycamore' trees. There is a legend that when the Romans came in here and established Aix in 122 B.C., the Caesar declared all the roads be lined with plane trees so his legions could march in the shade."

"Speaking of which, Dad, did you know how burned your neck got this morning?" Violet reached out to touch it and he flinched.

"Your face also," Charlotte said and smiled. "That will start to peel tomorrow. Turn there."

Emery wheeled left at the sign she'd pointed to. Lac Zola (Zola Lake). Mont Sainte-Victoire was now to their right and Emery realized he was completely turned around, distracted by his daughter touching him and Charlotte staring at him.

So he gritted his teeth and concentrated, taking in everything as he drove. He was going to get this all straight when he set out the next time by himself. Take a map if he had to.

"You know you don't need a map, darling," said a woman's voice as they drove in between the pines.

"Hunh?" Emery looked sideways at Charlotte, who was strikingly beautiful with the mottled light shifting and rushing over her wide mouth and pulled-back hair.

"Yes?" she said.

"Did you just say something to me?"

From the back, Violet leaned her head forward between the two front seats. "What is it, Dad?"

"I... Nothing," Emery said. *Just your mother again, presumably.*

They saw the dam, turned around and came back with Emery memorizing each turn, each road sign. Until they finally found the dirt drive that took them into the Avrochet farm and the round open space in front of the house itself. Emery pulled up to a stop beside Charlotte's lime green Peugot hatchback. It looked like a jellybean, Emery thought as they all climbed out of the larger Renault and walked Charlotte to her car.

"You have my phone number," she said as she keyed open her door to the jellybean and climbed in. "If there is anything you need I can help you over the phone, or come and visit, after six o'clock."

"We'll have you over for dinner, won't we, Dad."

"Hm?" He looked at Violet and realized he'd been staring at Charlotte, at the way her long body folded gracefully into her car seat, making her blouse gape and her tight business skirt ride up her thighs. "For dinner some night. Sure."

Violet laughed and reached her head in through the open window of the jellybean to air kiss beside Charlotte's cheeks – right, left, right again.

Charlotte then looked at Emery with her eyebrows raised expectantly. When he took a half-step forward, then stopped uncomfortably, she laughed, winked, waved at him, and roared the little car to life.

"Á bientôt!" she called—*See you soon!*—and was gone.

Emery, staring after her, realized that he and Violet would have to go out driving again. They had no real food in the house and he was suddenly very hungry. He'd skipped lunch. And while this was not usually a big deal for him, this time it was. His body needed fuel, he decided. It was coming back to life. The dead painters and Charlotte had given him something to look forward to.

Changes. Discoveries.

Like the voice of Mattie, or his own unconscious recreation of her, had said to him in the car, he *did* know where to go.

First thing tomorrow.

Face and nose peeling or not.

THE ROMANTIC

This time Emery left the house before Violet had even stirred out of bed. The air was cool, dew still on the grass, and the sun was still below the horizon so the sky ached with the palest eggshell color. The backlit Sainte-Victoire brooded in the distance.

Saying a quick apology to Mattie's memory for yesterday's lust over Charlotte, he set off through the still-wet grass, trying to retrace his steps from the day before. This time he'd prepared, wearing a broad brimmed straw hat he'd found in Avrochet's studio and one of the small backpacks he and Violet had used as carry-ons for their flight to France. He'd stuffed it with a water bottle, apple, sandwich, and, after much hesitation, a small sketch pad and pencils he'd found in the studio near the hat.

He'd worried, zipping up the nylon backpack, that such a clear article from the twenty-first century would somehow short-circuit the visions he was having and no dead artists would appear, no matter how far he walked.

But he remembered seeing faces in the Louvre, seeing Manet and Morisot in the d'Orsay. Those places had been rife with modernity –

electric lights and security equipment for one thing. It hadn't stopped the dead there. And if these dead were really his private hallucinations, why should *anything* stop them? They were his personal creations, his coaches, his avatars, whatever. Him talking to himself?

His ruminations took him through the fields, over the fences, around the swimming pool properties, across the roads and stream, through the forest and vineyard and field to the path where he'd met Picasso. He climbed to the top of the path where he'd lost that artist yesterday and did a slow three-sixty, trying to locate himself relative to the Avrochet farm and the roads he, Violet, and Charlotte had driven yesterday.

But damn it all he couldn't do it. Either the light was still too confusing—everything seemed shimmery gold now with the dawn sun above the horizon—or Emery was still confused about his directions. The one thing he *was* clear on was a need to go just a bit south. The angle he was seeing the Sainte-Victoire from was wrong, or at least not where Cézanne had usually painted it from. And the young Picasso had been walking south too, like he'd known where to go.

So Emery did an about face and walked back down the path, feeling the growing heat of the sun now as he passed the town to his left. He glanced casually down its streets as he went, amazed at how quiet and primitive it looked. No asphalt roads, just cobblestone and dirt. No Renaults or Fiats or Peugeots visible either. No tourists' Audis or Mercedes or *any* cars. Everyone apparently parked their cars indoors overnight.

He did see some farmers walking their horses out to the fields and shook his head. Too quaint. Cliched. He couldn't sketch that if he wanted to. His pencils would snap in protest. His throat would close up in disgust.

He passed the town proper and entered the silvery green light of an olive grove, smelling the dusty earth they grew from in long rows, unable to resist leaping up to snag some half-ripe brown ones from the lower branches.

It was while he bit into one of these that he noticed the slender man sitting with his painter's palette in front of him where the grove opened up to mostly parched grass and red, hard-packed dirt.

Then the extreme bitterness of the olive hit Emery's tongue and he spat the pulp out with a loud cry. He threw the rest of the bitten olive away too, screwing up his face and spitting over and over to clear the taste.

When he finally looked up again, he saw the slender painter looking his way with a wide smile on his face, rubbing his nose, then tugging on his thin mustache as he shook with laughter. Emery's anger flared...and died. Something in the man's laughter was actually welcoming. And so Emery brushed off his hands and approached, half-expecting to see the gypsy Picasso again, though the physical build didn't seem right.

It wasn't Picasso. It was someone older this time, perhaps in his mid-thirties? He sported a classic, flat-topped straw boater hat with a faded black ribbon around its crown, and a billowing gray cotton shirt with rolled-up sleeves. His body was a marionette of delicate bones and face hunched on the folding wooden stool. His eyes drooped with gentleness. His sensual mouth was encircled by the wispiest of orange-tinged beards, the neck and cheek areas of it shaved so close to the jaw line that they almost disappeared.

"I know you," Emery said in French, reaching him. "I just can't quite..."

"Hello, Sir," said the man, also in French. He stood at last and rubbed his nose again before setting his palette and brush on the chair and extending his hand. "Pierre-Auguste, at your service."

Pierre-Auguste, just as Max had said it, but with no pretension. Just a fact.

"Renoir," Emery completed it, too dazed to accept the handshake.

"Yes!" the man said, dropping his hand but smiling so wide now it lit his whole face. "Are you from Paris? Do you know of my work?"

"I'm not from Paris, but yes, I know of your work. More than you can imagine."

"Good! Good! And you don't know olives, so you are not from around here. But the way you look at my canvas, then at my subject, I guess that you are a painter yourself. Is it so?"

Emery blushed and nervously clutched the front straps of his backpack. Unlike with the young Picasso, he realized he was actually intimidated by this man. Or maybe not intimidated, but in awe. Renoir's craft, for one thing was obviously fully developed. Glancing at the half-finished canvas, Emery saw Renoir was capturing Cézanne's mountain in his own unique way, emphasizing the wind-silvered leaves of the olive trees in the foreground, strays from this very grove, swirling in front of the stodgier pines, both parting in the middle to reveal the distant majesty of the Sainte-Victoire.

Of course! Emery had seen this work before! Never one of his favorites, but maybe because he'd never studied it like this, half done. Now he could see how Renoir was making the trees like worshipers waving palm leaves and the mountain was the ineffable approaching. The olive trunks twisted. The trees seemed to dance and sway.

Emery cleared his throat. "I'm... I was... I mean, I used to paint. Yes."

Renoir looked at him keenly, waiting.

Emery stepped closer to Renoir's work in progress and pretended to study it closely. "You normally do human subjects, don't you?"

Renoir smiled obliquely, then shrugged and tugged on his

mustache in embarrassment. "One uses what is present, yes? And my friend Paul..."

"Cézanne?"

"Yes. He puts such stock in this mountain. I had to see what the fuss was about." He turned to regard his canvas as well. "It would be better with some naked women, I think. Laughing. Dancing in the fresh air. Big busted women."

Emery found himself smiling too now; Renoir so obviously enjoying skewering his own predilections. "But you *have* put naked women in it," Emery said.

Renoir turned and raised his eyebrows. "How so?"

Emery stepped closer to the canvas and leaned down to see the familiar wash of unexpected tints playing through the olive leaves Renoir had done, much of the paint still wet. And the ground, the impressionistic dashes making up the grass and the clouds in the sky. "The trees. You see? Versus the mountain, which you have made a stone God in the distance. They dance. He watches."

"Yes! Exactly!" Renoir laughed again and clapped a hand on Emery's arm. "You have the painter's eye at least, whether you paint or not. What is your name?"

"Emery Lake." A part of Emery hummed, waiting for some recognition, some sign that the man was a fraud. Something.

But all he got was another open smile. "Lake. Lake. Did you paint here, down in Aix? Do you know Cézanne?"

"I'm an American."

"Ah. This explains why I have not heard of you. Our friend, Durand-Ruel, Paul Durand-Ruel, have you heard of him? He wants to take our work to America. To New York! And Edgar's Mary... You know her? Mary Cassatt? She is American."

"I've seen her work."

Renoir nodded and picked up his palette and brushes again, reseating himself and starting to paint again as he spoke. "Very good painter, Miss Cassatt. Very skilled. As difficult as Degas himself. As difficult as Berthe, heaven help us. But she also believes we would do well in America."

Emery surprised himself by slinging his backpack off his back and stretching out on the ground beside Renoir, strangely comfortable in the man's presence. Not to mention giddy to be able to watch him work. "I suspect you *will* do well there. Very well. Make your fortunes. Become internationally famous."

Renoir sat back a bit on his stool and looked steadily at Emery to see if he was serious. Then his mouth again broke into a smile. "Ah, Aline would like that. Yes, I'm sure she would. Her mother too."

"Aline?"

"Aline Charigot. The most beautiful woman in the world, I think. She is the reason I left Paris. And the reason I am going back."

"To marry her?"

Renoir tilted his head to the side and looked off to the blue sky. "One day, perhaps. The *Montmartroises*, you know, we do not always marry."

"*Montmartroises?*"

Renoir nodded. "Those of us who live in Montmartre. Paris, yes? With the Sacré-Coeur at its top?"

"I know it."

"Very poor. Everyone there. But we are all very happy. There is no pretension. We live lightly."

"While you paint the rich? You exhibited a portrait of Madame Charpentier and her children at the Salon, I believe."

Emery held his breath, hoping he had his time periods straight and would not scare Renoir off with fortune-telling, as he'd done with Picasso. Particularly speaking of Paris's infamous *Salon*, which in Renoir's day was the only place an artist could exhibit and be actually seen by all the public. But also a place governed by archaic, set standards of what constituted art. The Salon's naturalistic, religious or mythological-themed works were an anathema to most of the impressionists' fresh air studies and experiments with color. So when Renoir had gotten his paintings accepted there, he was kicked out of the impressionists group for a time. If that had not already happened...

Renoir grinned, nodded, kept on painting, and Emery breathed a sigh of relief.

"I think I like this painting better than the Charpentier portrait," Emery said.

Renoir paused and considered his own work, then the nature that inspired it. "Every work has its own voice. Here the air is arid but alive in the trees, the pine smell in the air. At the Charpentiers, people were the soil and the sun and everything. Did you know I met the Russian, Turgenev, there once? And Maupassant, Flaubert, Daudet, Zola. All the great writers and artists passed through the Charpentier salon."

"Ah, but are they your people?" Emery said, leaning back on an elbow.

Renoir looked at him and shook his head with a wry grin. The Montmartroises are my people."

"And other artists."

"Of course."

"*That* I understand," Emery said, not exactly sure *why* he understood it. He'd never been great friends with other artists. There'd always been too much competitive angst, especially as he grew more successful. The people he'd gravitated to, other than Max, had all been outside the artistic community – an engineer, a man who owned an electronics dealership, a sports psychologist, and of course Mattie, a flautist with the figure of a Boris Valejo warrior goddess, pint sized.

But with Renoir it was different, he thought as he took off his own straw hat, lay back on the dusty grass with his hands behind his head, and squinted up at the blue sky. With Renoir he understood for the first time what it meant to have instant understanding.

There was a rustling sound and he realized Renoir had reached over, figured out the zipper on Emery's backpack, and was now rustling through his things. Emery's heart stopped, remembering Picasso's frightened retreat from modern things that didn't fit his understanding of the world.

But before he could reach over to take the nylon pack away from him, Renoir looked up with calm curiosity.

"You have a sketchbook and pencils here," Renoir said. "You must set up beside me and draw."

"Right. I could draw you painting."

"Certainly. Why not?"

Emery actually laughed for what felt like the first time in years. "Why not...?"

"Yes, why not?"

"Like I said, I don't paint or draw any more."

"Why is this?"

"Because..." He almost blurted out the whole story of Mattie, of his deal with God, of his disillusionment with art in general, but all that came out was, "It's too difficult."

Renoir tut-tutted, tugging on his moustache and stroking his nose. "Can I tell you what my last painting was before I left to travel?"

"What?"

"A very hard piece. Complicated. Fourteen people in a tight veranda. Originally fifteen! They are eating and drinking. Laughing. Long grass and sailboats in the background. The wind is blowing. There is a little dog being kissed by my beautiful Aline. They are boat men and men and women who have come here on boats. A Sunday afternoon away from the city. But at first none of it would come together, you understand?"

Emery nodded with a grunt, careful to stifle his excitement as he stared up into the cloudless blue, picturing the commotion Renoir described. This had to be *The Luncheon of the Boating Party* that Renoir was talking about. It had always been Emery's favorite Renoir. More than *The Umbrellas* or *The Bathers* or any of the portraits or nudes. Only his *Le Moulin de la Galette*, with all its plain folk dancing and talking, came close in its celebration of life.

"But I had to do it!" Renoir swooshed his long thin hands together in front of him as if to pantomime giving birth. "Before I got too old. I had been itching to try this. And it is good thing from time to time to attempt something beyond one's powers."

"But it wasn't beyond your powers," Emery pointed out.

"It was! I could not do more than get the general idea at the hotel where I set it up. All my friends. Aline. The other artists who modeled for me. I had to bring it back to my studio afterwards to work and work. Take this woman out. Change the position of this man, this woman. I realize at some point that I need an awning. To define the space, you know, to pull these people together so they do not appear random against the grass and trees and sky. This must be an intimate *group*. And the light! And the wind! I wanted the viewer to smell the *sweat* of the men who had rowed them, taste the wine and bread and grapes they ate. Feel the quick little heartbeat of the terrier Aline held in her hands. Hear the murmur. Feel the ease of the summer day. *All* of this!"

"I'm glad to hear you set your standards so low," Emery quipped.

"Exactly."

"You bit off more than you could chew."

"Yes. But I kept chewing and chewing and chewing."

"And...?" Did he know he had created one of the world's great masterpieces then?

Renoir smiled and shrugged. "Then I finished and sold it, as I did many other pieces, to Durand-Ruel. I think he still has it."

"That's it?"

"Yes." Renoir was tugging on his mustache again agitated.

"You didn't know what an incredible piece you'd finished?"

"It was...good. I knew that. But the technique, impressionism, I was not sure... And Aline wanted me to move with her to Burgundy. I was not sure where I was going with my painting..."

"So you left for Algeria."

Renoir stopped his mustache tugging and stared at Emery, dumbfounded. Finally he shook his head. "You are trying to distract me from yourself, aren't you, Emery. The point of my story is that you must paint or draw even when you are afraid you cannot. You must keep working. There are things to discover. There is beauty and joy to bring out."

"Hunh." Emery did not stir from the grass. Beauty and joy? He didn't think so. If there was, take a photo. Digital.

A second later his sketchbook and box of pencils had landed on his chest. Emery grunted without shifting. "I don't want to get up."

"Then draw from the ground."

"Draw what?"

"Draw the sky."

"In black and white."

"Why not?"

"Seriously?"

"There is always a way."

And just like that, Emery picked up his pencils for the first time since Mattie had died. Because he was intrigued by the challenge of painting blue nothingness with a graphite 2B, and maybe a 6B, pencil and eraser. No chalk. No sanguine crayon or colored pencils.

But if Pierre-Auguste Renoir thought it could be done, who was Emery Lake to gainsay him?

Which is how he became so intensely engrossed in the study of the sky's clear colors, its slightest gradations and the way the sun *moved* them in long seamless tones of light from the void of white to the depth of blue—refractions; light as colors sliding through and only the blue spectrum bouncing back; seeing that; feeling that; turning it into shades of gray exploding from a common point on his paper—he dug in his pack for an apple and some bread at one point; shared it with Renoir—the light *becoming*—that he completely missed Renoir finishing his work for the day.

It wasn't until the painter had cleaned his brushes, scraped off his palette, and stood to fold up his stool and easel, making a trio of birds fly out of the nearest tree, that Emery blinked and rolled up to sitting.

His arm ached from supporting this sketchbook up in front of his face for hours. He once again felt sunburnt, even his eyeballs, so his vision was a little blurry. His head shot with pain as he tried to focus on something other than sky. Violet would probably screech with concern when she saw him. And his sketch of the empty sky he had done, while interesting, was only that.

But Emery didn't care. For the first time in a very long time, his soul felt soothed. Almost – excited.

"Will you...um...be coming back here tomorrow?" he asked Renoir.

"Of course. I'm not finished yet. Will you come back here yourself and spend some time with me?"

"I'd be honored to. At sunrise?"

Renoir looked aghast as he set one end of his canvas-in-progress on his boot and leaned the other against his thigh so he could flip his easel closed and up under his left arm with the stool. "To get up at sunrise, one cannot go out drinking the night before. Besides, the light is all wrong then. We'll meet closer to the time we met today. Around eight-thirty or nine. I will bring the food."

"Perfect," Emery said, deciding he would still bring something. He had no confidence either that Renoir would ever be here again, or that anything he brought would be of substance. How could it be? How could this legend be anything but a ghost?

And as if he read Emery's thoughts, Renoir extended his paint-smudged right hand again and held it there until Emery managed to grunt and groan himself to his feet and hesitantly reach out his own hand.

They shook and Emery felt sold flesh against his palm, in his fingers. The man was real. This was real.

He shook again, harder, returned Renoir's beaming smile, and watched him turn with his stool and easel clattering under his left arm, his half-done painting swinging on the fingers of his right. Renoir paused one more time and nodded at Emery. "Until tomorrow, my friend." Then walked off to the east, across the field and into the trees.

Except it wasn't just "my friend" he'd said, was it. It was *"mon ami"*, with all its reverberations of camaraderie and kinship that the English phrase could not hope to capture.

À demain, mon ami.

Until tomorrow, indeed.

CLUTCH YOUR CHEST AND DROP TO YOUR KNEES

As expected, Violet had a hissy fit when Emery walked in through the front door. She was in the kitchen, sipping red wine and chopping vegetables. She turned to see him and set down her wine glass.

"Where have—? Oh, God, Daddy! Your face!"

"It's only sunburn, Violet."

"Skin cancer waiting to happen." She came across the living room tile, wiping her hands on the apron she wore. "You're burnt underneath your peel, for God's sake! What did you do? Leave with a hat then stuff it into your waistband for the rest of the day?"

"Kind of." Emery grinned. He pulled the hat off now and tossed it to the floor near the patio doors.

"And you didn't wear sunscreen."

"Can't stand the stuff."

"You look horrible!"

"I'm not that—"

"Terrible, Daddy! It was horrible what you did! How could you!"

Emery took a step back, blinking, and slid his backpack off and down to the floor. His daughter wasn't just being prissy or concerned, she was truly upset. Her face was all twisted. She was crying. Her dried hands were now clutching her apron spasmodically.

"Violet," he said in his calmest tone. "What is it?"

"You *left* me here this morning with no idea where you'd gone! You're gone all day! You didn't even want to *come* to France! What am I supposed to think!"

"I left a note." He had, hadn't he?

"The 'Gone for a walk. Be back this afternoon.'? *That's* supposed to cover it? And it's not 'this afternoon.' It's nearly dinnertime. *French* dinnertime. Do you know when that is?"

Emery glanced behind him and realized he couldn't see the sun because it was too low in the western sky. "Um...six o'clock?"

"It's almost eight o'clock! Did you even eat? And we're having company!"

"Yes, I.... We're what?"

Even as he asked it, he heard the distinctive roar of an underpowered French car crunching to a halt on the front driveway. Violet's chin jerked up. "Charlotte."

Chalotte?

Violet saw his face. "You *said* we could invite her. Now go clean up. You smell of sweat and your face is half peeling off. Fix it."

Then she'd sniffed, wiped her eyes, and hurried back to the front door to welcome their guest.

Emery ran for the upstairs bathroom.

* * *

CHARLOTTE BOULAIN LEANED close to him over the corner of the dining room table where the three of them sat, the French doors to the patio open, the cooler evening air blowing in the smells of pine trees and sweet hyacinth. "Tell me about the great painters you've met," she said.

"What?" Emery clattered down the knife he was buttering his piece of baguette with and looked at her wide-eyed. Then at Violet.

Violet shrugged broadly and poured herself some more wine. "I told her you knew everyone in the New York art scene. Or at least you used to."

"The New York scene." Emery looked from Charlotte to his daughter and back again. Charlotte wore her blond hair down this time, held back on one side with a sparkling hair clip, a butterfly. And she'd had her hair lightened, it seemed, so it was truly blond. For him? Strands of hair on the non-clipped side kept falling around her eyes when she leaned forward. Emery wanted to brush them back, to see her face. The minimal makeup. Deep tan that had taken its toll around the corners of her sparkling dark eyes. Her sensual mouth.

"Yes," said Charlotte. "Did you ever meet Mati Klarwein?"

Emery blinked at the name 'Mati.' Then took a deep breath when he realized it wasn't *his* Mattie. It was a male Mati. "Mati Klarwein. Surrealist. Album covers."

"I was a big fan of Santana. Their *Abraxas* album cover..." She turned to Violet and gave a self-deprecating smile. "This was a rock band back when they still had vinyl records, you understand."

"I was a child," said Violet and raised her wine glass. "I don't remember that."

"Klarwein painted the album cover," Emery said. "Yes. I met him once. Nice man. He died awhile back. In Majorca, I think. Of cancer."

There was a long silence in the room. Emery went back to eating the buttered bread with the pesto pasta Violet had prepared. He also eyed the bottle of Merlot that Violet and Charlotte were consuming between them. Did he wish he could join them in that?

Once he would have. For almost sixteen months, ironically just a year before Mattie had been diagnosed with her own 'wages of sin' disease for all the youth she'd spent smoking, Emery had climbed into wine bottles, beer bottles, vodka and whiskey bottles, to avoid the struggles he'd been having *out*side the bottles. He'd hit what everyone said was the pinnacle of his career with a series of paintings on the ends of wars – great, monumental canvases that he'd had to paint in a specially rented space downtown Manhattan. The canvases had been too large to fit in his lake house studio.

Yeah, he'd hit the peak and believed everything after that had to be a slow slide to obscurity. He'd started to drink to hide from that. And from the person his fear revealed him to be – needy, petty, small, a casual drunk. He'd had to hide all that from Mattie and Violet, too, which meant lies. And more drinking.

Until Mattie managed to finally break through his wall and actually threaten to leave him if he didn't stop.

Which amazingly stopped him. Cold. Got him painting again. Then Mattie got sick. Was there a link to all the stress he'd caused her? Of course. It was another reason he would never touch alcohol ever again in a hundred million fucking years. Not even an option.

And neither, he decided now, should he let himself get caught up in his old game or self-pity.

He swallowed the bite he'd been chewing and looked back and forth at his two companions. "I did meet Matthew Brannon and Mika Rottenburg once. Matthew does things like a letterpress rendering of a shrimp cocktail and gets everyone excited by slapping a dirty title on it. *Slut Best Friend,* for that one. Mika does videos of repeating futility and calls it art. Look it up on YouTube. My favorite was the one where a fat woman pedals a bike to light a lamp that helps some woman's hand grow her painted fingernails long. Then they cut off a ruby red fingernail, throw it through a hole in the floor, and another fat woman pounds and mashes it until it becomes a maraschino cherry which she adds to a bowl of them."

A pause, then Violet asked, "What does that mean?"

"How the hell should I know?" Emery said. He took another bite of pasta and spoke before he'd finished chewing. "How about Damien Hirst? Stuffs and pickles a shark, mounts it, and sells it for twelve million dollars. Or Jamie Isenstein? She has herself shut up inside a wall so only her hand sticks into the gallery display space. And the hand *moves.* Takes different shapes. Whoever buys the piece, and if I recall correctly she had a lot of bidders for that one, gets to call her up whenever and have her come and perform it for them."

Charlotte had sat back in her chair and now smirked at him. "I gather you do not approve of this new art?"

"Is that what it is?"

"Isn't it?"

Emery deliberately laid down his knife and fork. "Look, Pollock spattered paint on giant canvasses and convinced people it was all about the process, not the product. Warhol churned out color-modded prints of Marilyn Monroe and soup cans and made a hundred million dollars. Hell, way back in 1917, Marcel Duchamp took an industrially manufactured *urinal*, signed it, called it *Fountain*, and made it art. You don't have to even *create* anything. You just point to something, say 'See it this way!' and you're an artist. You tell me how to identify real art."

"No, you tell me," Charlotte challenged, leaning forward on the corner of the table, exciting his senses despite himself.

"There's no *form* today!" he said. "No respect for tradition! For learned craft! For real talent!"

"Like the old masters," squeaked Violet from across the table.

"Yes. Ingres. Or Delacroix," teased Charlotte. "Weren't those the painters who ruled the Salon back before the impressionists?

Wasn't it because of their work that new artists like Monet and Manet could not get in?"

"*That is not the same!*" roared Emery.

Charlotte didn't even blink. "And how is it different? They saw that photography was making naturalistic realism obsolete, yes? No more reason to paint to simply capture a likeness or record of the world."

"Yes!"

"So the impressionists try to grab something a photograph could not grab – the *spirit* of what they see, the ephemeral essence. Now the artists use photography, sound, texture, all to capture it in another way, yes?"

"Signing a urinal is not art!"

"Again, why not?".

"It's... It's..." He turned back to Violet, deep into her wine now and hopelessly out of her depth anyway despite having attended two dozen or so of his openings through her childhood. So he turned back to Charlotte. She was hanging on his words but obviously ready to give back as good as she got. She might be a peddler of fragrance, but had obviously picked up a decent art education somewhere as well. *And* played the flute. The eccentric combination was intoxicating enough that Emery not only felt himself getting swept up, but let it happen.

He said, "Okay, it's like this. It's like this. Good art has everything come together in a way that, when you see it, you feel the completion, the emotion or intention of what the artist was feeling. Or at least what he was trying to say."

"And Duchamp's urinal? You don't think people felt that? Just seeing it like that in an art gallery..."

"It's cheap. It's easy. And it fails the second test."

"That only the particular artist could have done it," Charlotte said.

"Exactly!" Emery said. "Otherwise, why not elevate every two year old who looks at things in a way that adults have forgotten how to do? Why not make *them* the millionaire celebrities?"

"But there *have* been children!"

"Sure, Joshua Johnson."

"Jordan Cook."

"Oh! Oh!" Violet interrupted, spilling her wine. "I saw one on Oprah! A little blond girl who did these amazing portraits!"

"Akiane," Charlotte supplied, pronouncing it *Ah-kee-ah-nuh*..

"She didn't have a last name," Violet said.

"Akiane Kramarik," Emery said, rolling his eyes. "Home schooled. Swears her talent is a gift from God. Yadda yadda. Apply the second test, remember? These kids all do beautiful painting, but nothing a reasonably competent adult artist couldn't do. Hell, I was drawing and inking entire comics for Marvel at sixteen. I was a 'child prodigy.'" He made air quotes around it. "But it didn't make me an *artist*. More to the point is a so-called prodigy like Marla Olmstead."

"Who?" Charlotte said it peevishly. She'd downed her last glass of wine and poured herself another, Emery noted.

"Doesn't your cooking class start tomorrow?" he asked.

"You're taking a cooking class?" said Charlotte, turning to her. "In Aix?"

"Shut up, Daddy, and tell us about art. Mara whatever."

"Marla. Olmstead," Emery corrected, frowning.

Then Charlotte's fingers were on his arm, sending little electric tingles through it. "Please tell us," she said.

"Just another kid painter prodigy," Emery said. "Except that she does abstracts."

"Like what? Colors all over the place? Finger painting?"

"Finger painting. Brush painting. Supposedly started when she was two. Very emotionally free or emotionally immature, depending on your point of view. Not a lot different than what a lot of five, six, or seven year olds would do, except that her parents give her expensive paints and canvases to play with, and videotape her working, and sell her end product for thousands of dollars. 'Such a control of color balance and tone!' 'Such an intuitive understanding of light and meaning!'"

"You don't agree?" said Charlotte.

"Google her. You tell me. I gave up on that one. But I do offer the second test."

"Which is?"

"Repeatable results. Almost anyone can, if they fiddle with artistic media enough, create something that will make a viewer clutch their chest and fall to their knees in wonder. Why? Damned if I know. Humans seem to have an innate need and appreciation for wonder and truth. So much so they can find it in signed toilets, okay? The trick is for someone to so hone their craft or their eye or both, that they can make viewers fall to their knees *consistently*. Not every time, maybe. But often enough that you get them coming back for more, like junkies looking for a fix. Or like an alcoholic..."

He reached out and grabbed Violet's hand as she started to raise the wine bottle to pour the dregs into her again-empty glass. By Emery's count, Charlotte had drunk maybe one-and-a-half glasses. The rest had all been Violet's.

"Daddy, let go." It was almost a snarl, not looking at him.

"It's past ten, Violet, and you've just drunk most of a bottle. And more before I got home."

"I said let go!"

Emery did and the released arm jerked across the table, clinking over her glass and thumping Charlotte's bowl almost off the table before Charlotte grabbed it and her glass.

"Fuck!" Violet said.

"Yeah," said Emery.

"It's alright," Charlotte said. "Let me clean this up. Then, perhaps, I should go." She began picking up the mostly-empty dishes.

"No!" Violet said, jerking to her feet and shaking her head, then stopping and widening her eyes as if everything had just gone swimmy. "No, you stay. You stay and talk. Just me. I gotta... You're right, Daddy. Too much to drink. Long day tomorrow. I gotta...go. Upstairs."

Emery stood. "You need any help?"

"I'm a big girl, alright?" She caught his eyes as she said it, and he shivered at the pain he saw in there.

Note to self, he thought angrily. Get your act together, Emery Lake. Learn how to be a father somehow. Violet was what? Twenty one now? And you always assumed she'd managed Mattie's death better than you.

Then Violet was stumbling out to the stairs and up, and Emery was left alone with Charlotte. She stood with three stacked plates, her eyes watching him with compassion.

"I do have work tomorrow as well," she said, "but I can stay if you need to talk."

There was such a shiver of invitation in that, an almost tangible velvet cord wrapping around both of them and pulling them together across the tiled floor.

Too much, too soon.

"Another night, maybe," Emery heard himself say.

"Tomorrow?"

He opened his mouth to say yes, but heard himself suggest Wednesday.

"I'm out of town Wednesday to Saturday. Saturday night?"

"Yes. Here?"

Charlotte nodded. "But talk with Violet first. I don't want her to feel she has to go to great effort."

"The cooking class. You think she'll feel compelled to show off?"

"Yes."

"Maybe I'll cook."

Charlotte's eyes widened. "That would be interesting."

He'd walked towards her as they talked and now took the dishes from her, brushing her fingers with his as he did so. "I'll finish the cleanup."

She laughed lightly, suddenly skittish. "Nonsense. We can do it quickly together." She bustled back to the table, gathered the glasses and napkins and baguette basket, and almost beat Emery to the kitchen sink. Together they rinsed and stuck everything in the dishwasher and she showed him how it worked.

Then he walked her out the door to her green jellybean car and waited while she unlocked the door and opened it. She turned to him, standing very close.

He could smell her perfume, a fruity scent that blended somehow with the cool night air. And her warmth. The curves of her. It was like they were already pressed together in passion.

"The French kiss this time," Charlotte said with a twinkle in her eye. "Not the American version, but this – cheek, cheek, cheek, yes?"

"Okay," Emery said, and did it. A kiss beside her left cheek. A kiss beside her right. A last beside her left again. Each time their cheeks touched and dragged just a bit. Each time their lips just missed touching.

Then she had pulled back and dropped down into her tiny car. "Saturday," she said, closed the door, and pulled a sharp turn in the driveway and was gone into the night.

Emery! Said a voice from somewhere.

He ignored it, clutched his chest, and fell to his knees in wonder.

A STAIN ON HEAVEN'S DRESS

At first, it seemed as though things were only going to get better.

If Renoir perceived the change in Emery over the next few days, he made no comment. But Emery saw it. He felt it in himself when he hiked out in each morning with one of Avrochet's old wooden-stick easels, canvas, and painter's boxes strapped onto his backpack much the way painter's in Renoir's day would have gone to field.

He headed directly to where he knew he would find Pierre-Auguste. His step was lighter. His face, brighter. He found himself noticing the birdsong. And because his time with Renoir was impossible, something that couldn't really be happening, he let himself paint again. He delighted in arguments over whether creating your own paints with pigment and linseed oil produced better results than modern-bought tubes, or whether cotton duck canvas or primed linen allowed better expression of color and light.

Even Violet seemed turned around after her crash on Monday night. Tuesday morning was rough, but she'd come back from her first day full of energy and eager to share with Emery what he'd learned.

He was apparently forgiven, and she was apparently not an alcoholic after all.

Emery did, nonetheless, start paying attention to his watch and got back Tuesday, and Wednesday around the same time Violet did, shortly after six. True, he couldn't share with her the insanity of spending time with a long-dead master painter, but he could listen to *her* day, and he could finally make her face light up when he showed her Thursday the canvas he had begun – a pastorale of the Mont Sainte-Victoire, a shepherd in the foreground.

"Oh, Daddy, I'm so happy for you!" she gushed. "You're painting again!"

"Not seriously. Just while I'm here."

"But...but..." She burst into tears again, making Emery wonder just how much of the strong daughter he'd seen after Mattie got sick had been an act. Violet had given up piano and moved from Julliard to NYU business, brooking no argument. She'd toughed out her boyfriend's abandonment. And even when Mattie died, she'd been furious at Emery, but she hadn't broken down once at the funeral. She'd been tough as nails.

Now this?

Emery cleared his throat, still more comfortable talking with the impossibility that was Pierre-Auguste Renoir than with being a father. "Uh...what is it, Violet? Really."

She looked up at him with her eyes brimming but her face radiant with happiness and Emery realized he should have taken her by the arms when he asked. Or drawn him in against him. Provided fatherly comfort.

Instead he now just stood awkwardly watching as she cried and beamed at him. "Daddy, I'm *expanding* myself here! So are you! Don't you know how *rare* that is? I feel like...like...I'm on the cusp of finally finding something big in my life!"

Emery frowned. "Cooking?"

She laughed, sniffed, and swiped at her eyes. "No, not cooking. I mean, yes, I love it, but it's just...driving into Aix each day, speaking French nonstop, meeting all these people. If Mom's parents were alive, it would be so perfect. Are you going to show me where she grew up while we're here?"

"We'll see." In fact he had no particular desire to track down that little country house again. When he and Mattie had gone there after their wedding, her parents hadn't exactly welcomed him. He hadn't been heartbroken when they'd passed on.

"It's just..." Violet spread her hands out to feel the air around her. "I feel like anything's possible here. That we're on the cusp of magic happening. Don't you feel it?"

Her eyes sparkled so like her mother's that Emery felt his own eyes water in response. Even more when Violet saw, laughed again, and leapt forward to give him a quick kiss on the cheek.

Incredible, he thought, stunned. Perhaps the happiness that had drowned with Mattie's diagnosis might resurface in some form after all.

* * *

FRIDAY.

Renoir had just finished his Sainte-Victoire painting so that it looked as Emery remembered it from his early studies of the man – the dancing olive trees, the victory of the mountain touching God in the distance. But having seen Renoir actually paint it, stroke by loving stroke, with Emery creating his own landscape from a standing position beside him, it was hard not to feel an ownership of it. The "cusp" of magic, Violet had said. No, Emery was smack in the center of it and it felt wonderful.

"You know," Emery breathed as he and Renoir examined the finished picture, "I once almost gave up on landscapes completely."

"Because you cannot paint nature," Renoir agreed and pointed to the olive trees. "A gust of wind and everything changes. Happy, sad, silver, green. But you must try. That is what Claude taught me. You must try."

"Claude Monet?"

Renoir nodded. "His trip to Le Havre. Our time painting the Seine to—"

He snapped his thin mouth closed and his eyes became hard.

"Pierre?"

Renoir was staring past Emery to something and would not take his eyes off it. Emery turned. There, ambling cocksure through the thicker part of the olive grove, came the short, burly youth who had called himself the Gypsy. Only he wasn't a youth any longer. He looked to be Renoir's age. No, older. In his forties like Emery. His hatless hair was still as dark as his eyes, much receded from the top, but combed over and forward and glistening in the sun. His face, brown as a beech nut was lined in furious furrows down around his wide mouth, his spread-out nose.

But then he caught Emery's eye, smiled, and his entire face transformed, appearing at once innocent, warm, and thoroughly engaged.

"*Hola!*" he called out and raised the nubbly arm of his incongruously-fresh linen suit jacket as he approached. Then, in much more polished French than the first time he and Emery had met, "I see you have found the Romantic! Yes! Almost as obsessed as the Master with this mountain. Almost! And you!" He had gotten close enough now to see Emery's painting. "You *are* a painter, I see. One day you may even be a good one!"

It was a mark of the man's charisma that Emery laughed, rather than growling.

Renoir was obviously not so charmed. He did not rise from his stool but simply began cleaning his paint brushes, his eyes hooded. "Hello, Pablo. What are we today? The gypsy? The rebel? The magician? No. I see you are much too old for that now. Too much living with the *beau monde*."

"Yes, yes," said the man Emery now obviously had to call Picasso. The man tossed back his lanky shock of combed-over hair, patted the breast pocket of his suit, then reached inside to pull out a cigarette. He lit it with a box of matches pulled out of another pocket, then sucked on the tobacco like it was the sweetest air this side of, well, the Provençal countryside.

"Genius," he said.

Renoir snorted and Emery raised his eyebrows.

Picasso puffed. "That's what they call me now. I could shit on a canvas, hand it to them, and they'd convene two dozen of Paris's best art critics to analyze and fawn over it."

Emery furrowed his brows. "You're past your blue and rose periods then. Into cubism?"

Picasso sighed and waved his cigarette about. "Braque is cubism. A charming diversion. I paint whatever the subject demands."

"Like *Les Demoiselles d'Avignon*?" Emery asked. "Tell me what subject demanded to be four whores standing together in distorted chunks."

Picasso froze, staring at Emery with eyes so black they seemed to suck the sun out of the sky. Then the man took a long, deliberate drag on his cigarette and blew it out in Emery's direction. "I like you, but you know nothing. *Les Demoiselles* was an exorcism painting."

"Ah." Emery knew he should have been fawning and sucking up whatever this man had to say. Picasso was, after all, probably the most famous painter of the last two centuries. But just as Renoir was clearly not enchanted by him, Emery found that Picasso's arrogance simply rubbed him the wrong way. "So you were, you're saying, basically full of shit and in need of a good dump onto your canvas. And the critics ate it up, as you knew they would."

Emery deliberately turned his back on the man and went on finishing his own canvas.

This time, though, Picasso was ready and laughed explosively. Emery's peripheral vision saw him throw his cigarette to the dry ground without bothering to stomp it out. Then he walked over to stand behind Emery, so much shorter that he was breathing into the middle of Emery's back.

"Art is war," he murmured.

There was a small tug and Emery spun around to see that Picasso had lifted his wallet from his pants pocket as deftly as any street urchin. He was flipping through Emery's photos, thankfully ignoring his driver's license with the impossible (for Picasso and Renoir) dates.

"Give that back," Emery said and stepped towards him.

Picasso danced backwards, holding up a family photo of Emery, Mattie, and Violet. The last one he had of them all before Mattie got sick. Taken by the lake out front of their house.

"Very pretty women," Picasso said. "Your mistresses?"

"My wife and my daughter. My *dead* wife. Give it back *now.*"

Picasso held it a moment longer, then shrugged as if it were of no consequence and handed it to Emery, who returned it to his pants pocket. Picasso spun on one foot and made to walk away, but then scooped up Emery's backpack and began going through it as Emery shook his head in disbelief. The squat Spaniard pulled out Emery's green, neoprene water bottle, the apples and sandwiches he had packed in Tupperware, the foil-wrapped granola bars, and Emery's spiral-bound sketch pad and pencils.

"Ha!" he said, remarking on none of the modernities, just as Renoir had not.

"What in hell do you think you're doing?" Emery said coldly, inclined to lunge at the man and thrash him once and for all, but he was stayed by the subtle shake of Renoir's head.

"I will draw you!" Picasso said. "The two of you! The Romantic and the what? The Challenger! Yes!"

"I don't think..."

"Nonsense! Don't you know that if I draw you, if I sign my work and give it to you, you will become part of history! You can sell this for thousands of American dollars. You can tell it to all your painter friends, that you were the subject of the Genius!"

And again, despite all the distaste the man produced in Emery, Emery found himself getting swept up in the man's sheer force of personality. Not to mention an intense curiosity in what the man would produce. Of course Emery selling it was impossible. Somehow they'd date the work and declare it a fraud. But if Picasso truly did draw him and Renoir and then kept it for himself, what would that mean? Could Emery then track down the drawing in the various Picasso collections scattered around the world and *see* what was done here this day?

Or would it only (and here Emery found himself rubbing his head in alarm) establish just how profound a delusion Emery had created for himself here, blending fantasy with all that he knew of Picasso's *oeuvre*, and Renoir's?

Then he realized that what he thought was irrelevant, for Picasso had already taken Emery's sketchbook and taken ten steps back from Emery and Renoir. He was circling them both now like a vulture, kicking at the dirt with his fine leather shoes, and studying them keenly. He laughed and muttered to himself until Emery began to feel faint watching him.

Just at the point when Emery was about to insist on the return of his materials, Picasso suddenly sat on the dirt, his feet splayed out, half-bent before him. With one hand he tugged open his silk tie and popped loose the top buttons of his shirt. Off came the suit jacket. Down came the suspenders.

And suddenly he was sketching with such frenzied concentration that Emery doubted his pencil ever left the paper.

Except that these were still his earlier years, weren't they? The one-sketch style was Picasso's later period. And even as Emery thought it, Picasso had his rubber out and fingers, erasing, shaping, redoing his lines.

"When will you take me to the Master, Pierre-Auguste?" Picasso called as he sketched.

"Not soon, Pablo," Renoir responded. He had finished cleaning his brushes and palette and was packing everything up for the day – paints and brushes in a burlap bag, easel collapsed down. All done much earlier, Emery was sure, than he would have if Picasso had not shown up.

"Have you taken this Challenger?" Picasso said, indicating Emery.

"No. Paul does not like meeting new people. I've told you that." He looked at Emery. "I'm sorry."

"That's alright," Emery said, though he swallowed disappointment as he did. For how could he be here, in the shadow of the Sainte-Victoire, and not meet Paul Cézanne? He grinned a little at the craziness of it. "But I think it's probably time for me to be getting back too." He began cleaning his own oils and brushes as Renoir had done.

"Could I just follow you?" Picasso said to Renoir, still sketching fiercely and not taking his eyes off his work except for quick glances to his subject matter. "You're staying with him, aren't you."

"You could try," Renoir said.

Emery looked at him closely. Somehow the connection of these painter ghosts to the land was different and they knew it. Different rules of reality, where intention, need, and acceptance played greater roles. Emery had *needed* to find Renoir. Renoir had accepted him. Picasso wanted to find Paul Cézanne, but could not.

But even that made Emery's head swim, for these two had none of the characteristics of ghosts – no ethereality or lack of substance. It was more that they had simply stepped through some skein of time to join him here. Or Emery was stepping backwards each day to join them.

Or he was crazy.

"I am done!" Picasso said, and turned his sketchbook around so that Emery and Renoir could examine it.

Which Emery could hardly resist. He put down his paints, palette, brushes, and cleaning cloth, and walked over, squatting down since Picasso did not seem inclined to stand. Renoir was at Emery's right elbow.

And the sketch?

A cubist joke, though not as blocked out and distorted as many from that period of Picasso's. With the deft touch of the skilled craftsman he was, Picasso had captured Emery's bearish physique in hyper-realistic detail, except that he was naked and excessively hairy, his penis erect and wagging like a snake towards an oblivious, rail-thin Renoir.

Both Emery's and Renoir's faces were a mass of blended perspectives in analytic cubist style, not recognizably either of them, except for Renoir's thin beard and mustache, yet somehow clearly them. Renoir, in all his distortion, was smiling at the world. Emery was gnashing his teeth like he was trying to make sense of his existence and failing miserably.

It was brilliant. Clutch your heart and fall to your knees brilliant.

It also made Emery want to smash Picasso's face in.

"My gift to you," the Spaniard said tossed Emery his spiral-bound sketch pad without ripping the masterpiece from it.

"Tomorrow," Renoir said quietly and turned from Emery to pick up his paraphernalia and leave.

"Tomorrow," Picasso said and jumped up to his feet. He brushed the dirt off his pants, turned, and walked back through the olive grove.

Then Emery himself turned to find Renoir packed up but not

yet departed. He looked unusually somber as he stroked his nose and tugged on his mustache. Like he had something to say but didn't know how to say it.

Emery waited.

"Be careful," Renoir said finally.

"Of Picasso?"

The Frenchman nodded. "He is a hungry man. Hungry for fame, for women, for followers. Never satisfied."

"Part of what makes him a great artist."

Renoir looked doubtful. "It makes him a stain on heaven's dress, I think."

"How well do you know him?"

"He has been chasing me for some time. Chasing Paul as well. Do you understand?"

Strangely, Emery did, because he felt the same hunger that he imagined Renoir feared in Picasso, the need to reach out and absorb the talents of his forerunners in art, to know what they knew, to fill himself with it so that his own work could be that much better. The never-ending conversations with the dead.

The fact that the forerunners were actually here, still living and learning themselves, Renoir and Cézanne both charting their own new paths that Picasso and Emery could build on...

"He won't swallow you," Emery said. "He can't, you know. We're all so different."

Renoir's face contracted in disappointment and he shook his head. "Be careful, *mon ami.*"

He turned and left. Emery watched him go, this slight figure, walking across the dusty red ground and vanishing into the arid pines, and wondered if maybe he had not understood what Renoir was getting at after all.

PAINTING THE NUDE

The days had faded together so that it was not until Friday night, late, eating a dinner of ratatouille which Violet had prepared for him to change his mind about the foods of Provence, that Emery remembered to tell her about Charlotte.

"She's coming for dinner tomorrow night," he said. "And before you say anything, I promised her that I would cook. Delicious as this is. Surprisingly. Even the eggplant."

Violet laughed, clapped her hands together, and brought them down into her lap so that her bosom pressed up and again Emery saw Violet's mother. The same dusky hair. Same flush that came into her strong cheeks when she was excited. But Violet was so young.

"Daddy, that's wonderful. That is absolutely wonderful!"

"Whoah. I didn't realize you were so starved for company."

"Oh, no. Not for me. For you! You like her, don't you."

"I... Yes, I think I do. I might."

"Good. Good!"

She jumped up from her seat, hitting the table clumsily as she did, and Emery wondered briefly whether she'd been drinking again before he'd come home from his time with Renoir and Picasso. She'd only had one glass of wine with dinner. Or had she stopped off somewhere in Aix for a shot or two? He knew how that could work.

"I'm *not drunk*," Violet said, seeing his face. "What I am is happy for you. And for me. Because... Because..."

"What, Violet?"

"I have a date for tomorrow night too!"

Emery blinked at her. "A date. Someone from your cooking class?" The thought suddenly struck him that it might be a woman. But in Julliard she'd been very involved with that boy, Benjamin Rand, a cellist, of all things. They'd slept together, Emery was pretty sure. True, she hadn't mentioned any romantic entanglements since then, but Emery hadn't exactly been in any state for her to confide such things in him.

Violet shook her head with a grin, seeming to see his thought processes. "Someone else. A man I met in Aix in a café."

"Whose name is?"

"Not something you're going to get just yet. No details. I don't want to jinx it."

"A nice man, though."

"Sterling, Dad. Even you would like him. Not that you get any say anymore, you know."

He held her gaze and saw the happiness in it, which, he figured, was ultimately what mattered. "Okay. I'm happy for you. And I look forward to hearing about it. Are...uh...you going to be back home on Saturday night, then?"

"Oh, Daddy!" She laughed and came over to give him a kiss. "I tell you what. If the date is crappy and I want to bail, I'll call up a female friend I've made in Aix, a girl my age, and crash there. Okay? The house will be yours all night."

Emery blushed. "You don't need to..."

"Three years, Daddy. God, I think Mom will be dancing

hallelujahs all across heaven if you get your ashes hauled with Charlotte."

Now he cleared his throat, his face so hot he thought it might explode. "There's absolutely no...um...no guarantee that..."

"Dad." Violet picked up his empty plate and glass. Her own too. "It's okay. It's pretty clear she's got a thing for painters, and more particularly for you. Be yourself. Enjoy it. Really. I'm going to. It's about time for both of us to start living again."

* * *

Saturday night.

Emery had visited the InterMarché, a bakery, and even a local butcher he had found, to prepare one of the few truly fancy meals that was part of his repertoire – rolled leg of lamb with mint jelly. There was nothing remotely Provençal about it, as far as he knew. It was just good food.

He'd cut his time in the fields short, which was just as well. Picasso had continued to show up wherever Emery and Renoir met. And he was a confusing presence, charming one visit, peevishly abrasive the next, goading Renoir to choose a new subject to paint, directing and belittling him in turn. Perhaps because of this, Renoir seemed increasingly distracted, ready to go back to Paris to find Aline. In fact he seemed to be staying mostly to protect Emery somehow, to absorb Picasso's combative energy or bolster Emery's own shaky return to his art. It made Emery feel foolish and weak.

But then Emery had come back from his food shopping this afternoon to see Violet pacing about waiting for him. She'd obviously wanted his reaction to her outfit, a tight little black dress that made his eyes nearly pop out of his head. As Emery stuttered, she beamed in confident satisfaction so profound that her eyes sparked. And all Emery could think was – all was as it should be. He was a widower who'd done good. Raised a happy, independent kid. Invited a sexy, intelligent Frenchwoman over for dinner. What more did he need?

Violet kissed him on the cheek and left. He got busy cooking and cleaning.

By the time he heard the sound of Charlotte's jellybean car in the driveway, everything was perfect. The sun hung low in the west. He'd put on a Diana Krall CD of slow jazz that he'd found in Avrochet's collection. The pot of green beans steamed. Lamb rolls almost done. Wild rice cooked in chicken broth and wine. Baguette cut up. Mozzarella and tomatoes drizzled in olive oil as an appetizer. Light green salad on the side.

The cooking meat smelled, even to his unrefined sniffer, heavenly. The vase of assorted wildflowers he'd gathered from around the property had mostly pink and purple tones, with asters and long delicate, violet-like blossoms, plus some yellow snapdragons and chrysanthemums for zest.

Charlotte stopped in the front door that he opened for her and looked past him into the main room with the table set up before the open french doors. Her nostrils flared, ears turned towards the music, every sense appearing to absorb and revel.

"Perfect," she said.

She didn't ask where Violet was. Had Violet called her about it? She simply walked through the main room to examine the flowers, then back to the kitchen to see what he had cooking.

And he watched her. Unlike Violet, she'd opted for an airy green dress that brought out her eyes and stopped well above her knees to show off her very toned, long legs. When she walked, her hips swayed so fetchingly it was hard, especially with his well-trained artist's eyes, not to imagine her naked.

She turned to see him studying her and smiled, seeming to know exactly what he was thinking. "The food smells delicious," she said, licking her lips. "We should eat it now, don't you think?"

Before they forgot to eat?

He nodded and served it in stages, small portions of a perfectly balanced blend of steaming and cool, complimented by a locally-produced red which the winery owner had made him taste test to confirm it was neither too sweet or too oaky. And they talked of her job, the places she traveled. Then of her relationship to art and artists – her former husband had been a collector and had required her to learn about art so she could advise him on his buying decisions. As the light of the day faded, taken over by the light of the candles at the table, she confessed she had been excited when Claude Avrochet had told her Emery Lake would be staying at his house for two months.

Emery ducked his head modestly, torn by conflicting feelings of wanting to bask in her praise and deny his old life. She covered for him by raising her near-empty wine glass to toast the meal they'd eaten.

As she clinked her glass of red with his own glass of Evian water, she leaned close enough to him that he cautiously moved the candles further to the side.

"So tell me now," she whispered intimately. "You do not drink alcohol? Ever?"

"I used to. I found it was something I couldn't appreciate in small amounts."

"Such a pity. Here in the south of France there is so much good wine."

"And chocolate. And cheese," he said.

"And bread."

"And beautiful women."

"Yes," she said. She was close enough for him to kiss her, so he did, tasting the perfection of wine and lamb and baguette in her mouth.

She had closed her eyes as he kissed her. Now she trembled a bit and sat back in her chair, regarding him with a wide, lazy smile.

Her dark blond hair, worn loose around her shoulders tonight, glowed and sparkled in the candlelight.

"I want you to paint me," she said.

Emery, seeing an easy move upstairs to the bedroom, twitched his head in surprise. "I'm...not sure I can."

Her smile didn't change. "I know you can. I told you I have studied your work. There is maybe no American artist I have seen who can capture women as you do. So I know you can. I don't know if you want to."

"My paints..."

"Claude left you his paints and blank canvases at your disposal. He told me."

Now Emery's throat was closing up and he felt his heart accelerating in an odd simulation of a panic attack. He looked down at the table and clenched his hands. "You don't know what you're asking."

"Yes. I think I do."

He looked up to meet her the candle-lit sparkle of her eyes. "It's been a long time. I'm not sure you'd want me to—"

She cut him off with another kiss, longer this time, deep-tongued and sensuous, that reached tingles deep through his body and galvanized his spine. When they separated, he stood up and held out his hand. "Come on, then."

He blew out the candles first and let their eyes adjust. Then in the dim light from the half moon, he led her south across the patio and along the stone path to the Avrochet studio and inside, since he rarely locked it, despite her earlier admonitions on the subject.

He found the lights without fumbling since he'd come in here frequently in the last week, seeking paints, brushes, and other supplies for his forays out in the olive grove. Now he walked straight to where he knew Charlotte would have to model, almost as if he'd been subconsciously planning this session.

It was an old couch that Avrochet himself had used in many of his paintings of Aimee, so it would be impregnated with that painter's love and sex. Not to mention its simple, solid construction with old-Empire claw feet and purple brocade covering.

Emery walked behind it and shoved one corner so it came more into the room and sat on a better angle from the window. It would be too harshly lit by the sun in the daytime, but now, in the softer light of the studio's adjustable incandescent bulbs, with the moon an eerie circle up high in the window behind, it would be perfect.

By the time he'd turned around, Charlotte had already removed her clothes and Emery felt a moment of excited weakness in his knees when he saw her.

She had to be almost his age. Forty-one? Forty-two? She had never had children and, like many French women, watched her weight. Yet she was not overly muscled like an American movie star trying to stay young. Her stomach hung low and soft. So too her breasts, with wide, dark nipples. And all but her triangle of her close-shaved pubic hair was as evenly tanned as her face. True southern French.

"I assume you wished me naked," she said.

For more than just painting, he wanted to quip, but knew it was redundant, so he simply nodded. "Here on the couch," he said.

She walked to him, paused with her body vibrating less than an inch from his, then stepped past him to the couch, turned and sat.

"Do you want me lying down?"

He studied her as she studied him. Her elbows were on her bare knees, fingers pressed together in semi-supplication, face angled, breasts half in shadow. A promise.

"Exactly like this," he said.

And like an experienced model, as practiced as ever Mattie had been, she simply nodded and held the pose while Emery quickly pulled over his easel, set up a fine linen canvas, and laid out his paints. Then he dialed down the overhead lights in her half of the studio to find the right shadows, went back to the easel, and began roughing in her form with a charcoal pencil, his hand deft and sure.

"May we talk as you work?" Charlotte asked.

He grunted.

"May *I* talk as you work?"

Another grunt.

"I've read a few of the interviews you've given over the years," she said. "I even found two issues of comic books you illustrated when you were still a teenager. *Wonderous Tales #15* and *Storm-Seeker #2.*"

"Good condition?" Emery said. The fall of her hair was too even, pulling down her head like a storm cloud.

"Very good condition. The boy who sold them to me had carefully preserved them in special plastic."

"Then they're worth quite a bit. Can you please carefully move one hand to scoop your hair back from the right side of your face and bring it over your head so all your hair falls down to the left."

"Like this?" She did as he asked, but now something was lost in the position of her eyes.

He put down his pencil and walked to her, conscious of the hard bulge in the front of his pants that was often there for him in the intensity of new discovery. He knelt before her, smelling the citrus musk of her skin, and reached a finger gently under her chin. He lifted the chin slightly above ninety degrees. Then he leaned in and kissed her tenderly on her lips so that her face opened slightly in surprise.

"Exactly like that," he said, stood, and walked quickly back to his easel to finish his sketch in a few quick strokes.

Then he paused, eyeing the tubes of oil paints he'd laid out in first instinct, but seeing the scene now as a possible acrylics wash in cool, moonlit blues.

"Not an abstract," Charlotte said, without losing the surprise from her face. "I want to glow like the woman in *The Diver*."

The Diver. He'd done that one shortly after the Beijing Olympics, transposing the political fierceness, the single-minded obsession of what he and Mattie had watched on television, to their little floating dock on Long Lake. There Emery had painted a tiny Chinese body builder tanning in a bikini. All her muscles had been clenched off and on for hours. Intense concentration. The perfect suntan position. Score – ten point zero, across the board.

"Oils then," he told Charlotte now. "Hours. Both tonight and tomorrow."

"I am yours for as long as it takes."

And no longer? Almost as pressing was the question of what Renoir would do if Emery did not show up in the olive grove tomorrow. Would he vanish and never return? Would even Picasso disappear?

"Tonight and tomorrow night," he said, unscrewing the caps from his paints and laying out a cool palette of Prussian blue, ultramarine, cobalt blue, emerald green, permanent green, alizarin crimson, raw umber, and yellow ochre, which he began to mix with his . "Only in this light."

"Making love to me with your paints."

Emery's chin jerked up to look at her, still studiously holding her pose. It was what Renoir had told him just the other day as the man admitted figure panting had always been not only his greatest tool to seduce women, but also an act of making love in itself. *For every time I paint a woman, she is Venus, or Nini*, he said. *And the painting is not done until you want to reach out and stroke her breast, squeeze her behind.*

"Yes," Emery said, to both Charlotte and Renoir, and began.

SHADES OF DORA MAAR

By three a.m., the moon had shifted out of sight above the roofline of the studio and Charlotte, for all her determination to be Emery's first figure model since Mattie's death, was visibly sagging.

Without notice, Emery wiped and cleaned his brushes in turpentine, scraped his palette, and came to Charlotte, pulling her up to her feet and helping her unkink her muscles with a vigorous stretch.

Then he spun her in his arms so she ended up pressed to his sweaty chest and he could feel her heart, too, thumping in excitement.

They kissed deeply and stumbled back to the couch she'd sat on for so long. Emery shed his clothes. They laughed and sighed and explored each other, though Emery felt he already knew each smooth curve and hidden shadow of her. This was merely his hands and mouth confirming what his eyes had taken in.

While she, in gripping his chest hairs, then moving her hands lower to grip the hardness between his legs, seemed to be taking ownership, claiming the rights she had earned in her steadfast modeling. Until their mutual claiming of each other brought their connection – he inside her, their sex parts hooked and sliding like they were suddenly both one of Avrochet's horrific flesh-machine constructs, and simultaneously the oldest of the old beasts dancing in the wild wood together.

Their sounds, their juices, mixing and thumping on the old, overstuffed couch together in ways both traditional and gymnastic, came finally to a series of climaxes, first for Charlotte, then for Emery, that squished and squeezed a gush of satisfied grunts from both.

It left them both spent. Panting.

Ten minutes later, inspired by some vague recollection of a Picasso painting that Emery did not even want to think about, he untangled himself from Charlotte's limbs, slid off the couch, and scooped her up in his arms as if she were not a full grown woman, but a nothing waif and he, a giant bear. Bull? His mind was confused. It was far too deep into the darkest time of night.

He turned with her in his arms and walked with supernatural strength out of the studio, hitting the lights off with his elbow as they left. Along the stone path, into the house, up the stairs. He carried her to his bed, Claude and Aimee Avrochet's bed, and laid her down.

There he lay down beside her. They kissed and stroked her passionately until they connected a second time and drove with more deliberate concentration to a mutual climax. Then they both fell into a sound sleep.

For Emery, the sleep was only two hours.

Something was awake and goosing him into action. Not to finish the study of Charlotte, though he would surely do that at the end of this day. Something *else* drove him. Something *critical*.

He slipped off the low queen-sized bed where Charlotte still slept, her long dark body a study in sculptural loveliness. Pulling on a fresh pair of underwear and socks, he tugged on his jeans and donned a tee-shirt and fleece before creeping from the room.

Downstairs, he found his running shoes and a piece of paper and pen. He left a note for Charlotte, telling her he would probably be out for much of the day. She should make the house her own or drive home as pleased her, but in the evening he hoped to pick up where they'd left off.

Then he grabbed a pear, baguette, cheese, and a water bottle to add to his backpack, walked out to the studio through the early glimmers of dawn to retrieve a field easel, painting supplies, and his work in progress, and he headed out through the gardens and off across the fields and fences.

"It wasn't the painting which frightened me but the sex after," Emery explained to Renoir as the finer-boned man tackled his new subject, a pair of twisted olive trees, from a standing position this morning.

"Because the painting is *your* passion," Renoir said, barely pausing in his own work. Emery had barely managed to set up his canvas beside the man before abandoning it to pace and confess what he had done. "And it is your craft. You control the composition, the colors, the textures and what the viewer will see. You lead them to the beauty you wish them to find."

"Not spontaneous. Not out of our control."

"Of course not! Unless you are a boy or young man. Great art is not an accident."

"And great sex?"

Renoir shrugged, but Emery saw him grin underneath his thin mustache and rub his nose. "Much of that lies with the woman, I think. At least it lies as much with her as with you." He laid down a few more dabs of color. "*Was* it great?"

Emery laughed. "Yeah. More than seems decent."

"Because of your dead wife."

"That's right."

As Renoir nodded, Emery smiled, amazed at how good it felt to unburden himself like this to another man. Not that he'd ever been shy around other men, but they'd never been his close confidantes, with the possible exception of Max Hebbler, who was more father-confessor than confidante. But Emery *trusted* Renoir. Not just because his paintings seemed to all find the best, the happiest, the strongest parts of life and people, but because even Pierre-Auguste battled through a surprising amount of self-doubt about his talents to keep on exploring, sharing, changing...

"God in Heaven," the thin artist now muttered under his breath.

Sure enough, when Emery raised the brim of his straw hat to see better, Picasso had arrived. No warning this time. He was somehow right there behind them, like he'd crept up on them, tree to tree, then jumped out like an overgrown garden gnome in a loose shirt that showed off his chest.

"So early this morning!" he boomed.

He said it as a criticism, as if it were Emery's fault. Which made Emery suddenly wonder if it were. Emery, after all, was the one who'd felt driven to come out at the break of day because his time with Charlotte unsettled him. Yet Renoir had already been here when he arrived, set up and waiting for him. And now Picasso was here too, hours earlier than usual.

Then Emery consciously noted the Spaniard's age. Despite his physicality, he looked brown as a beech nut with a more lined face. His hatless head sported hair gone a gunmetal gray in a U-shape around a slick bald pate. Older than Emery then. Maybe...fifty?

It somehow pushed at Emery as much as Charlotte's lightning

intimacy had. So much so fast. Like time was driving him forward and even coming out here at the crack of day was not going to save him from its march.

The effect was heightened when Emery saw Picasso had brought along his own canvas, easel, and paints. Did this mean a truce? He was going to paint alongside Emery and Renoir? Or did it mean something more dire? That he too felt their time slipping away, *his* time at least? He had to paint now or vanish forever with only the two sketches he'd done of Emery – one by the wall before Emery had met Renoir, and one of he and Renoir as cubist idiots – left behind him to mark his strange existence here.

"Get much older and you'll just vanish away," Emery said to his face.

Picasso blanched. "The sketch I did of the two of you. Where is it?"

"Why?"

"I want it back. It's mine."

"What?"

"You heard me. I loan this piece to you and you think you can just take it from me?"

He said it with such conviction that for a moment Emery wondered if he was remembering it wrong. He looked at Renoir for support but the thinner artist, also the youngest of the three of them, was stroking his nose and tugging his mustache, not looking at Emery.

"Why are you just standing there?" said Picasso, planting his fists on his hips and thrusting out his lower lip. "Didn't you bring the sketchbook I did it in? You did, didn't you. Because you hoped I would do another picture and you could steal that one as well. Isn't that so?"

The artist began to move towards Emery's knapsack and finally jolted Emery into action. "Stay out of there!" he roared, rushing past Picasso and grabbing the knapsack up from the ground.

But his roar, his height, his glower, only slowed the Spaniard down. He circled Emery now, with nostrils flaring and shrinking as if looking for an opening to charge.

"*My* art! *My* drawing! You would try to steal it from me? Sell it? It's not signed. If you show it anywhere I will say it is not mine. It is a fake."

"And no one will know, will they?" lied Emery. "Because there's nothing distinctive about it. Nothing that any young art student couldn't have done."

That rocked Picasso back for the first time and he crossed his arms over his chest, considering, his eyes coal black and deadly.

"Maybe," suggested Renoir, "what Pablo needs is a gift in exchange. You could paint a portrait of him. An original Lake for an original Picasso."

Emery laughed at the ludicrousness of such an exchange, yet he saw a glint in Picasso's eyes and had a sudden flash of understanding. It wasn't about the art at all. Otherwise why wait until now, almost a week later, to bring it up. No, this was about power. If Picasso could force Emery to paint him, he had won. And he would be part of Emery's oeuvre forever, a more insidious victory.

"Okay," Emery said flicking a finger at the brim of his hat. "But a drawing, like he did of us. A sketch for a sketch."

Picasso's teeth clenched and his eyes narrowed, but he nodded. "How would you like me to pose? With my shirt off and my dick out?"

"Not necessary," Emery grunted, and unzipped his pack to pull out his sketchbook.

When he did, he flipped it open, stopped, and frowned. This was the same book Picasso had stolen from him last week and drawn his cubist double portrait on. Yet there were no drawn pages in it. Someone had ripped out Picasso's sketch.

Violet? Charlotte? Had Emery himself done it some moment he'd forgotten? Or had Picasso, in one of his goading visits here over the last few days, searched through Emery's pack when his back was turned and reclaimed his drawing? And then demanded its return? Yes. That would fit.

He looked up slowly at the short Spaniard's glare and thought, *Alright, you talented genius phoney.*

He pulled out a trio of pencils, found a place to sit with his back to an olive tree, and waited for Picasso to walk closer and pose. Then he began to draw.

* * *

"Hey!"

A female voice, calling from somewhere to the west far beyond the reaches of the olive grove, snapped Emery out of his artistic immersion. He looked and couldn't see the caller, which meant whoever it was couldn't see him and was calling for someone else.

He was done, in any case. The portrait was finished.

He smiled at it now. Picasso had drawn him in the style of one of his earlier periods. Emery had now returned the favor – hyper-realistic, with only the musculature exaggerated, maybe even in a way Picasso would appreciate. And different clothing, of course.

"You were always a student of Nietzsche, weren't you?" he asked Picasso now.

The man had turned his head towards whoever had been calling them. This was bizarre, actually, since Emery didn't think Picasso or Renoir interacted with anyone in this world except for him. Unless the caller was from *their* time period? That would actually be exciting. Another artist from the late nineteenth or early twentieth century? Who? Mary Cassat, perhaps? Degas's would-be girlfriend?

"Hunh?" Picasso snorted, turning back to Emery.

"Nietzsche. You studied him," Emery repeated. "*Man and Superman?*"

"Yes," Picasso said.

"Good." He turned the sketchbook around for Picasso to see, then ripped off the drawing and handed it to him.

The Spanish genius took it, and studied it closely, coal-black eyes raking over it, back and forth. "What is this clothing you've drawn me in, like a tight pair of long underwear and a bullfighter's cape? A diamond shape on the front with a large S inside it?"

"The 'underwear' is supposed to be blue, the cape and boots and S are red. The S stands for Superman. A Nietzsche Superman."

Emery managed to keep a straight face as he said it, wondering again at just how much these two characters knew. Siegel and Shuster's *Superman* had made its first appearance in the late 1930s. Picasso would have been late fifties by then, if he'd even have noticed it while he was bouncing back and forth between Paris and Cannes.

The corners of Picasso's mouth turned down and he nodded approvingly, obviously flattered by the portrait and clueless as to any cultural reference beyond what Emery had just told him.

"Gift repaid?" Emery said.

"Would this have sold for much to your collectors?"

"Oh yes," Emery said, clued into the game at last. The man liked winners.

"But not as much as my sketch."

"I won't be selling your sketch."

"Then," Picasso said and paused dramatically, "I will accept this as the gift of a friend who shares what he can."

And again the smile that, damn him anyway, made Emery actually feel favored.

"*Emery!*"

The woman's cry again, closer, familiar, and clearly directed at him. Emery scrambled to his feet in confusion, striding away from the tree where he'd sat until he could see the figure winding her way among the thicker trees of the grove, coming towards him.

Charlotte. Dressed in a set of casual, fawn-colored clothes that she must have borrowed them from Violet's wardrobe or had stashed in her own car, she ducked and wove her way through the olive grove, coming ever closer.

But how had she found the place? And how, for the love of God, was it that both Picasso and Renoir now seemed to watch her approach with interest? Or did this hallucination he let himself indulge in *make* it work this way? They were part of Emery's mind, so why wouldn't they—

"I almost didn't recognize you in that funny hat," Charlotte called out as she rounded one tree then vanished behind another. "Who are your friends?"

No. Emery was struck dumb. Charlotte Boulain, of the twenty-first century, a friend of the Avrochets, clearly saw Pierre-Auguste Renoir and Pablo Picasso. Just as they clearly saw her.

Yet Emery *knew* other modern people couldn't see Renoir and Picasso. They couldn't. It would be...too big a secret. Too improbable.

Charlotte cleared the thickest part of the olive grove, jumped over a tumble of grassy rocks near them, and trotted up to them. She stopped, sweating, face flushed in the late morning sunshine. Her smile ran almost ear to ear as she saw his expression. She pushed back a strand of blond hair that had slipped from her ponytail and laughed. "You're wondering how I found you."

"Among other things."

"Violet. She tried to call you this morning, and when I explained how you'd left me here, she told me you do this often. She skipped her class to follow you out a few days ago. She gave me directions."

"I see." The beginnings of a very bad feeling were forming like an acid lump in his stomach but he tried to simply look peeved, not terrified.

"I told her that you'd be annoyed and she said to tell you that you owed her."

Like he'd owed Picasso? The bad feeling just kept growing.

"But she didn't mention you'd found other artists to hang out with," Charlotte said, shifting her weight coquettishly to one hip and looking at Renoir, who'd put down his paints and walked up to stand beside Emery.

"Right. Of course. Charlotte Boulain, this is...uh..."

Renoir removed his boater hat and held out his hand to her. "Pierre-Auguste Renoir, Mam'selle. Enchanted."

"Like the artist?" Charlotte said. "I think you even look a bit like him, if I recall correctly. The self-portraits he did..."

"I have done a few."

"Very good," Charlotte said and laughed. "You're very good." She turned back to Emery. "And your other friend?"

Emery turned to see Picasso standing a few steps back, feet planted in unconscious mimicry of the Superman pose Emery had drawn him in, his chin forward, his arms crossed over his chest, his Lake portrait rolled and stuck into his front pants pocket.

Emery wanted to laugh, except for the flush of strained excitement on Charlotte's face. With no words at all, the Picasso was projecting his boundless confidence and voracious hunger onto her. It transfixed her like a deer in the headlights.

And of course now when he smiled—there it was!—the intense fear chunked into relief, which the recipient experienced as pleasure. Emery could feel it in Charlotte's quick release of breath.

Then she was stepping past Emery and extending her hand to Picasso. He was shorter than her by a good four or five inches but took her hand with both of his as if she were a supplicant.

"You know who *you* resemble, don't you," Charlotte said.

"Who?" said Picasso curiously.

"Someone I actually met once. I was a baby. He was an old man."

Picasso tilted his head to look up at her curiously. "I don't remember you."

"My father told me about it when I was a teenager. He said he was at a bullfight in Arles and when he was coming out, he bumped into this frail old man with his young wife. And who should it be but Pablo Picasso! My father said the man was about to be furious at him until he saw me in my father's arms. Then he became sweet and fascinated by me and begged to kiss me on the forehead. Somehow I grew up with the feeling I would meet Picasso again and I would be the one to kiss him!"

"Then here is your chance," Picasso said. He eyed her intently and Emery thought she was going to lean down to kiss him.

Instead she freed her hand from his grasp and laughed. "I grew up to discover that Pablo Picasso was a brilliant artist but not very nice to women. Are you like that too?"

Picasso shrugged.

"But you are him?" Charlotte challenged.

"If I am, will you kiss me?"

"What is your name?"

"He calls himself 'Genius,'" Emery interrupted, stepping up beside Charlotte to tower even more over the squat, balding artist. "Isn't that right?"

"No," Picasso said calmly. "It's not."

"No?" Emery said. "Then what is it now? Lord king ruler of all?"

Emery's tone was harsh enough that Charlotte glanced sideways at him and he at her. Had she read *all* of Picasso's history, his look asked. Had she recalled the fact he swung wildly from taking a seventeen-year-old innocent named Marie-Thérèse Walter as his muse-mistresses to wooing and destroying some of the continent's most intellectually gifted women? Like Dora Maar, a painter and photographer who was a key figure in the Surrealist movement. Bedded by Picasso and broken down to the nightmare he recorded in one of his most horrible cubist portraits – *Weeping Woman.*

Not very nice to women indeed.

Charlotte seemed to get it. She glanced back briefly at Picasso, then smiled and retreated. She walked over to Renoir's simple easel, with its dancing olive tree slowly taking form in a thousand dabs of almost-pointillist color.

"You have the style down beautifully, Pierre!" she called back to Renoir, who smiled and nodded graciously. She stepped sideways to Emery's easel. "This one I know..." Then she looked around and became disappointed. "Nothing by Pablo?" she asked.

With a flourish, Picasso pulled Emery's sketch out of his back pocket and approached her. "An experiment," he said.

She took it and sniggered. "Now *that* is vintage Lake. Not to mention the fact he's used you as a model."

Picasso caught Emery's eye. "She's very sharp, this one." Then back to Charlotte. "I would like to paint you. Will you come back with me to my studio?"

The uncomfortable ball in Emery's gut suddenly tripled in size and began twisting about. Charlotte would *not* become a Dora. He hurried over to her and wrapped an arm around her waist. "No. She and I have an appointment. A figure study already begun."

"Which you walked out on," she said sweetly, glancing up at him.

"I left you a note. And we agreed it would not continue until the evening."

"So then I have time to go with Pablo?"

"No!" Emery rubbed his forehead hard and looked desperately from Picasso to Renoir and back to Charlotte. "We have...other things we need to do."

"Such as?"

"Such as this!" he said and leaned down to kiss her sloppily on the lips, jerking her around to him as he did so, almost losing his hat, off-balance.

But she caught him, and her lips molded eagerly into his, finding his tongue and snaking her hands up around his neck, into the hair on the back of his head. Emery sprang an immediate erection that strained painfully against the crotch of his pants. The *taste* of her, the feel of her pressed against him out here in the sunlight of the magic olive grove. He could smell her sweat and his own desperation. He could see, in visceral memory, all the colors and contours of her naked body and wanted to take her right here, right now.

He was crazy for thinking that, he knew but his head still swirled with the need and he refused to let her go. Nor was it only him, for he felt her press her middle hard against him when he went to pull away. Her hands pulled his mouth so hard to hers that their teeth scraped and she moaned. Her fingernails dragged down his neck and back up. His own hands roved down her back and found her round little ass. Her fingers dug into his hair, into his shoulders, held him around his neck.

Until, almost as if on long-but-identical timers, they both surfaced with a loud, "Ahhh!" and stared wildly into each other's eyes.

"That?" Charlotte breathed at him.

"My God, yes," he said.

"Then I guess we'd better go," she said.

They both looked around. Picasso was gone. Renoir's easel and painting supplies were gone. About forty yards to the south, Emery thought he saw the flap of Renoir's shirt disappearing into the path through the pines that led down to Aix.

"Or maybe we don't go," Charlotte said.

He looked down at her and his mouth slid into a wide smile. "We'll have to find some shade and soft ground."

They did.

TOO MUCH TOO FAST

Despite Emery's fear that Renoir would vanish if Emery didn't show up at the olive grove daily, he declared Monday a day off. Both he and Charlotte were too wiped from their lovemaking and all-night figure-painting session to go anywhere. Charlotte called in sick. They stayed in bed.

Nor did Violet interrupt them. She'd apparently come home during their time in the studio and actually slept in her room Sunday night, but neither Emery nor Charlotte had even heard the car pull out in the morning. They only figured it out when Charlotte found Violet's note set out on the kitchen table.

"She says she won't be back tonight until late," Charlotte told Emery as he scratched his belly and rummaged through the fridge for something to make for a midday brunch.

"More time to fuck," he grunted back.

"For us, or her?"

He froze in his search and looked up in shock. "Hm. Both?" He resumed his search to cover the return of that little ball of uneasiness in his stomach.

* * *

FUCK THEY DID, Emery and Charlotte, for much of that afternoon. Though it seemed to Emery that towards the end, while he was still marveling in the wonder of it all, Charlotte grew distracted.

He mentioned it. Bluntness had always been something Mattie had prized in him.

Charlotte looked stricken, then offended. She rolled her lithe body off the kitchen countertop that he had hiked her up onto and went in search of her clothes.

She came back to the main room five minutes later fully dressed and announced she had to get to work.

"That sickness flew by quickly," Emery said.

"Sometimes they do," she replied.

Then she was out the front door and running for her little jelly-bean car before he even had time to find a dishtowel big enough to wrap around himself.

* * *

CHARLOTTE'S FIGURE STUDY.

Emery found himself studying it at eleven p.m. out in the studio when he heard the crunch and dull roar of a car in the driveway. Then the thunk of a car door.

Charlotte returning to apologize? He could imagine it was. The painting he'd done of her made her presence tangible before him. Like he could reach to the canvas and touch her tanned skin, feel its smoothness. Just like Renoir had talked about. Emery had achieved that here. Which meant that, for all his unwillingness to paint Charlotte, he was glad he had. This painting had proved to him that his skills had not vanished with Mattie's death. They might even have mysteriously advanced.

"Shine on, wonderboy," he muttered and tore himself away

from his self-adulation to hurry out of the studio, shutting off the lights as he went.

He knew it was almost certainly not a repentant Charlotte who'd just come back to the house. It had to be Violet. And Emery actually missed her, something he wouldn't have thought possible two weeks ago. In fact he not only missed his daughter, but worried about her. How parental was that?

Because he hadn't seen her in what? Gosh, two whole days.

Smiling at himself, he reached the French doors, entered the house, and immediately felt the hackles rise on the back of his neck.

Violet was there. She'd come in the front door and stood in the middle of the living room, the kitchen behind her. And she wasn't moving. She was just wearing a stupid smile and looking in his direction like she'd known he'd run in to find her. She wore a different dress than the one she'd left on Saturday in, but this one, in deep scarlet, was every bit as figure-hugging. And her hair was a ratty mess. Her mascara and lipstick were smeared. It was as if she'd gotten herself dolled up after cooking class for another date but then cried and chewed her makeup to pieces on the way back here.

"Violet?" he said, approaching her cautiously.

It seemed to jerk her out of whatever fugue state she'd slipped into, because her body crumpled a little and she turned from him to walk to the kitchen counter. She threw down her handbag there.

Then she spun around to him, face all bright and cheery, despite the ghastly make-up. "Hello, Daddy! So! I'm guessing you had a good time Saturday night! And this morning too!"

Despite her attempt to act normal, her eyes kept darting around, seeming to register and take in everything. The pillows bunched up on the couch? A stain on the kitchen counter?

"Violet, I'm sorry I didn't even say hi to you when you came back last night. I didn't hear you come in. I was in the studio, painting Charlotte."

He'd decided to tell her as soon as possible to get it over with, but seeing her involuntary gasp now, Emery wished he'd waited. She was just on the edge of tears, he thought. Just holding on by her carefully polished fingernails. Dealing with another woman swooping in to take her mother's place was the last thing she needed to deal with.

But she surprised him by turning the gasp into a manic smile and going to him, hugging him. "Oh, Daddy! That's good! That's really good! Can I see it?"

Then she was pushing past him to go and see it before he could answer.

"It's not completely finished," he said as he ran after her. I may have to adjust the light balance or dial it down. And there are finishing details on the hair, on the background, that..."

He let it die as he stepped into the studio behind her. She'd flicked on the light going in and stopped dead halfway across the floor, staring at the canvas.

Charlotte, he knew, had liked it. She'd wanted to take it from him right there, even knowing that was not how it worked. And Emery liked it. He liked what it said about *him* as much as her.

But Violet?

"Oh. My. God." She took another few step forward and finally walked right up to the canvas and reached out to it, stopping her fingers just short. "Oh. My. God."

"You hate it. You hate that she was nude. You hate that it wasn't your mother."

Violet spun around on him and he saw that the mania was momentarily gone from her eyes. "Emery Lake, this is probably the best thing I've ever seen you do."

He stared at her open mouthed, unsure of what to say to that.

Finally, he said, "Because it's been so long. Because you wanted me to paint again so badly."

She shook her head. "Maybe? But I just know I want to touch it so badly you've got me thinking I'm a lesbian."

And just the saying of it spun up the mania in her eyes again until she was smiling madly and hurrying past him, out of the studio, back to the house.

He followed, finally catching up to her at the tiled stairs leading up. He grabbed her arm so she skittered to a halt and half spun on the third stair.

"You're just going to go to bed now?" he said.

"It's late, Dad. It's almost midnight. I've got cooking class tomorrow."

"Like you had cooking class today?"

"Jesus Christ, like I had it today!" She shook her arm until he let go. Then she glared at him, hard. She stepped backwards up one step.

"Violet," he said softly. "I'm not the enemy."

"Like hell you're not! You're my father. You have to be."

"Because...?"

"Because it's your responsibility, goddammit!"

"To do what?"

"To fight me! To tell me I'm doing something stupid! The wrong thing! I'm going to get hurt!"

Emery furrowed his brows now to hide how the discomfort in his gut was changing to panic. "*Are* you doing something stupid? Are you going to get hurt?"

"*No!*" She banged her shoulder against the hard white wall to her right, then followed it up with her head. "Maybe! I don't know."

"Violet..." He reached for her arm but stopped. "I can't fight you. I'm not... I don't know how. You're mother might have. But...I'll listen."

Her teeth were still half-bared at him, but her eyes, angry and red, were at least *seeing* him now. The spinning had receded again. "You never listen," she grunted. "You never have."

"I know. But how's this? You told me you'd met some man in Aix, someone not in your cooking class. You were going out with him on Saturday night and thought you might end up sleeping with him. I'm guessing that, since you didn't come home on Saturday night, you probably did."

She chewed on her lips and said nothing so he continued.

"Then, after class, you went to see him again. Maybe you even bought this dress especially for it. But he wasn't expecting you and this time he didn't welcome you in like you expected him too. Maybe you even fought?"

"H-he said I was *pushing* him. That...that I was *clinging*. That I was asking *too much!*"

"Were you?"

"I'm..." She closed her mouth and looked at him, and it took all his strength not to turn away. Because at that moment she looked just like her mother had one time after a rare bad performance. Mattie had wanted to blame everyone else – the conductor, the pianist and cellist she was performing with, the lighting techni-cians, the audience – until she'd had just enough distance and safety to see that no, it had been her. She'd been so stressed by her mothering duties and the process of buying the lake house that she'd let her game slip. She'd been unprepared.

It had devastated her. And all Emery could do, as he did now, was watch his loved one crumble, hoping he'd be able to pick up the pieces when it was done.

"Oh God," Violet said in a little squeak.

In Mattie that had been followed by a heart-rending rush of tears and two days in bed. With Violet, her eyes went funny and it was as if Emery could see her reliving the entire afternoon and evening's fiasco through the eyes of her put-upon lover. Seeing herself appear unexpectedly. Feeling her push her way in, gushing and overpowering him. Hearing the too-high voice. Smelling the new perfume. Seeing the new dress.

Then she refocused on Emery, her eyes stricken. "God, Daddy, what I did... He must think I'm insane. I've scared him away forever."

"No," said Emery. "Scared him, maybe. We men scare easily. But I think we all believe women are inherently insane too. He'll need to meet you again at least once more to see *how* insane you are. If he really likes you, of course."

"He does. He does. I could tell he does." She nodded hard now to convince herself. "So I just have to act cool, right?"

"And don't call him. Let him call you. Or at least wait awhile. The party that screwed up can't jump back too fast. That's the rule."

He was thinking as he said it about how long he had to wait before he called Charlotte. Not too soon. That was desperate. But not to wait too long either, because then the awkwardness between them would just grow.

It raised a twitch on the corner of Violet's mouth. "Dad, you sound like a girl."

"I'm an artist. We're sensitive. You're hearing sensitive."

"About relationships? I don't think so." She sniffed and wiped her nose and eyes. "You messed up with Charlotte, didn't you."

He stuck his chin out, but nodded. "Yeah."

She laughed and sniffed and wiped again. "How come I got your genes and not Mom's?"

"You..." He cleared his throat and stared at the wall. "You got more of your mother's genes than you know. Her looks. Her fire."

"Your height."

"You taller than your guy?"

"Oh, yeah."

"Good. He gets out of line with you, you can slug him."

She gave a strained little laugh. "Right."

"Just saying. As a father."

There was a long silence, during which neither moved. Finally Violet sniffed and wiped her nose again. "Time for—"

"—bed. Yes." He waited.

"Thanks, Daddy," she said softly, and leaned over to kiss his forehead.

"Anytime, honey."

Then she headed upstairs to the bathroom while he went to his own bedroom, having a brief flash of what it had been like with Charlotte in here this morning. Then what it had been like for night after night, morning after morning, with Mattie and her long dark hair spread out over the pillow.

"I tried," he whispered to the empty bed.

And the memory of Mattie, as he closed the bedroom door behind him, seemed to whisper back, *It wasn't enough. It's going to get so much worse.*

COOKING WITH GARLIC AND TEARS

Before she left the next day for her cooking class, Violet gave her father a gift.

"A cell phone?" Emery turned the little flip phone over in his hands. "I already have a cell phone."

"But you don't use it, right? Too expensive. And it doesn't do the international chip thing, which is about as expensive as buying a whole new phone. Besides, I bought two, one for me, one for you, and got a great deal with a shared monthly *forfaits* of about thirty euros. Unlimited calls between our phones."

"I... Okay."

"You can't go off wandering in the fields out there without me being able to contact you."

Emery was thinking the same thing about her wandering around downtown Aix, seeing men he'd never met, whose name she hadn't even told him. "You're right. And maybe I'll take the bus to Aix today. Come and see where you're doing your class."

Violet turned away quickly, but not before he'd seen her blanch. "No, Daddy. Not today. We're working straight through lunch today. The teacher warned us. Make it tomorrow or Thursday and I'll meet you for lunch. Show you around."

"I went through the old city a lot with your mother. I think I could find my way around."

"Dad. No. Go paint in the fields. Finish your landscape. I'll be home for dinner."

Then she paused, pretending to be fixing a button on her blouse, but Emery knew she was waiting for his confirmation he wasn't coming. And bad father that he was, he gave it to her. She'd grown up all these years without him hovering over her shoulder. Surely she'd make it through a few more days without him. Especially since he didn't want to blow all his fathering credits now if the big storm was still coming.

Not enough, niggled in the back of his mind.

Then Violet was out the door and gone. And soon Emery was too, walking with his new cell phone out through the back garden, over the fences and stream and forest and fields.

* * *

PICASSO WASN'T at the olive grove that Tuesday, but Renoir was. He made no mention of Emery's Monday absence and the two of them simply painted side by side in companionate silence, with Emery fighting to convince himself there was nothing to talk about.

So too on Wednesday.

Violet made it home both days before him and cooked dinner, using many peppers and squashes and introducing him to seafood she claimed was fresh from the docks of Marseille where their teacher had taken them to shop. She seemed so happy and alive again. Her cheeks were flushed when she talked about her day.

She was still drinking wine with every meal, but that was the French way, she protested. She wasn't doing absinthe like the painters of yore, or whiskey like the rough types they'd met in Marseille, or even the hidden stashes of beer that Emery had been hooked on during his own slide.

And when Emery took the bus into Aix on Thursday, she met him at the splashing *Fontaine des Quatre Dauphins* (Fountain of the Four Dolphins) then wandered over to the cobblestoned Cours Mirabeau for some shopping and lunch before she had to drive back to her class in the southeast side of the city.

When she'd gone, Emery felt flush with the sense that things would work out after all. He pulled out his cell phone and the folded number he'd been carrying about in his jeans pocket for a few days now.

When the person he was calling answered, he could hear a dull rhythmic thunking in the background that made him think she must be on a train.

"Bonjour?"

Emery switched to French mode so naturally that he almost wouldn't have noticed it but for the silky husk of her accent. "Charlotte, this is Emery. Where are you?"

Her voice sounded wary. "I am halfway between Bern and Aix. You?"

"I am *in* Aix right now, looking at a lovely little hole-in-the-wall store that sells nothing but soap and spices in every color of the Mediterranean coastline."

"Both the soap and the spices?"

"They smell so good I want to wash my mouth out with them."

It was his clumsy attempt at an apology that he didn't expect her to get, but the pause in the line told him that maybe she did. "I won't be back for a few hours," she said. "Then I have paperwork to catch up on."

"How about tomorrow night. Friday. I think I might even persuade Violet to cook. She's been missing you too," he lied.

There was another pause. "Alright. But won't Violet want to see her man from Aix?"

"I'm going to try to persuade her to bring him."

"Ah." He heard the interest in her voice. "Okay. Yes. I'll be there around seven."

He hung up. Now he just had to convince his daughter.

* * *

"Do you understand women, Pierre?"

The Friday afternoon sun was so bright and hot that both Emery and Renoir had moved their easels into the shade and chosen new subjects – each other.

"What is there to understand?" the French artist said.

"Why they think how they do? Why they take offense? Why they fall in love or don't?"

Renoir's mouth twitched into a quick smile. "That is like asking why a deer runs at the sound of footsteps or the leaves blow in the wind. Women don't have such deep thoughts as we do."

Emery paused after his brush stroke and stared at the man. "You're serious?"

"You are thinking of Charlotte, are you not? You are thinking how she challenged Picasso, how we could see her and she could see us—yes, I am aware of more than you think, my friend— that this is because of her brain? Her thinking?"

Emery was speechless. Finally he said, "I wasn't thinking of that. But now that you mention it..."

"I think," Renoir said, stepping back from his canvas and comparing it critically with Emery's face, "that Picasso sees her only because she is so close to you. And she sees us with your eyes. You are the link here."

"The link between what?" Emery said cautiously.

"Between all of us." Renoir waved his hand around. "It's not natural. I know it. Your...backpack? Your clothes? I have met other Americans. You are not like anyone I have ever met. Except perhaps Charlotte. And I think that is only because she is with you."

"Which means my daughter could probably meet you as well."

"Yes. But do you really want that to happen? We artists are not always the best companions."

Emery chuckled. "At least she'd make you question your position that women don't think."

"You believe so?"

"Count on it!"

* * *

WHEN EMERY RETURNED to the house, it was barely five-thirty, but Violet was already there, bustling around the kitchen and living area as she cleaned and made things ready. She'd obviously already been to the InterMarché and purchased fresh food – a round of beef dripping blood through its wrapping, vegetables, different rounds of cheese, baguettes. Also a couple bottles of red wine, one of which was already open. A half-drunk glass of it sat on the kitchen counter beside the grocery bags.

"Your new beau," Emery called after her as she picked up a sweatshirt he'd left on the couch and carried it upstairs. "When's he showing up?"

"He's not coming!"

"What? How come?"

"He just can't!"

That didn't sound good. He climbed the stairs to find her going from room to room, distractedly. "I'm looking for my brush," she muttered when she saw him. "My hair brush."

"Your hair's fine."

She stopped and looked at him incredulously. "My hair?" She

grabbed a bunch of it, raised it, and let it drop. "My hair is dull brown and lifeless. Uninspired. But I'm thinking if I back-comb it and spritz it up..."

"You want to look like a eighties country singer?"

"I want to look *interesting*." she said and resumed her search.

"Anyone who doesn't find you 'interesting'," Emery said cautiously, "isn't really seeing you."

"Ohhh, Daddy. Ohhhhhh." She found her brush under a bunch of towels piled up on the dirty clothes hamper in the bathroom and she waggled it at him, her voice tight and her smile tighter. "If that is the best parental advice you have to give, you may as well give it up now, okay?"

"It's about your man, then."

She jerked away from him and found her hairspray on the long kitchen countertop. It was a French version of l'Oreal—they hadn't brought *any* liquids on the plane flight to Paris with them—which, from Violet's face as she read the back of the can, was not really intended for the maximum hold effect she had described.

Then her lips set in a hard line and she began the back-combing, spraying, treatment she'd described anyway. It wasn't long before Emery was gagging on the sharp smell and backing out into the hall.

"You know," he called back in at her, "there is the saying that there are always other fish in the sea. If this guy can't appreciate you for who you are, then—"

"Dad!" Violet slammed down her brush and hairspray bottle, then turned to face him. "This man is unique, amazing, gifted, funny, smart, and rich, okay? And he's a bit difficult too. It comes with the territory. Mom knew that when she married you! I know what I'm doing!"

Then she stomped to the bathroom door, caught it with her foot, and swung it closed in his face.

Emery backed away, turned, and went down the stairs. *Had* he been a difficult man even back when Mattie married him? Maybe. But he'd never for a moment let Mattie feel unappreciated.

Never.

* * *

BY THE TIME Charlotte drove up in her lime green jellybean, the entire house smelled of slowly simmering garlic and roast beef. If this had been the Catskills, Emery would have worried about black bears and cougars ambling in to check things out.

But here the patio doors and all the windows were open and the odor wafted everywhere. Emery even saw Charlotte raise her nose to sniff the air when she climbed out of her car.

Then he saw her and was amazed at how just the sight of her—she wore a white linen pantsuit this time, the bottoms rolled up her tanned calves, her sandals glittering and funky—sent his heart racing.

She'd touched him the last time she was here, not just on his lips and skin but on his heart. Not love. Not yet. But a very intense liking. The sense of possibility Violet had talked about. All part of the magic of the dead artists and this place. So whatever had really set her against him at the end of their last meeting was destined to crumble. She'd become part of his picture.

She saw him watching her and waved, then walked across the gravel of the drive to come to him.

She turned her cheek to him when he leaned down to kiss her and laughed nervously at his surprise. "Lipstick," she said. "I would like to look all put together for a little while at least this evening."

Her face was unreadable as she said it, so Emery didn't know if that meant she was expecting sex later or the crying fit of an argument. Or nothing at all.

God, he *was* turning into a woman. Just believe in the goddamned magic, Lake.

"Dinner's almost ready," he said. "Violet's in a bit of a panic because we had no basting tube or something, but it all looks good to me."

And without demanding any sort of response from her, he led her inside.

* * *

THEY'D FINISHED the main course at nine o'clock and were letting it sit a bit before Violet brought out the desert. Five candles flickered in a ring on the table, making their faces bright and flushed, making the dark outside twice as black.

Emery was clinging hard to his notions of fate and magic as he leaned back in his chair to study the two women of his life. Because even with every element of the dinner going like clockwork and surpassing Emery's idea of what home cooking could be, his daughter was still wired. On the edge. As brittle as her foot-tall hairdo. And this after at least three full glasses of wine. This was not the Violet he knew.

While Charlotte... She was as stunningly beautiful as he'd remembered, even with her blond hair pulled back and her smiles less frequent. Her years and minor wrinkles gave a character when she spoke that defied everything Renoir had said about women.

Her brain. Emery loved her brain. Her way of looking at things.

Yet where she'd been so immensely grounded before, where nothing could perturb her, now she seemed all surface and hidden. Case in point was how she had asked earlier on about the man Violet had gone out with last Saturday. Violet had basically told her to fuck off and Charlotte had immediately shut up. All of Emery's cajoling after that got her talking of the places she traveled for her work, the sort of people she met.

Surface! Fascinating, some of it, but all surface!

"You know what I think?" Emery cut in on Charlotte's discussion of the growing xenophobia in Switzerland and how it was affecting business with the rest of Europe.

"*What* do you think, Daddy?" Violet said too loudly. God, the hair was bigger than the early days of Shania Twain.

"I think someone at this table is hiding something."

Violet blanched and sat back in her chair. So did Charlotte, which hadn't been Emery's intention and threw him off a bit. Something to explore there. But first...

"Charlotte says you told her where to come and find me on Sunday. The olive grove just outside Le Tholonet. She said you'd followed me there one morning."

Violet grabbed her nearly-empty glass of wine and drained it.

"Well?" Emery said, casually taking the wine bottle off the table before Violet could refill her glass.

"Maybe Charlotte didn't understand exactly what I told her," she said in English.

"I understood," Charlotte said, also in English, with only the slightest accent.

Violet raised her eyebrows high and stared at her.

Charlotte switched back to French to add, "And your father knows I understood because I followed your directions and found him out there last Sunday."

"Alone?" said Violet, in French again too. Emery heard a quaver in her voice.

Charlotte shook her head. "You know he wasn't."

"I know," Violet whispered.

"Jesus!" said Emery and pushed back from the table. He stood awkwardly and carried the wine bottle and his own plate and cutlery back to the kitchen. The two women, he knew, were watching his back.

When he turned around again, though, they had both stood and were bringing over their plates and glasses and cutler and baguette basket as if nothing unusual had happened at all.

"It's not that big a deal, Daddy," Violet said now as she scraped her plate and began putting things away. Her voice was trying to be chirpy but it was too loud again. "So you've got a secret cabal of painters who like to gather and paint the mountain. So what?"

"Yes, Emery," said Charlotte, working beside Violet. "So they've given themselves dress-up names and pretend they're old masters. As long as you're all having fun, yes?"

"Exactly!" said Violet. "As long as you're all having fun out there. And God knows it's helped you get painting again. That and sex with Charlotte!" She turned awkwardly to Charlotte in the crowded kitchen. "I saw the figure painting he did of you. It is so good! You are so beautiful!"

"Thank you," said Charlotte tightly.

"You should pose for him again!" Violet said. "It's one of the best things he's done! You're his muse now!"

"I don't..." Charlotte began.

"Of course you do! My dad likes you, so you like him too! That's the way it works! That's how it's supposed to work! Don't you French people get that? My mom got that! She was French! She got it!"

Emery gently took Violet by both her arms but didn't let her shake him off this time. "Violet! That's enough. Calm down."

"Ungh! No! Daddy, you tell her! You tell her how Mom was! How a woman is supposed to be! Or a man! When someone loves them!"

"*Violet!*" Emery was physically struggling with his daughter now as she thrashed about in his hold, knocking dishes, elbowing Charlotte. One of the wine glasses that hadn't been put far enough back on the counter got brushed and tumbled off the edge. It smashed on the tile, spraying shards everywhere.

Emery wrapped his arms around his daughter and physically hauled her backwards out of the kitchen area until the two of them were standing in the middle of the tiled living room. As Emery planted his feet, twisting his head to avoid her hair and preparing for more struggle, Violet burst into tears and sagged in his arms.

Not knowing what else to do, Emery raised one of his hands to her hair and stroked its stiffness backwards and down. "It's okay, honey. It's okay."

Charlotte, he noted, had found the broom and dustpan and was sweeping up the glass in the kitchen. She looked like she had a cut on her leg from where a shard had hit. A little trickle of blood had started.

"Men are so...difficult," Violet said into his chest, still crying, but quieter now, her hands clutching his shirt as she wiped her nose on his chest.

"Love is difficult," he murmured back to her. But inside he was thinking, *Not like this, though. Violet, you should not even* think *of loving someone who makes you feel like this.*

Charlotte had finished her sweep and dumped the contents in the trash below the sink. She was now somberly watching Emery with Violet.

"I think it's time for me to go now," she said.

Emery shook his head and mouthed *no, no, no, no.*

"I have another train to catch tomorrow. Business in Paris."

"On Saturday?" Emery said.

She shrugged. "The store manager is leaving town for the summer next week. Beating the August rush."

"When will you be back?"

Another shrug. "Monday. Tuesday. I have other stores to visit as well."

Violet had gone still against his chest, listening.

"Okay," Emery said. "I guess." He looked down at Violet's head and wondered if he could release himself enough to walk Charlotte to the car. Violet seemed to sense his thoughts and clutched his shirt tighter.

"We will talk another time," Charlotte said and let herself out.

Talk another time? Not kiss another time? Not make love another time? He could the coldness in her voice. He remembered the way she'd blanched when he'd mentioned secrets. As had Violet. What the hell was going on around here anyway?

Violet must have felt his anger and suddenly released herself from his grip, staggering backwards, sniffing and wiping her eyes.

"Daddy... The clean up... I'll do't tomorrow. Gotta go t'bed."

"Of course you do."

He stared hard at her as she turned and wove her way up the stairs.

That wasn't his daughter, nor was Charlotte the woman he'd painted a few days ago. Who *were* these people and *what the hell was going on?*

THE MASTER OF AIX

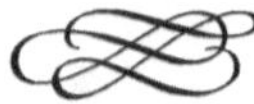

Emery had peevishly left the kitchen a mess when he'd headed out at daybreak. Violet said she'd clean it up? He'd let her. It was Saturday. What else did she have to do?

By the time he reached the dirt road that ran down out through the olive grove, he was so worked up his stomach was in knots and he realized he'd forgotten to eat breakfast. Or pack anything for lunch. Didn't even have his hat.

Well fuck it. The last thing you needed when your world was falling apart was food and shade.

He did have his easel strapped to the outside of his backpack. And his half-done canvas—How had he let Renoir convince him to paint a simple landscape?—as well as another blank one, larger, that something told him he was going to fill today. It was the kind of day he remembered leading up to Mattie's death. The kind where he splashed ugliness all over the canvas to get it out of *him*.

But something was missing too. Like knowing what was wrong exactly. Like being prepared for it. Emery needed something more.

It was in this state that he walked through the flickering silver-green of the grove, feeling it calm him a bit, or a least channel his discontent, making him note that once again he was coming out here earlier than Renoir said he liked to come in the morning. But he knew Renoir would be here anyway, wouldn't he. Because that was the way this insanity worked:

Emery needed. The world answered his need.

And there he was, just out the far end of the grove. Renoir stood in his usual boater's hat; his unbuttoned, blousy shirt; his simple trousers; his scuffed, dusty boots. But this time he also wore an old brown sports coat over his shirt as if dressing very formally for something. He also didn't carry his usual painter's stool or easel and painting supplies, but just stood there empty handed, waiting for Emery, birds chirping in the olive branches above him.

"What's going on?" Emery said as he cleared the olive trees.

Renoir's glance flitted from Emery to both sides of him, behind him, all around. Then he nodded. "I'm taking you to see Paul today."

Emery's heart skipped a beat. "Cézanne? Paul Cézanne?"

Renoir rubbed his nose. "He is...a difficult person sometimes, but a good friend. I have told him about you. If you want to come."

Emery nodded his head probably too vigorously. He needed the distraction. He needed *something* to change his head around so he could figure out what to do with Violet and Charlotte. An extra dose of magic, perhaps. Meeting the frigging Master of Aix-en-Provence himself. The precursor of cubism. The painter who probably shook up the art world more than anyone else after the impressionists. The gateway to modern art.

Renoir was already past him, walking through the olive grove like he was heading straight back the way Emery had come.

Emery hurried to follow.

And for a time he walked in contented distraction, thinking

about Cézanne and art and discovery. Trying, basically, to think about anything except his troubles back at the Avrochet farm. Until Renoir led him straight through the middle of the little village he usually avoided, the one bounded by the stone wall where he'd first met Picasso. He tried not to stare at people too much to see if they were seeing just him or Renoir too, but the few people out wandering about seemed to be ignoring both of them.

Primitive place. No cars. No kids playing on their PSPs. Nobody calling on their cell phones. He distractedly patted the French cell phone Violet had bought for him. It had been used all of once, to call Charlotte. Not an unmitigated success there. Should he call Violet now to see how she was doing? He didn't even know if she'd have her phone turned on in her class. Maybe he should call Charlotte and ask her to look in on Violet.

Renoir turned him east along a dirt road leading out of the village, heading them logically right past the Avrochet farm and on towards Aix, except...

Wait a minute. The time when young Renoir and Cézanne hung out, wasn't Cézanne living in the country estate of Jas de Bouffan with his family? That was on the far side of Aix. Too far to walk, and probably a tourist trap now anyway, so what...?

Oh. Right. Le Tholonet. Cézanne had rented place or two in Le Tholonet, too, hadn't he? Back in the 1880s? Emery remembered the personal stories well. The dates, not so much.

Besides, Picasso was only *born* in the 1880s and he'd shown up here, and kept aging dramatically. So time wasn't being rigorously observed here.

Well, obviously. All these painters were supposed to be long dead.

Still...

"Are we going to pass through Le Tholonet?" he asked Renoir and almost stumbled on a rut in the road.

The thin painter stopped and looked at him, surprised. "But we already have."

"What?"

"Back there." Renoir pointed. "It is not a large village."

Emery spun around and stared at the cluster of white stucco houses that spun out to farms and vineyards, the same small town he'd been passing by every day for over a week now. It was *not* the tourist town Charlotte had directed him by in the car on that first tour he took. And the paved road they'd driven that time, that ran along the north side of town...

This road? This hard-packed dirt and stone road he and Renoir stood on now?

No. Where were the telephone lines? The cars? The country mansions in the distance with their swimming pools and fifty-inch plasma televisions?

Emery's heart was pressing up to his throat in a vague panic. Renoir was watching him with an expression of curiosity.

"The...Zola dam," Emery said. "Which way is that from here?"

"You know of the dam? It was built by Émile's father, yes? Paul said he and Émile used to—"

"Which direction?" Emery dragged both hands over his face to calm his breathing. "Sorry, Pierre. I have to know. Which direction is the dam from here?"

Renoir pointed. "Just that way. Along this road. Then another one that turns off to the left."

"Is there a sign there? A road sign?"

Renoir thought hard. "I don't think so. The people here just know."

"Oh God." Emery's knees suddenly felt weak as he tried to process things. He pulled out his cell phone and turned it on. No signal. They were in the middle of an open road, not more than a couple miles from a pretty major town – Aix – and he was getting no signal. Where was he exactly? *When* was he?

He turned off the phone and swallowed hard. In the middle of magic, right? Had he been doing this all week? Walking into the past, then out of it again, into the real world. Did it require him walking *that exact route* to get back to Violet?

He suddenly couldn't breathe. Renoir placed a hand on his shoulder. Real? Solid? "What's wrong, my friend?" he said.

"I'm..." Emery took a deep breath, cleared his throat, and chewed his tongue to evoke some saliva so he could speak. "I'm not sure I can visit Paul. I think I should go back to the olive grove." Then walk back to the Avrochet farm by his usual route and stay the hell there!

"You are scared."

"Scared?" He looked down at Renoir then at his own hands. They were shaking and clammy. He felt his entire body covered in a cold sweat. Which was amazing really. A little over a week ago he'd been almost ready to leave the world completely. Now he was desperately afraid of losing the little life left that he had. His painting. Violet. *Violet.* She needed him. "I'm worried about my daughter."

"She is at home now?"

"No," Emery remembered. "She's in Aix. Studying cooking." Assuming that world still existed at all.

"As she is every day, you told me. But *you*, you need something, my friend. I've seen this too often in other painters I know. I've seen it in myself. You work and work, improving yourself, fighting for recognition and success, for others to appreciate your art. But once they do, once you have had that for a while, you begin to question everything again. Am I good enough? Does my work mean anything? Am I fooling myself and fooling others?"

"No." Emery shook his head hard. "That's not it. I lost my wife."

"And this means suddenly that your life is less sure? Your art, less important?"

"I'm not sure it ever *was* that important."

"Doubt! Yes. I understand that. Every artist understands that. Even Pablo."

Just the name pricked at Emery now and he reared his head back. "This isn't about my art, Pierre!"

The fine-boned painter stepped directly in front of him and looked up at him with his droopy eyes, dead serious. "Everything with us"—he waved a hand back and forth between him and Emery—"is about your art. Don't you sense it? A part of me wants to rebel like Pablo and say that *I* am the important one here. But I somehow know that is not so. I can feel it. This time, your entire journey, will only be worked out when you work out what your soul is going to do with your gift. Everything else, and every*one* else, waits on that."

"It's...why you're there each day in the olive grove. No matter what time I arrive."

Renoir shrugged and nodded. "It's why you must come with me now to meet Paul."

Emery licked his lips, his mouth bone dry again. He cleared his throat. "How much further do we walk?"

"Not much further." Renoir smiled finally. "We cross the field ahead as a shortcut, climb to a small road, cut back that way, and we are there."

"There where?" Emery said, but his mind was whirring through his memories of Cézanne's life, the time he spent near Le Tholonet. "The Château Noir?" The Black Castle.

"Yes!" said Renoir, walking again, so that Emery had to follow. "Although, with Paul waking up there each morning and grumping his way outside to paint, perhaps its other name is better."

"Which is?"

"Château du Diable." The *Devil's* Castle. "We turn off here."

✳ ✳ ✳

I T DIDN'T LOOK like a devil's castle. Or even a castle, for that matter.

When Emery and Renoir had puffed their way up the steep "shortcut" path that climbed the pine-tree bluff, through thick underbrush and over numerous boulders, they emerged on a simple packed-dirt path and stopped, breathing hard and swiping at their clothes to clear off the dust and pine needles. Along the path ahead was what looked like a small stone hotel that had no budget for grounds maintenance. The walls were two stories of unadorned, reddish-yellow stone. The only distinctive touch was the arched window openings.

"The owner painted it black," Renoir panted. "But he used a soot-based paint."

"It got washed away." Trying to sound normal.

"Yes."

"And he sacrificed virgins here. Under the full moon." Voice still tight.

Renoir raised his eyebrows, then got it and chuckled painfully, massaging his side like he'd gotten a stitch. "Oh, yes. The Devil's Castle. I think it was because this first owner was from Marseille. And because he painted his house black, of course."

Emery sniffed and nodded, then readjusted his backpack and its extra load for the twentieth time. He was no longer afraid, he told himself, but the fear had morphed into a kind of free-floating anxiety that was coming out as a really aggressive annoyance. Renoir! He usually liked the man. Considered him a friend. But the way Renoir had lectured him earlier? It was like he considered Emery a lost schoolboy!

Wiping sweat and dust from his forehead, he walked ahead by himself, approaching the château.

It wasn't as simple a building as he'd thought, he saw now. It actually had a higher section shooting up further back and it stretched left through the trees like it was multiple joined buildings. Probably had a dramatic view over the bluff, too. Whoop-de-doo.

Renoir hustled up to the front door beside him. "Have you ever seen a pistachio tree?" he asked and knocked on the heavy wood.

"A what?"

"There is a pistachio tree in the courtyard right outside Paul's room here. It is the first thing he sees when he gets up in the morning."

A wizened old man answered the door, puffing hard on a pipe. His back was so bent and deformed that he seemed to have a hard time raising his head to meet Renoir's eyes. Yet the thin painter seemed hardly to notice. He just smiled and leaned down to shake the man's hand and asked him about "the pirate who paints" who was staying in this place.

The old man nodded and disappeared back inside. A moment later he returned with the news that Monsieur Cézanne was on his way out.

Five minutes passed as Emery felt a growing need to kick something. Hard.

There was a rustle and clatter and Cézanne himself appeared with his easel and painting supplied strapped to his back. No mistaking the man Renoir had called "the pirate who paints" for that was exactly what he looked like. Cézanne was big and bluff around. Under a floppy black hat, his blood-shot eyeballs, pointed beard, and lower lip all jutted out from his head as he swiveled to face Emery.

"You!" he said. "You're the one Pierre talked about?"

Emery shot a glare at Renoir's placid smile. "I guess so."

"Waste of time! Waste. Of. Time. I have painting to do and it's already mid-morning." He waved his pudgy hand about.

Emery ground his teeth. "So? Go."

Cézanne stopped waving his hand and narrowed his red eyes at Emery. "What did you say?"

"I said go. You want to be a misanthropic hermit and have little children throw stones at you when you get older, you just keep doing what you're doing. Go off by yourself and paint. Go on."

Oh, that's smart, Lake. Get Cézanne to change and alter history, why don't you?

If this *was* history.

Ah, screw it. Emery was tired, hot, and disoriented, and the fat man was bugging him.

"Do you know who I am?" Cézanne said, glowering.

"Yeah. I do. You're someone who doesn't have a clue how good you are. And you're a big pain in the neck." He looked at Renoir after he said it, suddenly unsure if he'd used French slang for neck or penis. Well again, what the hell. Cézanne would get the general idea.

Emery expected bluster or laughter. Instead what he got from Cézanne was a look of carefully considered hurt.

"For me," the bluff man said, "it is always about the painting. That is all. Renoir told me you were a painter."

"I *am*," Emery said, to both Cézanne and Renoir. "But I'm tired of having pissing contests about it. With anyone."

Renoir, annoyingly, was smiling in private delight. Cézanne, though, was looking him up and down and nodding to himself like he might ask him to model for him at any second. Maybe his wife, Hortense, had gotten tired at last of doing so. Emery recalled that she was one of the only people who *would* model for Cézanne because the man was so difficult.

Emery shifted his backpack and easel on his back. Seeing that, Cézanne shifted his own load and nodded.

"Do you want to see where I am painting now?" he said in a suddenly much humbler voice.

"If I don't faint from thirst and hunger first, yes, I'd very much like to see that."

Cézanne looked distressed and Renoir waved his hand to indicate on Emery's behalf that the fainting was a joke.

"Good," said Cézanne. "Then follow me and I will show you a place where I am trying to change *everything* about art."

THE LESSON OF BIBÉMUS

Emery had thought the hike up to the Château Noir had been tough. Obviously he was soft.

Now, after half an hour of following Cézanne's twitching haunches up the rocky bluff, Emery was blowing and sweating like a sow in labor. While fat, middle-aged Cézanne, the ineffectual rich man's son, seemed barely winded. He wore a black suit jacket like Renoir's and a floppy black hat. Why wasn't he pouring down sweat?

"The quarries up here on the Bibémus," Cézanne called back as they climbed, "are one of God's greatest wonders. The orange rocks. The shapes. They are so simple that you can see them and put them together in your painting. Depth only with colors. Building a whole with pieces like you are a little boy with blocks."

"But why...ungh...do that?" Emery said.

"Maybe I'm just 'exploring', like you said," Cézanne called back, dead serious. "But it is like I can see each rock from every direction at once, they are so solid. It is that sense of heavy mass, a thing not danced about by light or wind or a person's eyes, that I try to catch."

"That's why...you outline...your stuff?" Emery had to stop for a second and steady himself against the rocks.

He didn't consciously see Cézanne pause ahead of him as if Emery's words had struck him upside the head. But when Emery looked up, the Master of Aix was looking down at him with an expression that flickered between hurt and open-faced surprise. Not a pirate at all in that expression; more a little boy who's just discovered he's not quite big enough to pee over the edge of the toilet bowl.

Renoir, climbing a short distance behind Emery, now caught up to him and also stopped to lean against the rocks. He was breathing so hard he sounded asthmatic. His pale, fine-boned face when he looked up and Emery could see it, was beet red under his boater hat. Emery grinned back at him with a shot of spiteful pleasure. There! Now he'd insulted *both* of these French masters. Maybe that hubris would help him burn off some of his bile. Let him just live the moment. Renoir said everything else would wait so...let it wait.

They all began climbing again and, twenty minutes later, the ground leveled out under their feet. Sort of. There were still solid banks of rock, mini-cliffs twenty-five feet high, cleft here and there where quarrymen had obviously blasted or chiseled out huge slabs of the stuff, all the same reddish brown as the Château Noir. Sandstone?

"This," Cézanne said as they walked through it, "is all sandstone."

There you had it.

The region's ubiquitous dry pines shot up here and there amongst the cathedral of rocks, clustering and leaning at crazy angles. Also sage and other less spiky bushes that gave the air an incredible scent of heaven as the wind blew over them.

Emery found he'd stopped to gawp. Okay, the bile was gone. It was too beautiful up here and he was too tired. But...

"Here!" Cézanne declared ahead of him and stopped to swing his easel, canvas, and paints from his back.

My God, Emery thought as he staggered to a halt beside him and looked. He knew this scene. In real life it was grayer than Cézanne's famous painting. The sun washed out the lighter red and golds. And the tumble of rocks, for all Emery's feeling of the child-block concept, were nowhere near as organized as Cézanne was going to make them.

But that was the organizing beauty he brought to it, wasn't it. That's why you couldn't just take a photograph, run it through a giclee printer that sprayed ink or paint onto a canvas "that painted look", and call it art. That was why this temple of brown-and-grey rocks topped by pines, when captured by Paul Cézanne, became immortal.

So as Cézanne began sketching the blocky shapes with a red pencil, Emery found himself holding his breath. He willed himself to see as Cézanne saw, flattening perspectives, giving each portion of the picture its own swath of strength, each outlined swath filled with close-spectrum rubs of color.

"This is something new, he's doing," Renoir whispered at Emery's ear. "Isn't it?"

"Yes," Emery breathed.

"But, like you say, he never knows how good it is. Nor, it seems, does anyone else."

"They will."

"Yes, I think so."

"Without him," Emery whispered, "Picasso might never have known to distort perspectives as he did, to show them all at once."

Renoir snickered. "Now you know one reason why I will not bring Pablo to Paul. If I could stop this madness…"

"But you can't stop art, can you."

"No. Not in ourselves. Not in others. But you can shape it. It only happens with the artist. Not by itself."

Emery found himself smiling. Hadn't he had just this argument with Charlotte on their first dinner? And hadn't he argued exactly the opposite of what Renoir was saying now, what Emery himself had just been thinking about giclee prints? Art was everywhere. And anyone could find it. "I'll grant you it's only the skilled, *consistent* creation that marks the—"

"Enough!" shouted Cézanne and spun his bulk around to face them. "If you are going to both whisper and whisper behind my back, then I will go somewhere else!"

He began to take the beginning of his Bibémus masterpiece off his easel and Emery leapt forward, staying his hand. "No! Please, Paul. Don't."

Cézanne glowered at him, but by now Emery saw beyond the glower. The pirate had the heart of a marshmallow. Or more precisely, the heart of a not-brilliant boy who'd spent his whole like trying not only to please, but also to pursue his unique style in painting, his own vision. It had made him conflicted, grumpy, and amazingly humble all at once.

Emery could relate, and just wished he had half the dedication in the face of all that.

"Please, Paul," Emery repeated again. "This landscape, this exact one, deserves to be painted by you. *Must* be. It's more important than what Pierre and I were talking about. It's even more important than my watching you work or talking with you. So you just go back to painting it, okay?"

And as Cézanne watched him uncertainly, Emery backed up slowly. He reached Renoir and took the skinnier artist's arm with his hand, pulling him back and away.

"Until next time!" Renoir called to Cézanne as he and Emery left, and Emery could have sworn the Master of Aix tilted his pirate beard a little sideways, watching them leave with all the vast understanding of an overgrown puppy dog.

* * *

"You know," Renoir said as they climbed down the way they'd come, Emery again leading, "about Paul's painting..."

"It's going to be great," Emery called back to him.

"It will. He's painted that very spot many times already."

Emery's foot stuttered and he almost slipped, grabbing a bush root from the rock beside him at the last second. Stones and dirt went skittering down below his feet in a mini-avalanche. He watched them a second then whipped his chin around and up. "He's already painted that spot?'

"And will again. Paul is a great believer in doing a thing over and over to find the right way because, I think, he does not know what that way is. He explores with his painting. He is not Pablo Picasso, who says people were buying his work before he was twenty. Me also, you know. I painted porcelain and... But Paul? No. He is only now starting to gain mastery. And because he has many friends – Zola, Pissaro, me – and a father who supports him, he can keep going until one day, I believe, at an age when Pablo will find people questioning the value of his work, Paul will create many fine masterpieces.

"Persistence. Perhaps that is the lesson of the Bibémus quarry, yes?"

Maybe, thought Emery, not sure how he himself fit into Renoir's model. But even more, he was distracted by the way nothing he'd done on this outing was going to change history in the slightest. This history might shape him, but it only worked one way.

Was this the real lesson of Bibémus? That whatever you do, it doesn't matter. Mattie's dead. Your life is going down and there ain't nothing you can do to change it.

Put that in your paintbrush and stroke it.

* * *

OKAY, happy man, what was that line from *Peter Pan* about how to find Neverland? *Second star to the right and straight on till morning.*

Except that Emery had felt that his way back to the Avrochet farm had to be considerably more concrete, especially as he was trying to *leave* the magic, not get there. So he'd had Renoir first walk him back the way they'd come, passing through Le Tholonet, through the olive grove, and right to the spot where they had met almost every single morning since he'd arrived in Provence.

And now?

Now Emery's forehead and nose and the back of his neck were once again seriously sunburned, and the sun was dipping low in the sky. Dusk. Everything looking gray. On top of that, the was lightheaded from the long day with no food.

"You could eat some raw olives," Renoir suggested as Emery oriented himself and prepared to leave.

"Funny. You *could* have bought me some food in Le Tholonet."

"Except that I never have any money."

"I remember reading that about you."

"Pardon me?"

"Never mind. You know what I wish, though? I wish I'd remembered to ask Paul why he painted...or *paints* the Sainte-Victoire over and over."

Renoir shrugged. "Practicing. Searching. I told he likes to paint some things many—"

"Times. Yeah. I got that. But over sixty times? No. It's something about the mountain itself. Like he believes the old stories of spirits residing up there maybe. Have you ever asked him?"

"No."

"Will you?"

"Maybe. Maybe someday you will."

"Right." Emery readjusted his backpack one last time. Enough stalling. "Wish me luck."

He did and Emery set off.

Through the olive grove, along the path that circled the east side of the village, across the field, the pine forest that was now full of threatening shadows and almost un-navigable, the gurgling stream, and then...then...thank God, the two properties with the swimming pools. One even had little party lights strung up around the pools; he had to shut his eyes and look away for a good minute before his night vision came back.

He crossed the road with telephone wires. The fences.

The vegetable garden.

The driveway.

The front door.

Open.

"Violet?"

A cry of anguish like someone being tortured answered him from the upstairs bedroom and he froze. Then it sounded again.

Violet!

Emery ran for the stairs.

VIOLET FALLS APART

She was in one of the kid bedrooms, the one with the ancient computer in it, sitting on the plastic-and-metal chair that faced the lit computer screen. When Emery ran in, her fingers frantically slid and clicked her computer mouse. The screen blanked and turned off.

"F-f—fucking *knock*, Daddy!" she spat at him. Her hands spasmed open and closed.

"Violet..."

Her face was a mess – mascara smeared down with tears, cheeks scratched like she'd been in a fight with a nasty cat. Her hair shot out in frizz and down around her face in chunks. The pink blouse she'd often worn into Aix for her classes was half unbuttoned with buttons torn off, so Emery could see her black bra underneath and more scratches on her throat and chest.

"Violet, were you in an accident? Did someone attack you?"

"Attack? Attack? Yeah. Attack. I was hit in a drive-by *heart* fucking attack!" Her head was going back and forth now, eyes squeezing shut and opening over and over like her fists, like she was trying to keep in an explosion. The cries he'd heard from downstairs.

"The scratches..."

"I fell down okay? Fuck." The last word caught in her throat and she clenched her whole body tight until she was panting and shuddering from the strain.

"You fell down," Emery said evenly, walking towards her over the thin area carpet. "And somebody attacked your heart."

Violet just grunted, her face squinched together, bottom lip quivering madly.

Emery knelt down in front of her, which put his head level with hers, and reached out to gently touch her shoulders. It set off a massive wave of shivering shakes. She opened her mouth and breathed out in high little cries.

"Is this about your man in Aix?" Emery asked.

Her eyes flew wide open and she looked at him, terrified. She whipped her gaze back at the computer and saw it was off. Then back to him.

"What is it, Violet?"

"He— He's—"

"What?"

"He's fucking someone else!"

It came out like a banshee cry and her mouth kept working after the words were out, gnawing at the air, her face a rictus of distress.

Emery didn't know what to say to that and his daughter's behavior was frankly terrifying him. If she'd been drunk... But she wasn't. He smelled nothing on her breath.

He drew back his hands.

Drugs? Maybe. Even living in and around New York most of his life, and hanging out with artists and people with far more money than sense, Emery's contact with narcotics had been minimal. Beyond a red nose from snorting coke or the air filled with the smell of cannabis, he didn't think he even knew what to look for. He tried to see Violet's eyes to see if the pupils looked like pinpricks or too large but she wasn't letting him catch her eyes right now.

"Do you know for sure?" he asked stupidly.

"Yes," she moaned.

"How?"

"He sent me pictures! By e-mail" She jumped up and began pacing the room, hitting her thighs with her fists. "I didn't think he even knew how to use a fucking computer!"

Hence her secretiveness about the computer. Emery didn't even realize she'd been checking her e-mails from here. She'd discouraged his own attempts to do so, arguing the Avrochet computer was so slow, the internet service ancient dial-up, that it just wasn't worth it.

Then the other thing she'd said hit him. Her man didn't know how to use a computer? Even for a Frenchman that seemed extreme. "How old is he, Violet?"

She froze and stared at him, her smeared mascara like raccoon rings around her eyes.

"Violet?"

Then she was shaking her head very tightly back and forth, harder and harder, almost out of control, until it got her whole body shaking and she wailed, "He loves somebody else! He loves someone else! He's supposed to love *me!*"

"Vi..."

But she wasn't even seeing him anymore. She'd thrown herself down on the child's twin bed and was sobbing hard into the bedspread. Emery stared longingly at the computer. If he just turned it on and called up the e-mail program, he'd presumably see what this bastard from Aix had sent his daughter. Emery could get his e-mail address and maybe even a look at the man's appearance. She'd said there were pictures.

As he stepped that way, though, Violet stopped sobbing all at once, rolled onto her back, and glared at him with murder in her eyes.

"I'll...go make some supper," Emery said. "Soup maybe? A salad?" His own stomach growled as he said it, suddenly remembering it hadn't been fed all day. He was lightheaded, in fact.

When Violet said nothing, he backed out and went downstairs to the kitchen, pulling out vegetables and the left-over roast beef, eggs, hot banana chilies. In five minutes he had a spicy egg hash going on the stove top and bread browning in the toaster. His mouth was watering big time. He had two plates out, table set, water glasses filled. No wine tonight. With the way Violet seemed to have been getting into it the last few days, he decided they could both go without.

Later.

He served up the two plates with buttered toast and egg mixture and called out to Violet to come join him.

No answer.

He took the plates to the dining room table and called again. Finally he went upstairs to get her and found she'd locked herself in the bathroom. After five minutes of negotiation, he retreated back downstairs and ate his dinner, which now went down like cold, tasteless lumps.

Violet would come around, though, wouldn't she. This was a woman thing. Probably partly PMS. Hormones were a frightening thing. It didn't mean the situation with her older man from Aix was okay, and Emery knew he couldn't downplay the excessive drinking Violet had been doing (particularly if there was some genetic susceptibility to alcoholism through him), but Violet came by her strong emotions honestly. She'd always been a ball of fire, just like Mattie. She experienced things intensely.

About halfway through his meal, he remembered the computer. If Violet was still in the bathroom...

But even as he thought it, there was a scuffling sound from upstairs. A door opening. Maybe Violet was going to come down and eat after all?

He waited. Then stood. Should he go up and talk to her?

A sudden crashing sound from outside made him jump. A burglar in the dark? His nerves were so jangled he couldn't think straight, but he did at least run to the fireplace and grab the poker that lay in the little black metal tray beside it.

Something else shattered outside. North side of the house. Emery hoisted the poker and sprinted out the rear French doors.

He almost tripped over the shattered metal box. His runners crunched over pieces of glass and plastic. He swung out the poker defensively, blinking hard in the darkness to make sense of it.

Then something like a stone and a hard snake came whipping down from above, thudding into the hard dirt and bouncing near Emery's feet. He looked up.

Violet leaned out the kid's room window, backlit so her face was dark but still clearly wild.

And Emery finally understood that the wreckage around him was the computer – the main case with hard drive and mother-board, the monitor, the keyboard, the mouse and power cord that had just whipped down at his feet.

Above him, Violet started to laugh.

* * *

She didn't stop moving about until almost one a.m., when Emery seemed to have succeeded in talking her into lying down and trying to sleep.

Emery crashed too, falling straight to sleep despite his worry.

In his dreams, he was part of one of Claude Avrochet's works of art, scrabbling to gather up pieces of his smashed computer as he laughed and encouraged him to gather them *into* himself, meld with them.

Then it wasn't Avrochet but Renoir urging him to pick everything up. While Cézanne painted him with a furious intensity, saying, "Hold still! Hold still!" And Picasso, eating an apple as big as his face so that juice ran down in rivers over his bare chest, laughed and laughed.

Emery woke up and jerked up to sitting. He'd heard something. Violet?

The bedside clock said three a.m..

He threw off his covers and rolled out of bed in his pajama bottoms and no top, the tile cold under his bare feet. There were no birds or cicadas sounds anymore. Just the sound of a night breeze through the pine trees outside.

He stepped silently into the upstairs hall and listened hard. There was a muttering coming from Violet's room and a dim light shone from under the closed door. Feeling like a sneak thief, he approached the door and listened.

Mumble...mumble..."goddamn, stuff an' pompous"*...mumble...mumble...*"fugger!"

And shuffling sounds. Gurgle of liquid. Swallowing. Wine. The wine! He'd completely forgotten to search and hide whatever alcohol was in the house.

Shaking his head, he quickly debated what was the best course of action here. For all he knew Violet was naked. He'd convinced her to go to bed earlier but hadn't supervised. And if he walked in on his drunk, naked daughter right now, however emotionally upset she was, there was just too much sexual weirdness that could result. Charlotte's sexual rejection of him... Memories of Mattie...

"Don't be a pussy, Lake," he muttered at himself. "Deal with it."

He turned the doorknob of Violet's room and stepped inside.

She wore a tee-shirt and panties, thank God, sitting back against the wall at the head of the bed with her sheet and comforter pulled up over one leg. As he entered, she turned her head to see him and her squinched eyes went wide. She swung her right hand, that held a half empty wine bottle, fast away from her mouth and under her sheets, neatly sloshing a huge red wine stain all over as she did so.

But Emery barely noticed. His gaze had shot to her bare left leg and the uneven series of red cuts that ran crossways up the side of it from six inches over the ankle, almost up to her knee. The bottom three or four looked freshly scabbed over. The top five were still trickling blood. Blood that also smeared the razor blade she held in her left hand.

"Daddy..." She looked at him in horror. In guilt. "I'm sorry."

"Honey, we've got—"

"I'm sorry," she said, over top of his words like she couldn't even hear them. "I'm a dummy. I'm so sooo dumb. So stupid. So worthless. Stupid."

"No, Violet. You're—"

"Stupid! But he's stupider! Tha' fugger!" She sniffed and wiped at her eyes with her razor-blade hand. Then she pulled up the other hand that was still holding the wine bottle and drank from it. She didn't even seem to see Emery anymore.

Swallowing hard, he walked to her and pried the razor blade out of her fingers. Then he took away the wine bottle and looked quickly around the room to see if she had replacements for either. Finding none, he left and deposited the confiscated items in his bedroom. Then he went to the bathroom and found some anti-septic and gauze and medical tape for her legs. He had to pull them out from under the covers when he got back to her room because she'd passed out on him. He cleaned and taped her left leg up. He examined her right leg and found one or two older looking cuts there too, but they were already scabbed over and he left them alone.

And now what?

Checking first to make sure Violet was truly asleep, he got up and went down to the kitchen. Turning on the light there, he found what looked like a guide to Aix and tracked down a bunch of medical clinics, none of them open twenty-four hours.

Which left the hospital emergency rooms.

He hesitated. If he took her in like this, in the U.S. anyway, they'd probably commit her. At least keep her overnight for observation and an interview. She'd be forcibly confined. Maybe even strapped down.

Memories of Mattie's last hospital days hit him, how desperately she'd wanted to be out of there and just be home. How Violet, too, had shuddered at the hospital and pushed him to set up the home care room for Mattie that one of the doctors said he could.

First his wife. Then his little girl.

No! This wasn't like that. And Violet didn't need to be locked up there *or* here. She just needed to be watched.

He put down the directory, shut off the kitchen light and went back up to Violet's room. He shut off her light and pulled the chair that had been for the computer up to the end of her bed. There he sat and put his feet up.

In tomorrow's light, he knew, everything would look different. Emery would keep her home. They'd talk. He wasn't good at it but he'd try. And he'd get her to agree to see a psychologist maybe. Surely Charlotte knew of a good, discrete, therapist.

It would be alright.

Why do you think that?

Because everything here was waiting on him to find himself. Renoir had said so. Nothing more could go wrong until he did that.

He was still fighting hard to believe that when, around four a.m., sleep overtook and he dozed.

When he woke up, the bed in front of him was empty.

Violet was gone.

THE LIMITATIONS OF MODERN COMMUNICATION

Charlotte's silky recording in French was brief and to the point: "I cannot answer the phone right now. Please leave a message and telephone number so I can return your call later."

Emery's response in her language was far less straightforward.

"Yeah. Charlotte. Hello. I know it's early. I know it's Sunday. I hoped to catch you in. I'm...trying to find Violet because she had a very rough time yesterday. A rough night. Some ongoing issues. You know about the drinking, I guess. And...other things. She left me a note before she headed out this morning saying everything was okay and she had a special end-of-session cooking class today. But it's Sunday. I think she's lying on both counts.

"She's not answering her phone.

"I can't find the number of this place where she's been taking her cooking course; they don't seem to have a phone. If I don't hear from her by noon I'd like to take a bus or taxi into Aix to look for her, except she specifically asked me not to.

"Could you please check up on her? At least see if her class is actually, running today? It's at 522 Chemin Jules Renaud.

"And even if you can't, can you suggest a good mental helper? I

189

mean a psychological counselor. I'm not even sure exactly what you call them over here. I found the names of some people in the phone book but they were divorce counselors or some such and nobody's answering the phone. Don't you people have any head doctors who work on the weekend?

"Please call me back."

He left the numbers for both the house phone and his cell.

* * *

At 9:30 A.M.:

"Hello! Dr....um...Sansolziskensen? Ziksensen! Yes. Sorry. You do counseling work, correct? Someone at the University of Aix-Marseille III gave me your name. For couples and families... Yes, I know. I know it's Sunday. But I have a daughter... Twenty-two. Yes, I realize that, but she won't *call* you herself. She doesn't have— what do you call it?—a lot of *insight* into her problems but she needs urgent— No, I recognize that it's not your standard... No, I can't take her to the hospital. It's complicated."

...

"Our names? Why?"

...

"You won't agree to see her but you want our names? Are you some kind of fascist idiot? More to the point, do you think that *I* am an idiot? See ya, Chuckles."

* * *

10:00 A.M.:

"The Serrut School of Cooking? Be still my heart, you do exist! Oh, you're the husband Serrut. No, I've just been calling around to get your number all morning. I think I had the wrong name. Look my daughter is taking a two week course with your wife, chef

Myriam, right? Learning how to cook in the Provençal style. That's right. Is she actually holding a class today?"

...

"She is? My goodness. No...it's just...on a Sunday. The last Sunday. I see. A special trip to..."

...

"Oh.

...

"Well how long will they be out collecting truffles?

...

"And there's no way...

...

"Jesus Christ.

...

"No, sorry. Nothing. Never mind, Mr. Serrut. Never *mind.*

* * *

10:15 A.M. (In English):

"Violet? Hi, it's Dad. Look, I'm sorry to keep calling, but I'm thinking I could have helped more last night somehow. Not sure how. It's not my specialty – the whole 'boyfriend left me' thing. I always figure that would be your mom's department. But I do have some ideas you might want to consider. So call me, okay? Call home, meaning here at the Avrochet's. Or call the cell you gave me. I'll keep it turned on in case I'm out in the studio or walking.

"Just call me, okay?"

* * *

10:25 A.M.:

"Charlotte?

"Look, on the off-chance you got my earlier message and went to check on Violet, don't bother. This Sunday class thing is amazingly legitimate, but they're "out in the field", digging up mushrooms. I'd still appreciate a call about somebody who might help Violet with some major issues she's dealing with right now.

"Or just call so I can talk to you. I know we haven't exactly...

"Look, just call. Please. I'm going out walking but I'm leaving on my cell. The number again is..."

THE MINOTAUR

There was no way anyone would be able to reach him, of course. Not once he crossed the stream. Or got into the pine tree forest. Or entered the olive grove. No, before the olive grove, because the modern Le Tholonet had always vanished by the time he'd reached the olive grove.

Emery kept pulling out his cell phone and checking for signals as he walked his route. Church bells were clanging somewhere in the distance. He was making good time with no backpack or easel or canvas or paints.

Oh look! Sure enough, the signal faded, then vanished when he was deep into the pine trees. And while normally he would have chalked it up to interference, he had no question it wasn't going to come back once he came out the other side.

This is the point of no return...

God, now he was even dredging up bad lyrics from Andrew Lloyd Weber's *Phantom of the Opera*. But everything had slipped into that kind of surreal, melodrama, hadn't it. Him out wandering in magic olive groves. Violet falling apart over some French lover doing what French lovers always did.

The thing was, Renoir's words to him yesterday on the hill up to the Château Noir kept coming back to him: *All of this will only be worked out when you figure out what your soul is going to do with your gift. Everything else waits on that.*

Which meant what, exactly? That his sadness would be cured and Violet's stability returned when Emery figured out what he wanted to paint? Or not paint? If he abandoned painting completely, like Violet had done with her piano, would everything finish then?

But how? By falling apart completely like in some little moral drama? After all, he had art. He had magic. He had dead people.

He coughed out a laugh at himself as he walked but kept going until he reached the stone wall that ran along the east side of ancient Le Tholonet. There he stopped.

A stone wall. What a perfect symbol. Dead stop. Meet rebel artist on a quest here. Get drawn looking lost. Duh. Maybe Emery should paint it too. Like that old Kliban cartoon that had a giant blank wall with a tiny little door that everyone was ignoring. The door was labeled "perception" or "truth" or something like that.

Emery turned right and began the descent around the south side of the village, into the silver-green light of the olive grove, half-expecting to finally find no one there. To be just in an olive grove in Provence.

But Renoir was there, his easel already set up, his close-up work on the two olive trees continuing.

Picasso stood behind him, watching each stroke keenly. With a sixth sense, he turned, saw Emery, and raised a hand, his expression sour.

Emery almost stumbled. The famous Spaniard, wearing leather sandals, rolled up cotton pants, and the horizontally-striped sailor's tee-shirt of his later years, had gone completely white on top – a fringe of short white hair around his nut-brown baldness.

His burly little body still looked tough, but shrunken around the neck, the bare chest, the legs.

"How old are you now?" Emery blurted out.

Picasso waved a hand in the air in front of him like he hadn't heard the question or didn't want to.

"I really want to know," Emery challenged, walking closer. He'd brought no painting supplies today. Not even a backpack. Because it was the magic he had to understand today and his painting was *not* magic. It was a diversion. It wasn't the truth.

"Like I told my grandson," Picasso snapped, "I am old. You are young. I wish you were dead."

"You told him that?"

Picasso raised his nose and stuck out his lower jaw.

"You're an asshole," Emery said.

"But a famous one," Picasso said. "More than either of you will ever be. More than Manet or Ingres or Delacroix or Dali or Diego."

"Yeah, you're the Genius. Right."

"I am the Minotaur!" Picasso exclaimed.

"The what?"

"Strength and virility. The beast who takes what he wants, full of rage and power. A monster, yet irresistible."

"Until Theseus slays him."

The older man sneered. "That myth is mis-told. It is all about a woman's string and magic. But Theseus never slew the Minotaur. He only pretended, while the Minotaur took his woman and sailed back the boats with black sails. *That* is what really happened."

"Pablo," Emery sighed, "you are so full of bullshit that it's leaking out your ears. Are you talented? Oh, yeah. But overrated. Because talent's only a part of it."

"Seeing *truth* is the rest."

"Seeing beauty and sharing it," Emery shot back. "Like Pierre.

Like I try to do. Like Cézanne. Like your friend Henri Matisse did. Does?"

Hearing the last name, Picasso jerked back like he'd been struck. He stalked over to Renoir, who'd continued painting throughout and pretended not to hear the two of them arguing. "Is today the day you take me to see Cézanne?" he demanded.

"No," said Renoir, without looking up.

It hit Picasso like a slap and the entire portion of his face below his nose was dragged down in deep frown.

"What?" said Emery, digging it in. "Why do you want to see Paul so badly? Why not your friend Matisse?"

"He's dead!" Picasso said.

Emery shook his head. What was this? God making it up as he went along? Concurrent timelines? One for Renoir and the people he knew? Another for Picasso the *post*-impressionist, and the few artists he called friends?

Picasso turned on him suddenly. "Do you know what your problem is? You and you." He stabbed a finger at Emery, then Renoir. "Both of you. You *think* you see the world, but you don't. You see just what you choose to see and nothing more. You are cowards who cannot face what the Minotaur rips through each day he is alive!"

Like a wife dying in your arms, you fucker? Emery stared hard back and felt his hands curl into fists. He turned away from Picasso.

But Picasso couldn't leave him alone. "You think it's not true? You think you can face the truth?" He poked him in his back each time he said it.

"Better than you," Emery muttered.

"Yes?" He poked him again. "Come with me, Lake, and I will show you the truth. And *then* we will see." Poke.

"Stop it, old man!" Emery roared and spun on him. He glared down into the Spaniard's hard smile, the coal-black eyes.

"You will come?"

Emery glared at him, then at the worried look on Renoir's face. He tugged his cell phone out and checked to see if it could find a signal here. Of course it couldn't. Which meant he should really head back. Whatever answers he'd hoped to find here weren't emerging. And what if Violet called home? What if Charlotte actually got his message, went to see Violet, and then called?

But...what if he got back home to find no messages, no one had called, Violet would not be home for six hours, and he was left to his own devices with nothing to do but worry or break Violet's explicit instructions and rush into Aix after her?

He started breathing hard. Sweating.

Everything waits on what you do with your gift.

Renoir's words sounded monomaniacal when Emery said them in his own head. Yet they somehow felt right. Maybe only in the sense that he wasn't much use to anyone until he had his own head on straight. And heaven knew right now his head was not on straight. He wanted to punch things. He wanted to go over to Renoir's canvas, pull it off the easel, and kick a hole in it. He wanted to find Paul Cézanne, drag him out of his precious château or Bibémus query and scream at him to get a life! Stop painting the same things over and over again! Take your bar admissions exam or whatever it is you have to do over here and practice law like your father wants you to!

Don't. Get. Hung. Up. On. Truth.

"So?" Picasso said.

"Is this another long hike like Pierre took me on?"

Picasso snorted. "It's much too far to walk. We take my car."

Car?

Then he was stomping off on a different path around the west side of the olive grove and Emery had to jog to catch up.

It turned out the path Picasso led him on ended on a pull-out from the southernmost road of Le Tholonet. There, parked close to an umbrella pine to take full advantage of the tree's shade, sat an ancient, large blue Peugot that looked like it belonged in occupied France during World War Two. A man who couldn't have been much taller than Picasso, but much skinnier, younger, and more pasty-skinned, stood by the rear passenger side, holding open a door for Picasso as he stormed up.

He kept the door open after Picasso was inside, looking expectantly at Emery, until Picasso stuck his head out and waved. "Come on! Come on! Marcel's been standing out here in this heat all morning. You want him to catch heatstroke?"

It made Emery wonder whether Marcel had been there with the car on all the other days when Picasso had come to ridicule Emery and Renoir for a good eight hour stretch. As he passed by the chauffeur, Emery looked up into the man's expressionless face and decided that yes, he probably had.

Then Emery was in, the door closed, and he sank deep back in the cloth of the back seat as Picasso banged on the top of the front seat bench. Marcel, climbing into the driver's seat, looked back with a nonplused expression. "Yes, Sir?"

"We're going to Arles!" Picasso said and grinned at Emery's surprise. "It's time to see some blood, sweat, and death!"

* * *

BULLFIGHTS, he meant.

Emery figured it out when they arrived in a small town on the Rhône River and were immediately plunged into a tide of revelers and posters announcing a "Corrida" with a cheap-looking lithograph of a matador waving a bull past his cape.

Marcel tried turning them onto secondary cobblestone streets bounded tightly by seamless walls of stone storefronts and apartments on either side. Emery assumed they also led to the central amphitheater, but they were just as crammed, people packed so tightly they rocked the car back and forth when Marcel slowed to a halt.

"Keep moving!" Picasso ordered.

Now Emery could hear a mariachi band playing somewhere ahead. No, *two* bands with competing Mexican rhythms. He could smell cooking lamb and, thanks mostly to the sweaty fat man with no shirt who couldn't seem to get past Picasso's car without slapping and sloshing wine on it, the cheap sangria that seemed to be flowing freely everywhere in the crowd. Emery was embarrassed at how it all made his stomach growl. He'd skipped breakfast this morning and now was paying for it.

"There!" Picasso commanded from Emery's right and Marcel cranked the wheel hard to turn into what looked like a private driveway whose doors to the narrow street, the owner had just opened.

"They'll be blocked from getting out," Emery said.

"No one 'gets out' of Arles today. And they will be proud I have chosen their space to stop."

It was yet more evidence that they'd entered some other realm of existence entirely. In this realm, not only was Picasso alive and able to drive Emery from town to town, but he was seen by everyone and believed himself a revered figure.

Which he apparently was, given the drastic change in the angry homeowner's face when the Minotaur actually stepped out of the car.

"Monsieur Picasso!" the bearded man cried in near ecstasy. "You are going to the corrida?"

"*Si,*" said Picasso. Then in French, "You can look after my car here while I am gone?" He looked around the tiny car courtyard. "And perhaps I can sketch something on your walls here before I leave?"

The bearded man nearly fainted in excitement. He slapped his meaty chest. "I cannot watch your car, for I too will watch the bullfights. But my wife and father-in-law will guard it with their life! Minoux!" he called over his shoulder. "I *told* you that you could not get out today!"

"Good," said Picasso with one of his dazzling smiles.

Then he turned and, with Marcel helping to break the wave of people in front of them, they walked up the gradual hill towards the arena.

It wasn't as large as the Roman coliseum Emery remembered seeing in *Gladiator*, but the smell of hot sweat, the sound, and the swollen bloodlust in the air, the stone bench seats – they must have been a bit like this. Picasso had gotten them places about six seats up from the boards that ran around the bottom of the bull-fighting sand. Far up behind them were the stone arches that ringed the upper wall of the amphitheater.

Bright blue sky behind. Limitless blue sky overhead. Was that the first thing the bull saw when it came into the ring? And the last thing?

"We have missed the *paseo*, where the riders and matadors and everyone come in and salutes the president of the bullfight," Picasso said beside him and Emery came back to earth and saw the crowd of costumed people in a tight huddle down in the ring. "And I think the first bullfight."

"Jose Castella," said Marcel, seated to Picasso's left. "French. The second is from Spain – Manolo de Paula. Also from Spain is the third, a young man – Antonio Bienvenida."

Picasso nodded. "They will each have two bulls to kill."

Blood, sweat, and death. "What happened," said Emery, "to the style where the fighters just run at the bull and try to grab the garland from between the bull's horns?"

"The *camarguaises* way." Picasso shrugged. "A pretty sport, but not as true as the corrida. Look. We begin."

Whatever the cluster of people had been doing in the ring was done and they'd all cleared out, presumably taking the first dead bull and the sand where it spilled its blood, with them. As they exited, an excitingly fresh young man strode out wearing the traditional matador's uniform of tight, knee-length pants with long stockings and dancing slippers below and a broad-shoulder jacket of sparkling brocade above, in his case red and black. All topped off with the black hat that Emery always thought looked like a Mickey Mouse hat where someone had scrunched the ears smaller and down.

Three other fit-looking men in similar outfits but with none of the flash or color, straight black and white, came running out behind him. Like the matador, they carried large capes of bright pink which they spun around a few times with their hands to excite the crowds.

"The *torero* and his *peones*, we say in French" said Picasso, who seemed to have decided Emery needed a running commentary. "Or you can call them by their proper names – the *matador* and the *banderilleros*, the baby matadors who set the flags."

Emery looked sideways at him, hearing, in Picasso's rolling r's and soft l's that sounded like y's, his love of all things Spanish. Because he'd been born in Spain, of course. But it was also, Emery remembered his history, because Picasso had sworn he would never go back to Spain while Franco ruled—that was obviously the time period they were in—and the only things Picasso truly loved were the things he couldn't have.

Emery looked back to the ring at the excited oh's of the crowd and saw that the second bull had been released. It came roaring into the arena and straight across the ring towards the crowds on the far side, swinging his huge horns and veering from the boards only at the last second.

Then it saw the banderilleros, who began dancing about to attract its attention, making it chase first one, then the next.

"The matador now studies his adversary," said Picasso. "A fine Camargue bull, you see? At least six hundred kilos of lean muscle. Fast and quick. Very noble. His charges are frank and direct."

"You admire the bull?" Emery said.

"Always!" said Picasso. "For him it is the fight of his life. He can die honorably. He can maybe even gore his enemy!"

"But ultimately he dies."

"Always. Yes. Always the matador wins. He has too many helpers."

The matador and the toro. Torero and the taureau. And watching, applauding, judging, was a painter who saw himself as the *Mino*taur – half man, half bull. What was that all about? Was he the killer or the one who was killed?

And what was Emery?

Down in the ring, the matador did a few practice passes, letting the bull run at his cape before he swept it aside and the bull thundered past and slowed. Turned. The matador stepped back, as did the banderilleros. A door at the end of the arena opened for a rider to enter the ring on a huge horse that was covered in what looked like heavy blankets or leather that reached almost to the ground. The rider carried a lance casually in his right hand like he knew how to use it.

That couldn't be good for the bull.

As if knowing that, the bull snorted and charged full-bore for the horse, digging its horns into the side-blanket armor and pushing...pushing...heaving...twisting...until the horse went down! The crowd gasped and for a moment Emery's heart beat with a wild hope.

But the rider had jumped quickly off the horse's back before he was caught and the banderilleros were all over the bull in seconds, waving their capes at him to distract him and guide him off so the other men running on could help right the horse.

They did and the picador leapt back up to the saddle, still holding his lance.

Too many helpers. Always the matador wins.

"The picador must stab the *rejones* into the bull...there! You see. In the top of the *morillo*, the big muscle on the top of bull's neck. Ah, but the bull masters the picador's horse, pushing him around. The picador must try for the vein again with his blade. No! He stabs but it is no good! Again. Yes! Now the bull bleeds. He gets weaker, damaged, and lowers his head. But he gets angrier too. He will keep charging now. That is the first act of the bullfight!"

Emery was glad he'd skipped breakfast after all.

"Now it is time for the second act," Picasso went on. "The *suerte de banderillas*. You watch and see as they each try to plant a pair of their banderillas into the bull's morillo. They have harpoon-ends, the banderillas, like fish hooks. They cannot be shaken out."

The first ran, jumped, drove in the two ribbon-fluttering sticks, landed and leapt away like some kind of Olympic gymnast.

"Second blood!" Picasso crowed, his dark eyes intense on the scene, his old throat swallowing hard, however much he might try to hide it.

But *all* the eyes of the crowd were intense now, Emery saw. Every eye was drawn to this formal dance of death that just went on and on, within its carefully prescribed rules that everyone understood except the wildly snorting, spinning, charging bull.

"Third stage!" Picasso said when the last of the banderilleros had planted his flags in the top of the bull's neck so that six flagged stick fell to either side but held on, bouncing up and down there as the bull trotted back in momentary indecision. The banderilleros had faded to the nearest gates and exited the ring.

"Now it is the matador's dance. He looks strong. He looks sharp. We will see." Picasso stretched out his right arm as if he wanted to grab Emery's knee. Then he saw what he was doing and grinned self-consciously and withdrew it.

Because he was usually here with whom? Wife? Son? Daughter? Mistress?

The bull had made two charges already and the crowd was getting excited. Was that because the matador had led him half around in a circle each time? Or was it because the bull had nearly gored the matador on that last one, swinging his horns unexpectedly to the side? Did the crowd *care* whose blood they saw?

"You see? You see?" Picasso was almost squirming up out of his seat. "The way de Paula holds his *muleta* out firmly and guides the bull in a smooth *molinete* around him? He has stopped the bull's head from swinging! He is mastering the bull! Now he has stopped it completely! Look, the bull is mesmerized!"

As Emery looked, he realized the entire crowd of what had to be a couple thousand people were leaning forward in their seats just as intently as him and Picasso. For what they saw was the oddest dance of death Emery could have imagined.

De Paula, his red muleta wrapped around him so that his whole body was offered to the bull as a target, had one foot directly in front of the other and he was *hopping* forward like a bunny rabbit, closer and closer to a beast that easily outweighed him by ten to one. A beast with snorting, sharp horns on either side of its head that could, with one charge or thrust, rip him from groin to chest.

The crowd held its breath. Emery thought he could smell the bull's breath, feel the heat of it on his face, as de Paula came within a foot and seemed almost to be cradled between the beast's massive horns.

The matador slowly unwrapped his cape, sank to his knees before the bull, and spun on those knees so he knelt there facing *away* from the monster.

Picasso's hand reached out and gripped Emery's forearm like a vise, his face frozen in a rictus of fear as he watched.

Emery heard and felt the bull hunch forward...

And as the bull charged, de Paula sprang to the side, flashing his billowing red muleta in a fluttering whirl over the bull's face and horns.

The crowd jumped to its feet, including Picasso, who released Emery and added his *Olé!* to the rest. While Emery, feeling his heart thumping loudly in his chest, pressure thumping in his ears, leaned hard onto his knees to understand if he felt like crying because of the audacity of what de Paula had just done, or its stupidity.

When Picasso retook his seat on the stone bench beside him, he turned and must have seen something in Emery's face for his own eyes filled with tears, a sight Emery had never thought he would see.

Again his hand gripped Emery's forearm, gentler this time. "We are both fathers," he said huskily, "and we have both been husbands. But before all this, Emery, we are men. Does this not make you understand that completely? The need to challenge and to push. The need to put yourself up against the black canvas that is the ultimate end and *be* something that others will not forget. But even more than that..."

"What?" said Emery, his breath high and tight in his chest.

"Look," he said, and gestured with his chin back to the bull ring.

De Paula was standing only about ten yards back from the bull now, facing the animal head on and staring it down. No hopping. No play. No delicacy.

"His right hand," Picasso said and Emery looked.

The sword. During most of the bullfight, this frightening implement had been hidden inside the red cloak, the muleta. Now it was out in the open and, as Emery watched, the hilt was raised up to de Paula's eye level. He sighted along it like a gun, aiming just over the bull's lowered, softly snorting head. At the gates around the ring, Emery saw the three banderilleros poised, ready to rush in.

Without a sound, de Paula rushed forward, triggering the bull's own last desperate rush. But the sword tip had already found its mark as de Paula raised the hilt and thrust it home with a yell, spinning aside to avoid the swinging horns.

The bull staggered forward. Weaved. Fell to its front knees. The crowd roared its approval.

And one of the black-suited banderilleros was there with his dagger up in his hand. He circled back and forth in front of the bull, still cautious even as the great beast faltered. Then he leapt, pounded the dagger into the bull's forehead, and jerked it out again.

Like a tap.

Like "Go to sleep now."

The bull did. It buckled completely and fell on its side.

Another roar of the crowd. All its sins were expiated. All it fears banished. All its wildest desires slaked in a mad rush.

"Do you see the truth now?" Picasso whispered beside Emery, driving the ice pick words through the noise of the crowd and into Emery's brain. "This is what it means to be a man. You fight and you fight until you get control over something and you *own* it.

"Then you must kill it. It's all that is left."

THE CRAZY MAN

They didn't stay for the third fight, or for the second bulls of any of the matadors. It wasn't necessary. Picasso had made his point and Emery was sickened. But it obviously wasn't all the Spanish painter had planned to do.

He led him out of the amphitheater and down the steps of its north entrance, walking so quickly even Marcel had to do a stuttering quickstep to keep up. Emery just lengthened his stride, but understood it for what it was – another attempt to "control" him, to "own" him.

Well, good luck with that, Pablo.

Emery stopped dead and sat down on the steps, forearms resting across his knees as he looked up at the blue sky. Eventually, he figured, Picasso would notice he wasn't keeping up. Or maybe he'd known immediately and just pretended he didn't. For all his talk about truth in art, truth in life wasn't Picasso's strong suit.

In fact, it took almost ten minutes before *Marcel* returned to stand by Emery's outstretched legs. "The monsieur would like you to come and join him," he said in his usual flat way.

"Do you always do what 'the monsieur' wants, Marcel?"

"Yes." Said simply. His face flat and untroubled. Just how long had he worked for Picasso, Emery wondered.

"Tell your boss that if he wants me to see anything more with him, he's going to have to come and get me himself. He can pretend I'm emotionally exhausted if he likes."

Marcel's eyebrows actually twitched down a little, but he finally nodded and hurried off. Emery resumed looking up at the sky, his eyes almost closed against the brightness. The heat, the rhythmic swells of crowd calls from the amphitheater behind him, and the ongoing mariachi music from the strolling musicians outside here, the tantalizing smells of cooking meat, were lulling him into an odd kind of dream. It had to be a dream. Because all these crowds still strolling and eating and drinking in their old-fashioned hair styles, the women almost exclusively in dresses, the men mostly in suits, leaning back against the dramatic grilles of their wartime automobiles – they didn't truly exist. They were part of a canvas Emery was putting together. And he was just so immersed in his creation that—

A man stood between him and the sun, looking down on him. A nut-brown, sailor-shirted, bald Spaniard. Particularly from this angle, Emery noticed, the bottom half of Picasso's face was so much more pronounced than the top. As if his being rested less in his brain, than in his voracious hungers, his physicality.

"Marcel says you are sick," Picasso grunted down at him.

"Does he?"

"He says the bullfight was too much for you and you needed rest."

"Hm."

"But there is someone you must come and meet."

"Who?" Though Emery just at that moment finally put it together and felt himself jolting out of his dreaminess with the speed of a double shot of espresso.

"The Crazy Man."

Exactly what Emery had somehow known Picasso was going to say. Because this was Arles, after all. And what was Arles known for but two things – its bullfights and its famous mad painter of sunflowers.

With exaggerated groaning, he stretched out his legs and arms, then stood up, staying on the step above Picasso so that he was tall enough relative to the Spaniard that Picasso seemed like a child to him, barely up to Emery's waist.

"Alright. Lead on, Pablo." Shake out that red cape and get me snorting along.

Picasso nodded grimly and began walking. Emery quick-stepped after him to walk at his side.

Traveling northeast, by Emery's estimation, they walked only about ten minutes with Marcel silently bringing up the rear before the streets seemed wider, the houses less frequent. Emery thought he could smell the Rhône through the tree to their left. And then the road underneath their feet was no longer asphalt or even cobblestone, but hard-packed dirt, separated from a similar side-walk now by a mound of packed dirt. A similar barrier, in fact ran all down the side of the street ahead as well. Something familiar about the scene...

The lamppost on the corner – it looked to be gas, where the ones around the amphitheater had certainly been electric. Then a clip-clopping and neighing sound made Emery jump and look behind him just in time to push Picasso over to the side of the road so the horse and cart could pass. Emery looked back the way they'd come and could have sworn the houses looked sparser than when he, Picasso, and Marcel had passed them.

Yet Picasso didn't seem to think anything was wrong. Emery turned to ask him, when the shorter man suddenly gripped his elbow and pointed.

"His shutters are open. You see? The green ones? I told you he was crazy."

Emery looked where Picasso had painted and the familiarity finally popped into focus. It was like he was looking at a familiar painting through a blue filter. The corner house with the shutters, joined onto a mirror of itself that looked like an operating grocery store. *Comestible* was written on a sign over the front door's awning. It was the yellow house.

Not *a* yellow house, but *the* one. The one Vincent van Gogh had painted during his famous nine month stay here with Paul Gauguin. The house was destroyed during World War Two, but apparently Emery wasn't in that time period after all. Or not any longer. The streets, the four-story building beyond, the stone railway bridge a short stone's throw further, weren't quite as yellow and orange as Van Gogh had painted them, but they were still unmistakable.

"Van Gogh's house," Emery said, almost daring Picasso to contradict him.

"Yes."

"Is Paul Gauguin with him?"

"No." Picasso spat into the dirt. "That pig took off back to Paris. Or some south sea island. Somewhere."

"Then shouldn't..." Emery shut his mouth, worried about disturbing history as he'd almost done that first day with Picasso. But it made no sense that Van Gogh should be here if Gauguin had already left. Because it was Gauguin's leaving that had triggered Van Gogh's famous ear-cutting incident, which had in turn led to his time in the hospital in Arles, then an involuntary committal to Saint-Rémy-en-Provence.

Unless this was just after he'd come back from the first hospital stay?

"And Vincent won't be out painting in the fields?" Emery said. Or down at the Langlois Bridge on the Rhône? Or further along the Rhône where he painted his *Starry Night*?

Picasso shrugged. "Let's go and find out."

Realizing his gut was clenched as much as it had been the first time he'd found himself face-to-face with Renoir, Emery accompanied Picasso across the side street and the narrow trench bounding this side of the yellow house.

Picasso stepped up and knocked on the glass portion of the thickly-painted green front door. There was a tumbling commotion from deep in the house as if someone had tripped over boxes or had tumbled down stairs. A moment later, the door was pulled open by a man with an intensity as hot as, but one-hundred-eighty degrees opposite of, Picasso's. Where Picasso's eyes were cold and concentrated, this man's were a bright and bloodshot green that darted everywhere.

His head had the reverse proportions of the Spaniard's too – a receding, narrow chin covered in orange stubble, that broadened up gaunt cheeks to wide cheekbones and a prominent, bony brow with receding orange hair.

Around his head vertically, like a giant chin strap, was wrapped a cotton bandage that held a thick piece of folded cotton in place over his right ear. The blood seemed to be seeping through it as Emery stared.

And Van Gogh stared back at his visitors, fixating on Picasso's eyes in particular and trembling like he was seeing the devil incarnate.

"Invite us in, Vincent," Picasso said and gave him a broad smile. "We've come a long way to see you. Especially Emery here. A long long way. All the way from America."

Now Van Gogh turned to Emery with his delicate mouth working silently, finally vocalizing with, "You're not an Indian." He looked Emery up and down, confused. "Are you?"

"I'm not a First Nations person, no," Emery said. "My great grandparents were from England."

"Can we come up, Vincent?" Picasso repeated.

"I'm not sure. Dr. Gachet doesn't like me to have visitors."

"Who?"

Gachet... Gachet... Van Gogh had done a painting of a Dr. Gachet, Emery remembered, but... Something wrong about that somehow.

Van Gogh himself was staring out beyond us at the fields, seeming just as confused as Picasso and Emery about the name. Then he seemed to drop it and stepped back inside, holding the door open for them. So Emery and Picasso entered, Marcel remaining outside.

The place smelled like turpentine, which hit Emery so thick and fast it bit deep into his throat before he blinked it off and stepped back to the door for some air.

By the time he'd ducked back inside to follow Van Gogh and Picasso, the two men had climbed the narrow set of stairs leading to the upper level. Emery held his breath and sprinted up after them to find two rooms upstairs. The first was abandoned in more ways than one. The drawers on the little dresser had all been pulled out and scattered about the wooden floor. The thin mattress was stripped and half-pulled off the narrow bed. As Emery stepped partway inside, his foot kicked an overturned metal washbasin.

Gauguin's former room?

He backed out at the sound of Van Gogh's voice from the next room over: "I told you, Paul, that I need to *see* a thing. I don't paint from my imagination."

Paul. Gauguin *was* here!

But when Emery hurried over, he found only Van Gogh and Picasso, the short Spaniard nodding at Van Gogh as if it had just been *him* that Van Gogh was addressing. And Picasso would do that, too, wouldn't he? Pretend to be someone else if it let him laugh at the mistaken person. Or if it gave him an advantage somehow. Any advantage.

Van Gogh's ear bandage looked worse now, with a spot of

blood the size of a quarter soaked through where Emery guessed his earlobe used to be.

Time to end this nonsense.

But just as Emery was about to address Picasso by name, he saw what Picasso and Van Gogh were studying. It was a canvas propped up against the end of Van Gogh's narrow, boxlike bed. Untitled. Unsigned. Yet one look at the thick brush strokes defining cobalt blue walls and brown vermillion floor boards of a small room with two chairs, two pillows on the bed, two pairs of pictures having over the east side of the bed, two brushes on the bedside table, two bottles...

"You only have one chair in this room," Emery said, surprised.

"I moved it and painted it twice," Van Gogh said, then smiled slyly at Picasso. "Even when you paint directly from nature, you must bring out the true feeling of whatever it is you paint. Sometimes with color. Sometimes with movement of the brush. Thick. Strong. Fast."

"I see that in your work," Picasso said.

"Yes. And sometimes you must stylize a little. You change reality to make it *more* real." He turned to Emery. "Do you understand?"

"I think so," Emery said. But even as he did, he thought there was something very strange about having the person who was maybe the most famous post-impressionist painter ever, explain expressionism to him so simply. "But how did you get there?"

Van Gogh thumped himself on his chest. "From here! And from Paris. The things they were doing with colors there."

"Renoir. Monet."

"And my friend Toulouse Lautrec. And a strange man named Seurat who was making formulas describing which colors together in which amounts would produce which emotions. Finally, of course, my friend Paul, here, who said I must paint also from my mind, not just what I see."

"Yes. Very clever," said Picasso and yawned. "What else do you have?"

"Oh. This isn't good enough?" Van Gogh's face went suddenly red. "You paint beside me every day, then you leave and... And..." He began shaking his head, trying to put it together.

Picasso cut him off. "And now I'm back. And I just want to see what you've done while I was away." So smooth even Emery almost bought it.

"My brother has most of my paintings. To sell, like I told you." He jutted his small jaw forward, challenging Picasso or Emery to disagree.

"I am sure Theo doesn't have *all* of your paintings, does he?" Picasso said. And only because Emery was as desperate as the Spaniard to see what else Van Gogh had around, he kept his mouth shut and waited for the answer.

"Downstairs," the red-headed Dutchman said, and led the way out and down. Thump, thump, thump, ker-thump. Van Gogh almost tripped on the stairs and Emery realized the man wore heavy, worn boots that were caked with mud and tied with laces that had been broken and knotted together many times. That had obviously been the clumping sound they'd heard before he'd answered the door.

Now they hit the bottom floor which was clearly the house's studio and Emery remembered too late to hold his breath. He put a hand over his nose and mouth and tried to take shallow breaths strictly through his nose as he stumbled after the other two men.

The stinging in his throat brought back memories of his own studio, of the noxious fumes he'd had once from a bad batch of turpentine he'd picked up on the cheap, of the air blowers Mattie had made him buy...

"This one!" Picasso was saying, pulling a canvas up from where it leaned against the wall with a dozen or so more of varying sizes. It was a bunch of sunflowers in a field. A familiar Van Gogh theme, a familiar thick paint style loaded with yellows and oranges, but Emery didn't recognize it.

And at that moment he didn't care. For, as Van Gogh anxiously circled Picasso, Emery wanted to feel what it was like to *be* Van Gogh and so stuck out his hand to stroke the end of a long roll of what looked like coarse canvas cloth. Jute? On the floor to the left was the curved knife like a hook, that Van Gogh and Gauguin must have been using to cut off canvas-sized pieces. It lay among stacks of neatly cut and mitered wood pieces to stretch the cloth over and tack into place. All very do-it-yourself on the cheap, which explained the bad turpentine and—

Emery's head shot up. Dr. Gachet. It wasn't only the portrait Van Gogh had done of him that was familiar. Dr. Gachet was the name of the man who'd taken Vincent Van Gogh in *after* the artist had finally been released from his involuntary committal to that place in Saint-Rémy-en-Provence. And Gachet had diagnosed Van Gogh's seeming psychotic breaks as resulting from turpentine poisoning exacerbated by absinthe abuse.

Time.

Van Gogh was thinking he was with Gachet but his ear was bleeding like he'd just cut it yesterday.

Mixed up Time.

Picasso knew Van Gogh and Van Gogh knew him, but in real life Picasso had been a little boy growing up in Spain when Van Gogh died.

And Picasso and Emery had just come from a bullfight held during World War II.

And somewhere out there, Violet was picking truffles with her class of twenty-first century wannabe chefs.

Maybe it wasn't Van Gogh who was confused after all but the whole frigging *universe* right now.

In a surge of frustration, Emery brushed past Van Gogh and pushed aside Picasso from the leaning stack of canvases the

Spaniard had been flipping through. Emery began his own review of them.

More sunflowers.

Wheatfields.

Wildflowers and thistles in a vase.

A green and yellow garden Emery was pretty sure was Dr. Gachet's.

A woman in front of a white house.

Then Emery stopped. Stared. He reached down and pulled the painted canvas out and put it in front of all the others. Then he turned to glare at Picasso, whose face had gone obelisk-unreadable.

"You know, don't you," Emery accused him.

Picasso shrugged. "What?"

Emery turned to Van Gogh and the Dutchman seemed to hunch more into himself, looking suddenly emaciated, his brow twice as protruding. His green eyes began darting again, his blunt, paint-spattered hands coming up to brush back his red hair but stopping when they hit the bandage.

"When did you paint this?" Emery said.

"When?" Van Gogh said, stalling.

"This. A wheatfield with a dark purply sky. Crows flying ominously overhead. Three paths through the wheat, representing choices. Maybe your last chance. You know they'll make a movie one day that makes this your last painting, a prediction of your death."

Van Gogh was shaking now, both hands up beside his head like he was trying to do Munsch's *Scream*. "What do you mean 'movie?'"

"A film," Emery snapped, knowing what he was doing but unwilling to stop. "A moving picture."

Picasso said solemnly to no one in particular, "I met Louis

Lumière one time before he died. He invented the motion picture camera when he was a young man like Vincent. In 1895."

Almost a decade after Van Gogh died.

"What are you talking about!" Van Gogh screamed now. His face was read and enough blood had soaked through his ear bandage so that it dripped down from his fingers. "You're not Paul! Who are you? You're not my friend!"

Again a Picasso shrug. "We're just admirers of your work, Vincent."

Emery just stared, tight-jawed. He had sympathy for the Dutchman, but none of this was real. It couldn't be.

As if he'd heard Emery's thoughts, Van Gogh gave a strangled yell and lunged for the hooked knife he and Gauguin had used to cut canvas. He snatched it up but stumbled in his big boots amongst the framing sticks and nails, a hammer, a ruler.

Picasso and Emery both ran for the hallway and out the front door, careening into the sunlight as the door slapped against the front of the house. Thumping hard behind them, panting and squealing like a stuck pig, came Van Gogh.

Emery turned to meet the rush, but Marcel beat him to it. As the crazy Dutchman roared from the house, Marcel hit him on the back of the neck with both hands joined together. Van Gogh flew to the earth, dropping his knife. Picasso ran to it and scooped it up, waving it in front of him defensively.

Van Gogh seemed barely able to see, much less acknowledge it. He ran at Marcel again and the Frenchman sidestepped him and punched him hard in the gut as he passed. Van Gogh dropped again. And again picked himself up, slower, still grunting and drooling now, the side of his head a mushy mass of bloody bandage.

"Marcel is trained in boxing," Picasso said fiercely to Emery and unconsciously stabbed and swiped the air with the knife he held. "Nothing to fear." He turned and shouted at Van Gogh, "You are not such a great one after all! No one buys your work, do they! You have sold what? One painting in your entire life! You failure! You incompetent!"

Van Gogh lunged at him but Marcel tripped him. The Frenchman stood back as once more Van Gogh struggled to his dusty, bloody feet

"I'm going," Emery said.

"What?" Picasso whipped around. "Where?"

"Anywhere. Back to Aix. Back home. I'm not going to watch this. I can't take this any longer."

Emery had been backing up slowly as he said it. And as Picasso held up a hand, "No!" and Marcel once more sent the sickly Van Gogh sprawling hard to the dirt, Emery turned and began to run.

A slow run. It would have been a jog except it had none of that grace. Because he didn't know where he was going or if there was anywhere *to* go. Instinct, though, headed him back the way they'd come, towards the amphitheater where they'd watched the bull-fight in what already seemed another life.

Yet as Emery jogged, the road seemed to get harder and he realized he was running on cobblestone, then asphalt. Then there were big-grilled cars and crowds and a major buzz of cheering from the pseudo-Roman coliseum ahead. A sustained ripping sound far overhead made him look up and he saw a passenger jet high in the blue, streaking southeast, probably for Marseilles.

With tears in his eyes and heart beating hard, he looked down and saw the cars were sleeker now. A SmartCar crawled past, careful of the crowds. He recognized the model of a parked Audi. And then a clearly-marked taxi-cab, a Renault model, stopped to disgorge its passenger about fifteen yards ahead of him, in the small parking area just to the right of the wide steps leading to the amphitheater's main entrance.

"Hey!" Emery yelled and began running again. The taxi was turning to pull out into the crowded perimeter road. "Hey! *Allo!*"

He leapt directly in front of the cab and slapped his hand on its hood.

The taxi stopped and he ran to its driver's side window.

"Can you drive me?" he said in French, almost out of breath.

"To where?"

"To...Aix-en-Provence. The other side of it."

The white-haired driver frowned and looked around, thinking to get out of it.

"I'll pay you double your normal rate!" Emery said. "Triple! So you will make a profit!"

"That will be expensive."

"I don't care! I don't care!" Emery strode to the back passenger door and pulled it open, spilled inside, and thunked it shut behind him. "Just take me home."

IT WASN'T until almost three hours later, when he walked for a third time around the deserted Avrochet farm, calling first Violet's cell phone, then Charlotte's, then seeking fruitlessly for left notes or messages, that Emery began to question the wisdom of every choice he'd made that day.

Things were not waiting on him. Not at all.

WHERE HAS SHE GONE?

Violet didn't come home that night.

Charlotte didn't answer any of his calls.

Emery went to bed hungry, his stomach too twisted in knots to eat, his mind too busy to sleep.

The next morning, the third Monday of the Lakes' house exchange, their fourth in France, Emery felt light headed but skipped breakfast anyway and caught the public bus into Aix, then a taxi to the Serrut School of Cooking, on 522 Jules Renaud Road, which turned out to be nothing more than an elegant stone home on a side street south of the Old City.

Chef Myriam herself answered the door as her two week cooking class had wrapped up the day before with the truffle hunt and a final use of what they gathered in a delicate soufflé banquet which the family and friends of the students had all been invited to attend as a kind of graduation celebration.

The middle-aged woman, her unruly gray hair held back on her head with bobby pins, smiled curiously at him as she described it. Her voice was a curious mixture of pride and resentment. Why? Because Emery hadn't shown up?

"I wasn't invited," he explained.

"Of course you were not."

"Uh...why wasn't I? Do you know?"

"The final dinner was prepared by the students, Monsieur."

"Like...Violet."

"By students who took the whole course and learned how to prepare all the dishes we served on the last day."

"You're saying Violet missed some of the lessons? Because she certainly seemed committed. If she missed a few, she must have—"

Chef Myriam cut him off. "She came only to the first week, Monsieur Lake. And not to all of that."

Emery felt his heart drop into his empty stomach. "What?"

The chef's husband was calling something to her from deep in the old house. The woman turned and shouted back, her south of France accent so strong that Emery couldn't quite catch it. When she spoke to Emery again, it was much more the French he was used to. And there was a compassion in her eyes that was explained when she said, "I have children too, you know. Two daughters. One in Paris. One who is helping orphans in Brazil." She shuddered. "They do not always do what we expect."

"But...she told me..."

"She said there was a man she had to meet. That was the first excuse she gave for not attending class. When she stopped coming altogether, I assumed it was for this man."

"Her 'man from Aix.'"

Chef Myriam smiled. "Is that what she called him? Did you meet him?"

"I never have." Emery looked down, his face twisting. A good father would have, wouldn't he. A good father would have insisted when he saw what was happening with his daughter. A good father...

"She has not come home." Chef Myriam said it with the gentlest of voices and a touch to Emery's arm that probably showed just how she coaxed truffles and souffles and other fine French foods to their fullest glory. In Emery, it conjured up images of Vincent Van Gogh lunging and being struck down, bloody and beaten, over and over. Or a bull lowering its horns because his shoulder and neck muscles have been stabbed and bled too much to support the horns' full weight any longer.

"Not since yesterday morning. And she was drinking, upset. She won't answer her phone. I don't know how to find her."

"You need to call the police."

He looked up to meet her eyes, expecting judgement, but found only compassion. It was an even heavier blow.

"I... Yes, I guess I do." He saw in his mind's eye flashes of police bursting in on her somewhere, ripping her out of the arms of her lover and either deciding she was crazy as she screamed and lunged at them, earning her an involuntary committal to some hospital in town or a stay in a holding cell for drunks, or profound apologies as they realized she was perfectly sane and in her rights to be wherever she wanted with whomever she wanted.

Chef Myriam echoed the last thought. "Or you can trust that she will be alright and come home in time. She is an adult, yes?"

"She's my daughter. She's my little girl."

"They stay that way always, do they not?"

The woman let the words hang and simply stood in the doorway, waiting for Emery to end their meeting. It was the last gift she could offer him.

* * *

CHARLOTTE LIVED in a small development just out of the west side of Aix that was called Les Milles. Unlike Chef Myriam and her husband's gracious and historic quarters, hers was a walk-up unit in a new-looking fourplex all in bright white that was nearly blinding in the sun as the taxi brought him close. He knew why she'd chosen it – just a short walk from a grocery store and more critically, a bus that went directly to the Aix-en-Provence TGV, from whence she could travel by high-speed train all over Europe.

That was Charlotte. Always on the move.

If they'd had even two more dates, Emery thought as he paid the taxi and asked him to wait, he'd have made her bring him here to stay the night so that she could get a sense there was something to come back to here.

As it was, he didn't even know which of the units he was facing was 301C, the address he'd scrounged off an old letter she'd sent to Claude Avrochet.

Emery hoped against hope she hadn't moved since then.

With a bleak sense of foreboding that had been growing ever since he'd come back from seeing the bullfights and Van Goghin Arles, Emery walked up a short flight of concrete stairs to the single entrance of the fourplex and found a buzzer beside the door for unit C. He buzzed.

There was no response so he buzzed again and, maybe with some kind of jilted lover's instinct, held down the buzzer. If she wasn't home, after all, who would care. If she was, then maybe she—

"*Quoi?*" The speaker crackled with the word like it had been attacked from the other end.

"Charlotte, it's me," he answered in French. He could hear her heavy breathing. "Emery."

The buzzing connection clicked off. But it wasn't followed by the click of the front door unlocking. Maybe she was coming down?

But he knew she wasn't. The foreboding in his gut told him she was running away from him like Violet was. How, why, he didn't know exactly. But at least with Charlotte he knew where she was right now.

At that moment, a young man in his teens came running out of the front door with his MP3 headphones jammed in his ears, his right arm clutching a pizza box like he'd just stolen the family's dinner and fled.

Emery caught the front door before it closed and locked. He ducked inside and went looking for Unit C.

It was on the ground level, rear left. Standing at the door, he could hear a commotion inside – muttering, slamming cupboards, toppling chairs. But it was only Charlotte's voice. Whatever going on it was her alone.

Significantly, a tied-up bag of smelly garbage sat just to the left of her unit door, like she'd put it here but hadn't yet had time to run it out to the general trash. Which meant maybe...

Emery tried her doorknob. It turned. Unlocked. He pushed it open, walked in, and a rush of discordance hit him all at once.

First – a dramatic color pallet. White carpet slid over blond hardwood and white leather sofas paraded before white walls and white melamine kitchen cabinets, everything jazzed with blood red and forest green pillows and curtains, original oil paintings, limited edition prints (including an early limited-edition Lake called *Beach Walkers*).

Then – chaos.

The air smelled both musty and crackling hot. Clothes lay scattered about the living room and further down the hall. A flute case sprawled open, flute half-assembled, by the bathroom door. And the air thumped with curses and knocks coming from the end of the hall.

Bedroom.

Emery walked to it and stopped dead in the open door because it was the madness of the yellow house in Arles all over again.

The woman he'd known as Charlotte Boulain – sophisticated, in-control, unpretentiously gorgeous – spun towards him in jeans and a tight tee-shirt with her eyes wide and staring, her clawlike fingers clutching a filmy purple negligee she looked poised to stuff into a small, already-stuffed hardback suitcase.

"What are you doing here?" she said.

"I'm looking for Violet."

"Well, she is not here. There is no reason why she would be here!"

She stuffed the negligee into the suitcase and slammed it shut, clicking the latches closed and spinning the locks on them.

"Charlotte, what's going on?"

"Nothing. Nothing nothing nothing's going on. I just have a...business trip to go on. That's all. That is *all!*"

The last word came out as a sudden shriek. She grabbed the handle of the suitcase she'd just packed and threw it against the wall. It hit and fell to the rug, not popping open. A glass-framed print of a small girl carting flowers in wheelbarrow shook off the wall and followed it down, hitting and shattering the front glass.

Nor was Charlotte finished. She'd turned to her bed now and started ripping off the bedspread, the two pillows, the blanket and sheets. Grunting. Her nails ragged. Her teeth bared.

"You must really hate your bed," Emery said.

"Bastard!" Charlotte cried out and kept ripping. Emery could see the sweat on her brow and staining her armpits. The smell in the room was bitter and hot.

"Who's the bastard? Me?"

"*All* men are bastards!" she yelled again. All the sheets were off now so she was struggling to lift the mattress itself out of the wooden box of her bedframe. "All of them...*ugh!*...cheat...*unh!*...and lie...and...*Holy Cross!*...steal your soul!"

"Well, I'm guessing it's not me you're talking about, then, since I never got that close. Which means you've got another man. You *had* another man when we slept together?"

She finally managed to raise the side of the mattress up and pushed it forward with a triumphant screech, running up onto the slats of her bed to push the mattress over and off the other side.

"Charlotte!" Emery snapped to get her attention. "Were you seeing this other man before we slept together?"

She turned around to face him, clattering precariously on her bed slats, her face still red and fierce, her eyes crazy looking. She stabbed back the sweaty strands of blond hair that had fallen over her face. "You introduced me to him, stupid man. You shot the drug of him into my veins. You were his pimp! His dealer! I had no chance!"

Emery shook his head. "I... Oh, God. You're talking about Picasso."

"Of course we are!"

"Shit."

"He came after me, you know. Him and his driver Marcel. They came here."

"I never gave him your address."

"I went to answer my door," she went on as if Emery hadn't spoken. "And there he was. The most famous artist of the last century. Of any century. With his eyes raking me over, so clearly wanting me. Do you *know* how powerful this is? It's impossible, of course. I told myself that even out in the olive grove with you when I *knew* who he really was. That he was real. That this was impossible but it was real. Which meant magic. Or that I was crazy. But my whole body responded, you know? And my mind. I wanted to *touch* him and have him *own* me, you know?"

Oh, yes. Emery knew. Like a matador mesmerized a bull. Or how the Minotaur, as Picasso had painted him, scooped up a helpless woman and carried her away. Endlessly powerful, the power all sexual. Because...why?

"No," Emery said intensely and walked into the room to the foot of her bed. "No, I don't get it. What the fuck did he have to offer you? You had it all together, Charlotte. You had your job, your love of art. You had me..."

She rattled forward on the bed slats until she was standing right at the end, towering over Emery. The light from the window behind her made her backlit like a deranged angel triumphant. "*You* don't know even know who you are, Emery Lake. *You* are still searching. But Picasso, he knows. He has plumbed truth with his art. He has a window to special truth, to things we all want to know deep in our souls. I wanted to be with him to touch that. Do you understand?"

The words stung and drove Emery backwards until he found his back against the bedroom wall. Picasso knew special truths? If so, they were only dark truths.

"So then what?" Emery said. "He dumped you? He decided to move on to another woman? Because that's what the *real* Picasso did in his life, you know – used up and destroyed one woman after another. Burned their cheeks with cigarettes, or hit them, or just messed with their minds. He alternated between the sexy stupid ones and the smart political or artistic ones. So after you, I guess—"

"Shut up!" Charlotte leapt off the end of the bed slammed both her hands against him to pin him back to the wall. "Shut up! Shut up! You don't know! You can't know what it's like!"

"So he *has* moved on?" Emery said, looking down at her fevered face.

"No!"

"Then what?"

"I... You don't..."

"What, Charlotte?"

"*He was already sleeping with someone else when he came after me! And he still is!*"

She pushed herself off him and began lunging randomly around the room, hitting things, sweeping and jerking her carefully decorated life from her walls, from her dresser and bedside table, from her closet.

Emery watched her, heard the wheezing whine building in her chest, and he stepped outside of his own anxiety a second to admire her stamina. If you were going to go crazy, you might as well do it big time.

"Other than the fact he's some kind of solid phantasm or something," Emery said finally, "I can't say I'm surprised. It's what he does. Not because he knows the answers, I think, but precisely because he doesn't. Because he's got this hole inside hi—"

"Stop!" Charlotte, on the far side of the bed, had spun to face him with her beautiful bare arms extended out, shaking her hands hard at Emery when he was about to speak again. "You still don't get it, Emery Lake. You don't understand the very worst part of it."

"Then tell me."

Charlotte opened her mouth and shut it again, shaking her head. She wrapped her arms around her and slumped back against the wall.

"Come on," Emery said, stalking around the bed to face her. "You've already told me you left me for a sixty-year-old braggart asshole whose best years of painting were long behind him even if he weren't dead and imaginary. So tell me what's worse!"

"The sixty-year-old asshole..."

"Yes?"

"The woman he was with before me, who he's still fucking every chance he can get..."

"Tell me," Emery said, even as he suddenly knew.

Charlotte looked up at him, her eyes were vicious, and she only had to say one word:

"Violet."

THE EMPTY OLIVE GROVE

Violet.

Emery couldn't breathe. The heat was suffocating him. His lack of food had drained all power from his limbs. He stumbled out of Charlotte's home and back to the cab. Ordered the driver to take him back to the Avrochet farm.

The thing was, Emery thought with his heart beating loud and painful in his chest, he'd known. Or, God, he should have known. He was her father. How could he not have known? How could he not have seen through all her facade of competence and satisfaction with her life when she was bringing him here to France? It was for Emery's search for meaning, she'd said. But it had been just as much for her own.

His little girl...

The cab swung onto the Autoroute and roared northeast, sinking Emery deeper into his rear seat.

When Mattie got sick, Violet had reacted so predictably, hadn't she? If Emery hadn't been so wrapped up his own fierce denial, he would have seen that Violet jumped ahead of him in the grieving process, straight to bargaining. It was why she'd given up her piano, the one thing she'd been so blessed with and in love with that her life path hadn't really been a question ever. And maybe losing her boyfriend of the time was even part of it. All a deal she made with God to save her mother's life.

And just as with Emery's pathetic little deal, God had said no. Mattie had died. It had swept Emery into a massive cycle of depression and anger that cut him off from the rest of the world.

But what had Violet done? Other than get angry at Emery, how had she coped?

Emery stared out the window at the clear blue sky rushing by. And the endless string of cars and electric poles and road signs and office buildings and life never ceasing or slowing down.

How had Violet coped? She hadn't. She'd covered up her grief, ignored how God had denied her deal, and gone on as if the perverted life path she'd chosen was meant to be.

She'd been a walking wounded who didn't even know how wounded she was until this voracious Picasso-thing had somehow latched onto her through Emery—the picture of her! Picasso had first seen her in that goddamned picture he'd pulled from Emery's wallet!—and swept in to fill the gaping hole her mother's death had created inside her.

The analysis felt right, but did it matter? Did it tell him how to find Violet now?

The cab had swung off the Autoroute and up the D7, then along the perimeter roads along the east side of Aix, and out into the country.

"Keep going out this way," Emery ordered the driver in French when he saw he was about to turn south on the smaller road to the Avrochet farm. "Take me to Le Tholonet."

Because just like Paul Cézanne had only found his way with the help of friends, it was time for Emery to do the same.

* * *

THE OLIVE GROVE on the south side of Le Tholonet looked all wrong.

More precisely, it was in the wrong place, considerably east of where it normally was. All of, trees, grass, the budding white rockets that had just begun to flourish in the last week Emery had been coming here, had all moved east.

And the trees were shorter, like they'd been genetically altered or selectively bred to have their branches closer to the ground for easier picking.

But of course that wasn't the biggest problem, was it. The biggest problem was that when Emery stood in the exact spot he estimated he'd been painting with Renoir for most of last week, we was in the corner of a ploughed field with a gravel road running along one side of it. And when he looked over his left shoulder he could see two in-ground swimming pools through the trees. Plus hydro and telephone lines, asphalt streets, a corrugated-metal shed, and two kids spraying each other with Master-Blaster water guns. Emery had made the taxi that brought him here drive through the entire subdivision twice before he accepted this was reality, while what he *remembered* was false.

Renoir was nowhere to be seen.

Emery kept calling for him anyway, finally walking across the field in the direction of the Mont Sainte-Victoire (the only thing that looked unchanged) until he reached the new olive grove with its freaky short trees.

Nothing except a couple of olive pickers who looked at him with mistrust.

Even moreso when he dropped to his knees and hands and began dry-heaving out his massive sense of panic.

When Emery was done, he picked himself back upright and

staggered back through Le Tholonet in mostly the direction he remembered taking with Renoir when they'd gone to see Cézanne in his Château Noir.

But half an hour later, walking alongside the Route Cézanne past the modern road signs, with modern BMWs and Renaults and even a couple GM vehicles speeding past him, he looked up at where the Château Noir had been and swore he could see, through the sparser trees, the top of a tour bus parked in front of its doors.

He finally tried hitchhiking, and was thoroughly amazed when a Mercedes-driving German couple picked him up and drove him all the way back to the Avrochet farm. "So clear you were American!" the husband with the dark sunglasses said when he climbed in the back. "We miss the talking in the English!"

Like Emery missed the talking of his daughter in any language, he thought back at them. But he smiled and thanked them for the ride before going into the house, finding no new messages, and collapsing in the living room armchair.

After a long pause, he got up and made himself a sandwich. But despite the hole in his gut, he couldn't bring himself to eat it. He walked out the front door to stare across the vegetable gardens at the Sainte-Victoire in the distance.

When he went back in, he looked up the phone number and called the police to report a missing vehicle.

EIGHT P.M.. 20:00 French time.

It was still bright outside, but with that kind of fragile thinness which said the day was slipping away. In fact, after four hours straight of sitting in a chair he'd pulled out into the driveway to stare at the Sainte-Victoire, his cell phone in his lap in case the police called, Emery could *taste* the night coming. There was a chill in the air that heightened the dusty smells of the garden and made them sit heavy on his tongue, trying to gently push their way in...

And just like that, he stood up, mentally smacking himself upside the head.

The reason Renoir hadn't been there, the reason the magic hadn't worked, had been because he'd invaded Le Tholonet by *taxi*. Not that cars in and of themselves were the problem. It was that the personal journey on foot was important. It spoke to the idea of going in naked. Or maybe to crossing some personal barrier. Or it simply gave his mind the time it needed to work up its hallucinations for him.

And if this all *was* some mental mind game he'd been playing with himself and sucking others into, well who better to help him figure a way out of it for Violet than the prime denizens of the game?

He'd have to hurry, though, if he was going to find his way before night fell completely.

Grabbing his backpack for familiarity's sake, he went to the kitchen to throw in a couple of dried-fruit energy bars and a filled water bottle. For a moment he considered packing his easel, canvas, and paints, but decided that was unnecessary. He hadn't had those the first few days he'd gone out, nor that last dreadful one yesterday that led him to Arles and Van Gogh.

So off he went through the front door, through the garden, the long grass, over the fences and roads, around the properties with swimming pools, across the stream, through the darkening pine tree forest and fields and vineyards, stopping at the mortar-free wall and making his way to the right in the gathering dusk to...an olive grove that was right where it was supposed to be.

But empty. Only fluttering leaves and deep shadow.

"Pierre?" Emery walked around the grove in the dark, finding the two twisted trees together that Renoir had painted, and the spot where Emery had lain on the ground beside the impressionist on his first day here to sketch the sky.

"Pie-e-e-e-re!" He called out. He thought he saw a light go on in one of the old farmhouses on the edge of Le Tholonet. Could an ancient-days farmer actually hear Emery? If they came out here, could they see him?

He put his hands around his mouth and turned a slow circle as he called out, "Pa-a-ablo! Paul! Vincent! Pierre-Auguste! *Anyone!*"

A small gust of wind through the olive leaves overhead was the only answer.

He called again and listened again.

Finally he leaned against the nearest olive tree, feeling its solidity and remembering how it hadn't been here earlier this afternoon. So Emery *had* to be back in the magic place, whether in his mind or not. Why couldn't he summon the others here? Did he have to need them more? Or was he needing too much right now?

Maybe...maybe he had to go to them. To where? To the Château Noir, where Cézanne was renting, where Renoir was probably staying too. Since the magic olive grove was here, then maybe he could get to the ancient Château as well.

Emery straightened up and tried to get his bearings in the dark, mumbling his directions to himself as he tried to line up the direction he had walked with Renoir just a few days ago.

Other mumbling sounded in the grove, so much like his own that it took Emery a moment to register then. Then his head jerked up and he looked around desperately.

The mumbling stopped.

Holding very still, Emery called out again. "Pierre? Pablo? Paul? Vincent?"

On the last name, a hunched black shape darted between the olive trees to his left and from that direction he heard mumbling again. Emery crept down the row of trees towards the sound, picking out more and more of the rough voice as he neared.

"...Theo...marriage will give you...Rey said most epileptics bite their tongue...but giving up hope...no, no, no...I exaggerate! My head! My brain!...How kind you are. In Auvers. Auvers?...this storm that threatens you..."

Emery rounded a set of two trees close together and suddenly saw the hunched shape. The bandage wrapped under the man's receded chin and up the sides of his head was visible even in the dark, but Van Gogh looked dressed for winter now. He wore some kind of dark fur hat on his head with a thick coat on, his arms wrapped around himself, and even when he saw Emery, he kept muttering to himself.

"I am risking my *life* for my work my work, which has taken half my reason, Theo. But we only make our pictures speak, don't we. And you've got Jo. She's doing well, thank God for that blessing. You must name your child Vincent. I love you. The fifty francs you sent me, I ate it, so to speak. Money and food and where I live. I don't know where I live right now, Theo. Auvers? Saint-Remy? I don't. Know. Where. I. *Live!*"

This last he shouted directly at Emery, then began running through the olive grove madly, striking a tree in the dark, bouncing sideways, but catching himself and moving on.

Emery, startled, took a second to follow, but then he was tearing madly after him.

Until he vanished.

Emery tore through a dark row of olive trees Van Gogh had plunged through and the madman was gone. Emery kept going into the next row. Nothing. Back. Nothing. He stopped dead and listened. Nothing.

"No! Oh, come *on!*"

Nothing. No sound but his own harsh breath. Emery sank down to his knees.

A sound behind him. Emery spun and saw the shadowed figure

running through the dark grove fifteen yards down, going the opposite way. Emery sprung to his feet.

And felt a hand on his shoulder and a voice said, "You won't catch him."

He spun around.

Renoir.

THE MIDNIGHT CASTLE

The French artist looked as he always did except for his expression, which was uncharacteristically dark and somber.

"Pierre! Thank God!"

"Perhaps."

"Listen," Emery blurted. "Picasso – he's got my daughter, Violet. I have to find her and save her!"

What Renoir did *not* do, which Emery would be forever grateful for, was ask how old Violet was or whether she'd chosen to go with Picasso of her own free will. Renoir knew Picasso. He knew what the man was capable of. And Renoir was Emery's friend, crazy as it sounded. His *ami*, who believed that everything in this world waited on Emery completing whatever journey it was he was on.

"He will have her in his castle now," Renoir said.

"His castle? Picasso owns a damned castle?"

"Not a big one with such a high wall as the Palais des Papes, but it is tall, all of stone, with a wall around its grounds."

"Wait! Wait." Emery was thinking furiously in the dark, unnerved as the wind swished suddenly through the olive leaves directly above his head. "You're talking about the Vauvenargues Castle, right? The one on the north side of the Sainte-Victoire."

Renoir nodded. "So that he could 'own Cézanne's mountain.' Yes."

"But he never really lived there. His last wife hated the place. He was mainly just buried there."

Renoir lowered his head and tugged on his mustache. When he looked up, he had no extra lines on his fine-boned face, but he looked older. Sad. "Maybe that is as you say somehow. Maybe it will be. But right now, my friend, I know he is there. He has boasted of it. It is where he would bring your daughter, I think."

"Then I need to go there. Now."

"It is a long way."

"How far?"

"Too far to walk. Five, six, seven hours? At night it would be more. And if you do not get there until morning, he will see you coming and set his dogs on you."

Emery dropped his face to his hands, massaging his forehead hard. There had to be a way. His brain wasn't working well, he knew. He should force himself to eat. Even just a bite...

"Do you know how to ride a horse?" Renoir asked.

"A horse? Not a lot of horses around where I come from. Well, no, actually there are, but I've only ridden one once or twice. And then only on horses that basically plant their nose into the butt of the horse in front of them and follow the trail until they're back in their paddock."

"The farmer over there, on the northeast end of the olive grove, keeps horses. We could borrow them."

"'Borrow.'"

Renoir shrugged. "Do you have money to pay him?"

"Not any he'd accept." Then the other part of what Renoir had said hit home. "You said 'we.' You're coming with me?"

"Someone has to show you where to go."

* * *

OF ALL THE insanities he'd encountered since leaving his lake house in the Catskills for France, 'borrowing' a bunch of horses in the middle of the night from a farmer who didn't even exist in Emery's real time and place was definitely the strangest.

And the most stressful.

Breaking into the farmer's small barn with Renoir made Emery reflect just what a frail physical specimen he had backing him up as a partner in crime. In the lovers vs. fighters dichotomy, there was no question where Pierre-Auguste fit.

Yet once Emery actually got them inside and they found the stalls in the back, Renoir surprised him with an obvious knowledge of horses and how to saddle them.

"I thought you were a city boy. Grew up in Paris," Emery whispered as Renoir pulled the leather cinch under the first plough-horse's belly.

"My time in the 1870 war," the painter said and gave another tug. "I trained horses in the Pyrenees. Far from the action, but I learned to ride, to groom, and to shovel much manure."

"A good thing for a couple of horse thieves like us."

"*Borrowing*, my friend. We are *borrowing*. And we are ready to go. Open the barn door. Quietly."

Emery did and returned to find Renoir already up in the saddle of the whuffling, more cantankerous horse, and holding the reins of the other ones, waiting for Emery. With a quick swallow, Emery stuck his foot in the stirrup, grabbed the coarse hair of the horse's long mane, and pulled himself up.

"Do you want to take the reins?" Renoir asked. "Or shall I hold them so your horse follows mine with his nose in my horse's tail?"

It was too dark to see the twinkle in Renoir's eyes, but Emery heard it in the voice and humphed. "Give me the reins."

"As you wish."

The next thing Emery knew his hands had the cracked straps of leather and his horse was heading off towards the fields in a direction opposite the one Renoir had indicated for them.

With a laugh, Renoir trotted after them, circled Emery's horse and nudged him in the right direction. "Like this," he told Emery, demonstrating an upright position and grip on the reins that looked different than how Emery had seen cowboys do it in the movies.

But when he tried what Renoir indicated, both in posture and firm guidance of the reins, he was amazed to find his horse actually responded. On Renoir's encouragement, he also slipped his nearly empty backpack off his back and used its straps to tie it to the front of his saddle.

"And now," Renoir said, "we must get out of here before the farmer or his wife comes out with guns."

"Farmers with guns or castle owners with guard dogs," Emery said. "Hm. Let me see..."

"Castle owners with guard dogs and with your daughter." Renoir hitched his reins and set off at a brisk trot.

"That does put things in perspective," Emery said grimly. And, as he gave his horse an extra kick to make it catch up to Renoir's, he added under his breath, "Hang on, Violet. Daddy's coming."

THEY DIDN'T FOLLOW the road, because Renoir said they could steer by the mountain. If they just circled the south slope, followed the trail around the Lac de Bimont, they'd be almost there.

It probably would have been a good plan in broad daylight. As it was, even with the full moon casting most of the dry landscape into an eerily sharp relief, Renoir and Emery still managed to almost run their horses off shallow cliffs not once but three or four times. Each time, it felt like Emery's heart was going to spin up out of his throat, his body broke out in a cold sweat, and his already sore and chafed legs got ripped and pulled as his horse scrambled for more secure footing. At least it kept him awake.

But by the time they splashed into the exit shallows of the lake that would one day be dammed up on the west end and made the source of Aix-en-Provence's drinking water, Emery felt like he'd been beaten thoroughly across the back of his legs and groin. He was also pretty sure he'd pulled a muscle in his lower back.

All of which paled beside the serious stomach knots of dread he was developing as they closed in on their destination.

He didn't doubt that Picasso had Violet. Nor that he had her in the Vauvenargues Castle, or Château de Vauvenargues, as they'd say in French. What he did doubt was that a) they'd be able to talk or force their way into Picasso's stronghold, and b) that Violet would be willing and/or able to escape with them once they had.

"You want to stop for a drink here?" Renoir called back as they came out the other side of the shallow river with their feet and lower legs soaking wet.

Emery shook his head. "It's almost eleven o'clock, right? How much farther do we have? An hour? Two?"

"Or more!" Renoir called back. "But we can pick up the pace soon, so maybe less."

"Make it less!" Emery called. And finally, forcing himself, he said, "I need to eat. You want to share some dried-fruit energy bar?"

"What is that?"

"Food of the gods, Pierre!" Emery said and trotted to come up beside him.

* * *

ON EMERY'S URGING, and with a temporary boost in energy from some actual food in his system, they went north until they found the main road heading into Vauvenargues and followed that. They met no one and made much better time.

Just past midnight, with the full moon past its highest point and sliding down to the west, seeming to grow bigger and brighter as it went, the two painters on horseback passed by the outlying farms and houses of Vauvenargues and could see in the distance the black block that rose out of one of the first foothills on this northern slope of the Sainte-Victoire. Unlike the houses of Vauvenargues, the castle showed lights from three or four of its windows. Probably it was Picasso up late, painting.

But the effect, given that this was the gentle side of the mountain that Emery had imagined like a giant rock wave sweeping south with other smaller hills following close behind, was that the castle was a twinkling buoy adrift in the ink-black ocean. It made Emery and Renoir sailors using it to navigate by.

"Do you want to just ride up to the front door of the gate and knock?" Renoir said as they clip-clopped ever closer.

Emery licked his lips. "Other ideas?"

"We could ride around the side and see if there is an easier entrance."

"I'm for that."

Renoir nodded and cut off the dirt road into a grass field, headed for the forest beyond that encircled Picasso's castle. As they approached, and before the forest swallowed them, Emery thought he could make out the basic shape of their objective. It looked like a thick stone mass, roughly square and three tall stories plus a double roof that sloped in from all four sides so the topmost point sat in the exact center, adding at least another story to the entire mass. The two western corners were rounded by turrets. The rows of tall narrow windows on each side were all bounded by shutters, which seemed to be open now to let in the cool night air. That much at least was promising.

Less promising were the lit windows – two on the north side

towards the Vauvenargues road and one on the down valley side from which Emery and Renoir approached. Also, as Renoir had remembered, the castle was ringed with stone walls that looked a good twenty feet high. If Emery had to guess, the guard dogs Renoir had talked about were probably patrolling the open space between those walls and the castle proper.

Emery bit down hard on his disappointment and fear as he urged his horse faster to catch up with Renoir. However they got in, it wasn't going to be as simple as their entry into the farmer's barn. This was Pablo Picasso's final defense against whoever finally found him out. You wanted to get in here, you were going to have to work for it, amigo.

Renoir had somehow quieted his horse as the ambled through the trees and up to the stone walls, then began circling the castle in a slow, counter-clockwise direction. Emery's hopes picked up. It was clear the initial purpose of the walls to repel invaders had not been kept up because numerous trees grew close enough to the walls that an agile or determined intruder could easily climb one and use branches to breach the perimeter.

It still left the problem of free-running dogs and penetrating the castle itself, of course, but if there was this lapse, perhaps there were others.

As they rounded the eastern side, Emery believed he saw two more. First was a rear gate. It was solidly locked, but had to be weaker than the surrounding stone.

Second, even as the downslope from the castle wall grew rockier and steeper so that the horses grew skittish and almost slipped a few times, the walls morphed into a kind of outbuilding (kitchen? livery?) that ran out from the main castle. It looked like it might have been built after the castle's initial construction, again believing that with no more German or Roman soldiers invading, the defenses could be relaxed. If Emery could climb this outbuilding and across its roof to the castle keep itself, he could avoid any free-roaming dogs and maybe find a way in.

He whistled softly to Renoir to stop and whispered exactly what he was thinking. Renoir agreed and the two began exploring the building for a way to climb. It took them twenty minutes before their hopes were crushed completely. The walls were smooth and windowless down low and for *this* section of wall, the trees had actually been cut back so you couldn't easily drop onto the outbuilding's roof.

"Let's keep going around," Renoir said when Emery kicked the stone wall in frustration. "Something may appear."

"What? Like knocking on the door politely and pretending we're really just friends wanting to visit in the middle of the night?"

Renoir shrugged. "If nothing else appears, yes. Someone is obviously awake inside."

* * *

THE FRONT GATE of the Vauvenargues Castle's perimeter wall was a flat-topped double door made of bolted wood designed to swing inwards. As thick and blunt as any steel portcullis Emery could have imagined, it had one profound difference. There, set into the stone on the right hand side, was a lumpy box with a heavy black matte finish and an obvious speaker grille and button.

Picasso's world, of course. Emery and Renoir had somehow ridden from the 1880's into the mid 1900's. Here there were cars and electronics, however primitive.

Renoir, who held both their horses some ten steps back, looked curiously at the door. "Do we bang loudly on it?" he said.

Emery shook his head and stepped over to the black box. He pushed and held the button. Waited. Punched it again. He should have eaten more. The energy had worn off and he was feeling both weak and annoyed.

Finally the speaker crackled to life, but not with Picasso's voice. Instead it was woman, her voice sharp, no doubt annoyed at having been awakened. *"Qu'est-ce que vous voulez?"* she snapped.

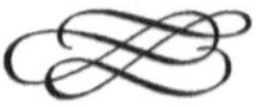

Emery kept the intercom button depressed and forced himself to speak his clearest French, "We want to see Monsieur Picasso. We're sorry for the hour but we are good friends of his and must see him tonight."

"My God, my God," muttered the woman's voice in French. "Are you crazy? Are you a madman?"

Renoir had pushed up beside Emery. He still held the reins of the horses and Emery felt their hot breath wet on his neck as they nuzzled him.

"Jacqueline! It's me, Pierre! Pablo will want to see us, truly! Please let us in!"

There was more muttering and the electric connection cut off for a moment.

"Pablo's crazy wife," Renoir muttered.

"His wife?" Emery said. "His last wife, Jacqueline? I read about — She was nightmare. She let *no* one get to him."

The speaker came back on with a sizzling crackle and the woman Jacqueline said, "You are not coming in tonight. Go away."

"No!" Emery said, pushing Renoir away from the speaker. "Listen, Madame Picasso, my daughter is in there! Surely you don't want your husband seeing another woman under your own roof!"

"Go away or I will send out the dogs."

The speaker cut off. Emery jabbed his finger into it, making it buzz again and again, until Renoir put a hand over it. "She will do what she says," he said. "She will release the dogs."

Emery stared at him coldly. "Good. That means she'll have to open the gate to do it, right?"

Renoir was about to respond when a door slammed from somewhere inside the wall and a loud voice that was half croaking mutter, half wail, filled the air.

"...a fall of damp and melting snow. I saw it, Theo! I never thought I would, but I came out and... People's superstitions! About my painting! I wanted to shout and shout at them but I couldn't and now I'm so afraid! Afraid that I will lose hope!"

As Van Gogh's wailing moved closer, Emery tensed, ready to push through the gate as it was unlatched. But suddenly the sound of his voice was to the right of them, on the outside of the wall and moving away.

"Gauguin doing 'Christ in the Garden of Olives'! No! Rembrandt! Delacroix! They were the ones! Theo, don't let Paul continue in this vein! Don't let him..."

"Wait here," Emery told Renoir and began running after the receding sound.

He caught up to Van Gogh just as he was stumbling through the stumpy pines separating the castle from a farmer's wheat field. Emery lunged forward and caught Van Gogh by the tail of his thick coat. He dragged him backwards and spun him around. The bandage wrapped under the Dutchman's chin and up around his receded hair, hatless now, looked fresher than it had before. Newly wrapped. The right ear still bled through it, though.

"Y-you're not Theo," Van Gogh sputtered at him, bony brow poking forward.

"I'm Emery Lake! I met you in Arles! In the yellow house!"

"The yellow house. I lived there. And Auvers. Paris. Saint-Rémy. I don't know where I live now."

"That's because you don't live anywhere, Vincent!" Emery said, shaking him. "But you were staying with Picasso, weren't you. You were in that castle over there. How did you just come out? How can I go in?"

"I gave my ear to the young beauty inside," Van Gogh said, eyes suddenly wide and childlike. "I told her to look after it for me."

"The young beauty? Where was she? Is she alright?"

"The whore of Vauvenargues. A sweet prostitute. Sweet flower."

Emery shook him again. "What was her name?"

"Her name?" Van Gogh suddenly seemed to focus, his eyes boring into Emery's in the darkness. "Her name was Violet. Violet Inviolate. And she has my ear!"

"Can you help me get into the castle? I need to save her. I'll give you back your ear. I just need to know how to get in."

For a second it seemed Van Gogh understood, then his eyes drifted. He ripped himself out of Emery's grip and went running out into the wheat field. *Swish! Swish!* His long coat fanned the wheat about him as he ran towards the farm houses of Vauvenargues, his arms high, calling, "Theo! Theo! I see colors everywhere! The trains to Paris are only twenty-five francs! I'll come and see you!"

Then he staggered to a halt so quickly that Emery, chasing after him, nearly bowled him over.

"Vincent...?" he said, taking a step back.

"There's no way in," Van Gogh said. "Don't you understand? No way in. No way back."

"What? What are you saying?"

"I see black crows over a wheatfield at night," Van Gogh whispered

Emery stupidly looked up.

When he looked back down, Van Gogh had a small pistol out in his hand and Emery's stomach dropped out. "No, Vincent. Please. I need your help. You have to help me save my daughter. Don't do this."

But even as Emery prepared to leap and wrest the pistol from Van Gogh's grip, the bandaged artist raised the gun to his temple and pulled the trigger.

* * *

"No-o-o!" Emery screamed over the bang.

Time fractured.

Always with Van Gogh, it seemed, time fractured. Like a Picasso painting. Like Picasso was painting this scene or painting Van Gogh's whole life.

"It didn't happen like this!"

Emery had rushed forward and caught Van Gogh's body before it could fall. Now the artist's body was sagging in Emery's arms. Emery, still shouting, his face red and mind spinning, sagged with it.

Because this couldn't be happening. Van Gogh shot himself, yes, but in a field outside Auvers, not here! And the shot was to his chest. It let him walk back to Dr. Gachet's house, back to his room. It would have let him walk with Emery back to the castle to show him the way in!

Emery tried to shake Van Gogh's still body now, even with both of them on their knees in the scratchy wheat. But the body was too heavy. Emery's limbs had lost all their strength and will.

No food. No sleep. No hope. No way in.

And from the dark, starry sky above, he thought he saw an

entire murder of crows fluttering down at him and Van Gogh. They hit and knocked him over, swarming his eyes with their feathers and beaks. His nose. Cawing. His mouth. He couldn't beat them back.

They pushed their darkness into his brain until everything went black..

THE THINGS WE LEAVE BEHIND

How long Emery was passed out for, he didn't know. But when he came to, Van Gogh's bloody head was resting on his chest. Emery's hand cradled it by the man's bloody ear and temple. The smell was rank and cut through with the metal tang of blood. Emery's mouth seemed full of it.

He rolled Van Gogh's head and torso off him and sat up, then almost fainted from the dizzy feeling in his head. He blinked hard to focus.

The dark wheat field. No sign of the crows he'd remembered attacking. Or had that been a hallucination?

A distant caw sent a shiver through him and said maybe it wasn't.

He shivered again, chilled to the bone. Whatever fever had gotten him here, had driven him for two days straight, looking for his daughter had burned through everything inside him. He had nothing left. Nothing but a dead man at his feet who told him it had all really happened. And Emery knew if he turned around he would see the moon lower in the sky and the black hulk of the

Vauvenargues Castle still looming at the base of the Sainte-Victoire.

"I can't...figure it out," he murmured. He was a painter, not a knight. And he'd never been much of a father or a fighter. He just wasn't up to this. He had barely begun to understand himself, much less Picasso and this crazy half-world that had let him steal Emery's daughter away from him.

"The one rule is to never give up," a voice said in front of him. "No matter who tells you to."

Emery looked up to see Pierre-Auguste Renoir walking towards him through the wheat field, still leading the two horses he and Emery had rode here on. But he had another friend with him in the darkness too and it was this man who'd spoken.

"Paul?" Emery said.

The gruff, bearded head of Paul Cézanne nodded.

"How?" Emery said. "Did you walk here? Ride? How did you know?"

Cézanne's face frowned so deeply it was hard to see in the darkness. "I felt...called," he said. "Needed."

"Like I said," Renoir said and smiled as he tugged on his mustache. "We're all waiting on you, my friend."

"To do what?"

"To rescue your daughter and yourself. To move on. To find what it is you were meant to do with your gift. I think that is why we've been here, Paul and I. Vincent. Even Pablo. We are helping a fellow painter to find his way."

Emery snorted. "Yeah, I'm sure Pablo's eager to help me. That's why he's trying to destroy my daughter. That's why he's so eager to let me waltz into his home."

"Or maybe he is showing you the final challenge you must face," Renoir said.

"What? Scaling the walls and fighting my way through a bunch of guard dogs? Oh, then breaking through the locked shutters on the ground floor, foiling any other protections he has inside, and doing that all before he can quietly slip out the back with Violet and just drive off to someplace I'll never find him?"

"Maybe those things are only a challenge if you let them be," Renoir said.

"And just what the hell does that mean?" Emery looked at the darkness on his hands, the stickiness of Van Gogh's blood and began rubbing them hard against his jeans, then swiping at his eyes. God, the stink of it was everywhere.

"Think it through, Emery. Like a painting. Some things only exist when you put them there. And all the problems they cause in the composition – those too are only there because of what you've created."

Emery shook his head and finally leaned forward to press his hands to the ground and get his feet under him. He staggered up to his feet and stuck out his chin at Renoir and Cézanne. "So what are you saying? I just scrape everything off, paint it out, and start over? And then what? Violet will be back in her bed at the Avrochet farm? I'll have never come out on this mad rescue ride? Picasso never led me around by the nose in Arles while secretly screwing my girlfriend and daughter? Presto, wipe-o, it's all gone!"

Cézanne shook his head at Emery as if he considered him a child. "What's happened has happened. But there are always layers of truth. Different ways to approach them."

"I DON'T GET IT!" Emery shouted, waving his bloodied hands about. "SPELL IT OUT FOR ME!"

Cézanne frowned and retreated a couple steps like he was going to leave, but Renoir caught his sleeve and looked calmly at Emery.

"You have to give us up," he said.

"What?" But he knew. Instinctively, he knew exactly what Renoir meant and it made his breath hitch in his throat.

"All the barricades Picasso has put up – the locked gate, the dogs, his wife Jacqueline – exist in this world with Paul and me and Vincent. Maybe they don't exist in your world."

In his world? But how could he go back to that world now? Back to a world where Mattie was dead and there was no magic? No meaning? No goading of Picasso and Van Gogh, the mystery of Cézanne, the intense happiness of his *ami* Renoir who painted trees as dancers and rays of light in blues and purples?

Emery lowered his head, blinking hard. Maybe he'd known, riding out here, that it would come to this. Maybe that was the real reason his guts had been twisting so.

Because he couldn't do this banishing halfway, could he. Picasso had shown him that. If Emery simply walked out of this world, somehow held it in abeyance again so that tomorrow or the next day or week he could get back here by some special path, then Picasso could get *out* too. The Spaniard was as strong as Emery. Stronger maybe.

To banish Picasso and save his daughter, Emery had to give it all up irrevocably.

His breath was loud in his own ears and his senses swam with the smell of blood from the suicide at his feet.

Give us up.

No.

The only way.

No!

Daddy...

Emery's face grew hot, his eyes wet, and he blinked hot tears into the earth before he raised his head.

Renoir, Cézanne, and the horses were gone.

* * *

ALSO GONE, Emery realized after a moment of letting his decision sink in, was Van Gogh's body and the blood from Emery's hands.

As a final check, Emery used trembling fingers to pull the cell phone Violet had bought for him out of his pants pocket. He flipped it open and turned it on. After it dinged to life, it spent a moment searching for a signal and...found one.

There were no left messages.

He dialed Violet and was automatically transferred to voice mail, so he disconnected, flipped it closed, and slipped it back into his pocket.

Then he took a deep breath of the cold night air and turned back towards the Château de Vauvenargues. As expected, no lights broke its black profile.

He began walking towards it.

RESCUE MISSION REDUX

Standing on the asphalt paving at the front gate of the chateau, Emery wasn't surprised to find the heavy wooden gate that had been there before looked older and weather beaten, but otherwise unchanged. It was also still locked.

One new thing was a sign posted where the old intercom box had been. It read: "The chateau is again closed. No visitors are allowed ever. Do not ring. Do not knock." Small print at the bottom indicated a museum in Paris that he could call.

That wasn't good enough at three in the morning.

Despite his generally run-down state, Emery began jumping and thumping himself into the black walls and gates with gusto, and finally got some purchase with his foot in the crack between the gate and the wall. Using it as a springboard, he managed to snag the top of the gate with his fingers and physically haul himself up and over.

He dropped onto the asphalt on the other side with a grunt and fell over onto his hip. Then he scrambled to his feet, unconsciously bracing himself for the attack dogs Picasso's wife, Jacqueline, had promised.

Of course there was nothing.

No. Wait. There was a dark shape over to the left of the front door of the chateau. A car?

He walked quietly to it and confirmed it was indeed a car. A Renault Laguna. The Avrochet's car that Violet had been driving into Aix for the last few weeks now. Whether Picasso had been here at all in the last thirty-plus years, Violet Lake certainly had. And almost certainly still was.

Filled with purpose again, Emery stepped back and scanned the chateau itself. Smooth stone made up the walls and they didn't look chinked enough to climb, despite their age. The shutters all looked closed. Emery had a vague recollection that Jacqueline's daughter, Catherine something-or-other, had inherited the chateau from her mother, but it didn't look like anyone was living here right now.

Still, Emery thought as he walked to the front door, if Violet was inside, it was just possible that...

He creaked down the metal handle on the front door and the door swung open.

"Violet?" he called into the musty space.

There was no answer. No sound. Emery stepped into the darkness and fumbled around near the door until he found a light switch. But when he flicked it, there was no result and he wondered if whoever owned the place simply shut off all electricity for the times they weren't going to be living here.

His eyes were trying to adapt to the darkness, but there was too little light. He felt his way cautiously along the right hand wall—not stone but some kind of material covering it and wooden wainscoting coming up to the height of Emery's chest—until he reached the west wall, outside of which the moon would be sitting. Feeling along that wall, he found a window and, after fiddling for a few moments with the latch, swung it inwards. Then he found the bar that held the outside shutters closed. He detached it and swung the shutters out wide.

The moonlight that flooded the entry hall actually made him wince. It revealed white sheets covering the furniture, the mirrors and pictures on the wall. What had probably been a large area rug, easily twelve feet wide, was rolled up and pushed against the wall facing the front door. Beyond that a hall curved around, presumably to further halls and rooms beyond.

He was about to plunge in when it occurred to him to look for footprints. Dust and cobwebs lay heavy on everything. Emery's own prints clearly tracked the entrance wall and ended here.

He saw no others.

His heartbeat threatened to run away with him but he forced it slower, coughed once on the dust, and began walking through the downstairs, west side of the house, opening windows and shutters as he went for their light.

"Violet!" he called and threw open another shutter with a *BAM!* "Violet!"

Ten minutes later he'd cleared the downstairs. Even the dark outbuildings which were, indeed, the kitchen for this chateau. Violet wasn't here.

So Emery found the stairwell and climbed, remembering only now that the lights he'd seen on here, when the chateau was in its other time zone, had been on the middle. Where? Towards the front. One near the back, the south side.

He did these rooms first, feeling his way in, finding the windows and opening them to the moonlight.

And so doing, he found Violet.

She was in none of the rooms where the lights had been on. Those were mostly filled with old paintings and sculptures covered over with sheets, presumably areas where Picasso had actually worked and stored his art. And not sold them? Emery was tempted to pull off the sheets and see why.

He didn't, though, particularly when he finally walked into the south room to find a dusty bed with its covers pulled back like someone had been sleeping there.

"Violet?"

There was a moaning sound from the corner beyond the bed and Emery quickly walked over. With a practiced hand, he first opened the room's window and shutters to let in some light and cool night air. Then he turned to see his daughter curled on her side, wrapped around her purse, her back against the wall. She was dressed in the same shorts and tight blouse he'd seen her drive off in a number of mornings since they'd been here. He knelt beside her and smelled vomit and booze. An empty bottle, possibly wine or port or even the mock absinthe he'd seen when he and Violet had gone food shopping in Aix, rolled away from her hand and under the bed as Emery pulled her up to sitting.

"Wha...?"

"Come on, honey." He strapped her purse crossways over his back, then pulled her left arm over his neck and wrapped his right arm around her waist. The muscle he'd pulled in his back earlier felt like someone was sticking in a knife as he awkwardly lifted her up to the bed.

She began to fall backwards but he caught her, holding her up in a sitting position.

"Violet? Violet! Look at me!"

Her face looked run over by a truck. Her eyes flickered open and tried to focus. "Da-Daddy?"

Then the eyeballs rolled upwards again and her lids closed. Emery ducked his head in next to hers in fear but could hear her breathing. Just drunk then. Massively. And when she woke up, would she be a drunk or just someone who'd had her soul flattened by an encounter with bad magic.

Or with life.

He let her fall back onto the bed and for a moment had absolutely no idea what to do next. Renoir said that he and Cézanne and Picasso and Van Gogh had been sent (or called?) to somehow help him on his journey. But he felt no different than he had been back in his lake house in New York. Mattie was gone. His world was empty. He was weak. He didn't know where to go.

Yes, said a small familiar voice inside him. *You do.*

He did?

Raising his head, he looked out the room's window, a south window, and saw mostly blackness. It was a hillside, he remembered. A mountainside. The Mont Saint-Victoire.

What had he felt about this mountain from the beginning? That it was an artistic nexus? A place of spirits? A place Cézanne painted over and over again looking for answers?

Find it.

Emery swooned a little, placing a hand on his head. There were so many degrees of hearing voices, so many ways, but this one had to be the most persistent. And that was what it wanted? To get him to the top of the Sainte-Victoire? It was going to have to wait.

Priority was getting Violet home. Safe. Come on, Lake. You *do* know what to do.

With a deep breath held against the inevitable lance of pain in his back, Emery scooped his arms under Violet's knees and back, straightened his back as much as possible, and lifted.

Ugh. God, he wished at that moment that Violet had taken her height genes from her mother, not him.

But he shifted the dead weight in his arms, trying not to jounce Violet's hanging head too much, and walked slowly out of the room.

Walking down the stairs was agony, with his biceps beginning to scream and his pulled back hurting more and more. This was ridiculous. How could—

His foot missed a step and he slipped forward, running down

with his arms clenching and unclenching on the shifting body of his daughter. Don't drop her! Don't drop her!

He made the bottom landing and went stumbling forward to brace himself against a wall with Violet still in his arms. His heart was pumping and he was wheezing hard. He needed to sit down. He needed to put Violet down. Just a short break. Just a minute.

A sound from the front of the chateau jerked his head up. It was the door opening.

Had he left it open so the wind could have...?

"*Allo?*"

A woman's voice, calling from the front. And not just any woman. Emery was ninety-five percent sure it was Charlotte.

He was about to stagger to her with Violet in his arms and ask for his help when he recalled how he'd left Charlotte the last time.

I hope he tears apart her soul! she'd called after him when he'd left her quarter of the fourplex in Les Milles. *I hope he* destroys *her!*

Breathing hard, his arm and back muscles straining, Emery thought a second. He could hear Charlotte moving into the house. She'd see his footprints in the dust and know he'd been here. She'd have seen the Laguna sedan outside. She wasn't just going to go away.

Fine.

Quietly inching around the corner into a dark room on the east side of the chateau, Emery set Violet down out of sight of the door. Then he came quickly back out, crossed to the west side and approached the front.

He met Charlotte halfway back.

They rounded a corner at the same time and almost hit each other in the gloom, both jumping back with a jerk and nervous laughter.

"Couldn't stay away, hunh?" Emery said in English.

"Nor could you," Charlotte answered in French.

"I had a daughter to save." He kept it in English out of perverse spite.

"And I, a lover." Still in French.

And so their bilingual conversation went as they slowly circled each other, taking in the sight. Because where he had been put together last time and she a total mess, this time it was the reverse. Emery was scraped and sweaty, covered with dust and cobwebs; Charlotte was perfection. She'd dressed in what, even in the moonlit gloom of the chateau's interior, Emery could tell was a chic business dress. Her blond hair, often worn back in a ponytail, had been styled loose but perfect down around her shoulders. Her lipstick traced a perfect definition of her lips. Her eyeliner made her eyes seem like orbs of feline intelligence in the night.

"Did you find her?" Charlotte asked.

"Maybe." He was painfully aware of Violet's purse strap running across his chest.

"Did you meet with him?"

"You mean Picasso? He's not here any longer."

She stuttered to a halt. "Where has he gone?"

"He's dead, Charlotte. You know that."

"You killed him!"

"No." Emery narrowed his eyes at her, seeing the sophisticated veneer she wore was just that – a surface. Underneath she was every bit the desperate woman she'd been out at Les Milles. So he spoke carefully, even shifting into French to be absolutely sure she understood. "Pablo Picasso, as you met him that day with me, and as you loved him in the days following, was not real. I know he felt real. He spoke real words to you. Maybe he even touched you and drew you and won you over with his artistic genius. But—and I don't know how to explain this, exactly—he was never really there. Deep in your heart you know it."

"That's not true! You're a demon. *You're* the one who's not real."

"Charlotte. Pablo Picasso died over thirty-five years ago. He's buried beside his wife, Jacqueline, somewhere out behind this castle. The grave has a bronze cast of one of his sculptures, 'Femme au Vase' I think it's called, though it probably doesn't look much like a woman with a vase. You can go and see for yourself. You're here."

"That's...that's...a *different* Picasso."

Emery blinked, not quite sure how to handle that one. It actually made more sense than what Emery had just proposed. It just wasn't true. And unfortunately Charlotte seemed to know it as well as he. She was chewing on her carefully made-up lips as she glared at him.

Finally she pushed past him and a moment later he heard her running up the stairs.

Had she been here before with Picasso? If so, how did *she* explain all the cobwebs and dust? How would she explain when everything she'd seen here with him was gone or old or covered in sheets, its master absent for decades?

A part of Emery actually cared. He'd actually thought that Charlotte and he...

Forget it. Weakness again. He had to put that aside. It was time to go.

Retracing his steps quickly to where he'd left Violet, he found her and pulled her now snoring body away from the floor and up into his arms. Jesus, the car key to the Laguna had better be in her purse.

He staggered to the front door.

Only to be stopped dead in his tracks by a screech from above. Charlotte, no doubt. She'd be finally facing the same loss Emery had faced out in the wheat field. And it wasn't fair, really. Emery had at least been given a choice.

Then there was something he had not expected – the flashing blue lights of a gendarmerie van and car both pulling into the front drive of the castle.

SPIRITS OF THE MOUNTAIN

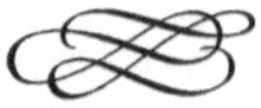

Emery retreated quickly into the shadows of the chateau as vehicle doors opened and slammed.

Oh, shit. The car. The Laguna. He'd called in about the car to see if they could find Violet.

Then he shook his head. No, that didn't make sense. It was the middle of the night. How could they possibly have tracked it here? Anyone who'd have seen it come in would have called hours ago. Unless...

"I called them here," Charlotte said, coming into the entrance hall behind him, but still staying out of sight of the outside. Her body looked hunched and hurt, but her voice was steady. "I finally figured out this is where Pablo would take her. And I knew you'd be looking. You'd have called the police. I just wanted them to take her *away* from him. Do you understand?"

"What? By having them charge her with break and enter?"

"I didn't know it would be that." Charlotte was clutching herself now, trying to hold herself together. "I didn't know..."

"But you do now," Emery said quickly. It would only be a minute before the gendarmes moved their search into the chateau.

"And you know there's no way she's going to be able to explain what happened. Not in a way that anyone will believe."

"No."

"She was just as trapped as you, Charlotte. Maybe more."

"Yes." Her voice was hitching, almost a whine.

"Then you have to go out there and distract them. Tell them you came here to find Violet first, because you're a friend of hers and you were worried about her. That's pretty much what you told them when you reported the car was here, wasn't it?"

She nodded, hanging on his words now as if he, at least, made sense.

"Then you say that when you came here, there was only the car. It looked like someone *had* been in here, but whoever it was wasn't here any longer. Can you tell them that? Convincingly?"

Another nod. Charlotte began taking deep breaths, straightening herself out. Damn, she had grit. And damn Picasso for being attracted to women exactly like her.

"Where are you going to be?" she said. "They'll still want to search."

"You leave that to me," Emery said with more confidence than he felt. His grip on Violet was slipping. Her dead weight seemed determined to push his arms to the floor. "Just try to stall them for five or ten minutes if you can."

When she nodded this time, she was fully Charlotte Boulain again, sales rep for a *parfumerie*, master of five foreign languages, both lover and survivor of Picasso. Emery figured you could count on one hand the women who could claim the last of those distinctions.

As she walked proudly to the front door, Emery turned with Violet and began hurrying as smoothly as he was able towards the back. His earlier exploration of the house had turned up a door that led out of the kitchen. In the darkness of what still had to be before four a.m., he should be able to slip out quietly enough.

A few minutes later, he had, cursing quietly at himself for bumping Violet's swinging head on the door as he slipped out.

Then it was a careful creep along the path by through the back grounds, quiet enough not only to hide from the French country police, but also from the ghost of Picasso and his nightmare wife who were both buried nearby.

He located the rear gate and laid Violet down on the grass, checking quickly to make sure she was still breathing normally, then turned to examine the lock. It was, of all things, a primitive swinging latch made out of dark, heavy steel. It took Emery five quietly-cursing attempts before he managed to bang it upwards out of its locking slot with a rock and a sound-cushioning stick. Then he threw his entire weight into pushing the heavy door outwards across the sucking grass and creepers.

Thinking he heard the sounds of a gendarme coming out back to check things out, Emery dispensed with picking Violet up and instead just dragged her outside by her armpits.

Then he closed the door and took a long, quiet breath.

So far so good. But it was still the middle of the night and they no longer had access to a car. Besides which...

Find it.

Yeah. That.

He craned his head back to look up the slope of the Sainte-Victoire, seeing what looked like a winding path leading up right from this very gate.

In the dark? Carrying Violet? Insanity.

He laughed quietly, feeling his sore back and arms, his swimmy head, and his general lack of physical ability. Then he looked down at his sleeping daughter and thought about how it was going to take something very special to bring her out of the nightmare he'd unwittingly dragged her into over the last few weeks.

Squatting down, he pulled her furthest arm up and over his neck and shoulders. Holding it there tightly, he slipped his other hand around her nearest leg, and with a solid weightlifter's grunt, raised her up across his back in fireman's carry.

One step at a time...

That voice in his head – he didn't know if it was still Mattie or just himself acting as his own minimalist cheerleader. But he took the advice and began climbing.

* * *

ONE STEP.

Another step.

Just keep going.

A sign on a rock read "facile." *Easy.* Sure. Easy enough for them to say. Maybe when he'd been thirty. Shortly after the rock, he lost the trail completely amidst the short, spiky bushes and rocks. He slipped on loose earth at one point and bumped into a pine tree.

But kept stumbling upwards.

Far out to the east, the sky seemed to be lightening. Was it? The top of the Sainte-Victoire, in any case, seemed easier to pick out. The sky was getting vaguely purple versus black. The moon had to be low and huge in the west.

As he looked to where it must be, on the other side of the mountain from him and Violet, he saw what had to be their final destination. Because it was probably every climber-of-the-Sainte-Victoire's destination.

A cross against the sky. He could just make it out over to the right, the westernmost peak of the top ridge. It had to be massive.

Violet gave a little moan near his left ear and he shifted her on his back. His legs were beyond pain now that he was into his fifth or sixth wind. He might collapse, but he wasn't going to stop until he got up there.

"You just hang on, Violet," he said and resumed climbing.

* * *

A CHILL MORNING wind was whistling along the top ridge as Emery mounted it to head for the cross at the west end. He staggered along the ridge with his daughter over his shoulders. His head hung low, unable to rise any higher under the weight of his load.

All of Provence spread out darkly ahead and left of him, he knew, far below. It seemed to call to him. *Just step this way. Let yourself fall. Let it go...*

His foot slipped a bit on loose rock and he caught himself with a small whine.

He could no longer feel his feet. He'd slipped right to his knees at least six times or more and had the scrapes all over his arms and face to prove it. But Violet he'd kept safe and *would* keep safe, he swore. Her stomach and chest would probably hurt like hell tomorrow from the bruises of the ride, but she'd be in one piece and not in jail.

Another gust tried blowing him left, down the sharper face of the mountain but he caught himself and pushed onward. At least he could finally see the rocks underfoot as the dawn crept up behind him. Long of pale light were dancing out across the valley, illuminating Aix en Provence in the distance, Le Tholonet down there somewhere..

And ahead, the cross, Christian symbol of death and resurrection.

Emery's faith might have dropped from him with his childhood, but his understanding of symbols hadn't. Nor had his yearning for what they promised. He'd already died at least once down there in the wheat field with Van Gogh. He might very well pass out up here once he actually reached his destination. A rebirth for him and one for his drunk, troubled daughter would be welcome.

On the other hand, he thought as his foot slipped again on

some gravel and he fought to keep his balance, if he fell down the sheer rock face here, the whole exercise was probably moot.

Just put one...foot...in front...of the other.

And again.

And again.

Until finally he reached the large base of poured concrete under the cross. It cut through the uneven rock to make a platform. On top of it rested another form of poured concrete, white, rising up square then cutting in to make a bench for exultant hikers. Then another block of concrete that shifted to brown brick with a dirty white plaque. Topping that was the huge cross—twenty feet tall?—made of metal girders that let the early dawn wind cut through it, unhindered.

Seeing it rise above him, seeing the level hardness of the high-altitude platform under his feet, Emery collapsed, letting Violet fall on top of him.

* * *

FIND IT.

I did, he thought back at Mattie's voice in the blackness he floated in. I'm here.

"But have you found it?"

Emery opened his eyes to see her backlit against a blue-gold sky in a simple summer dress. *It's still dawn,* he thought. *I've barely been out at all.*

Then Mattie smiled at him as he lay there on the rocks and concrete with Violet's snoring head resting on his chest, and the beauty of his wife's smile was so heartbreaking that Emery's eyes crinkled up with tears. They streamed down his cheeks, pooled in his ears, mixed with the dust and sweat of his hair.

"Are you like the others?" he asked her. "Like Renoir, Picasso, Cézanne?"

"Don't forget Vincent."

"Are you like them?"

"I don't paint," she said with a smile that quirked higher on one side of her mouth. A mouth wink.

"I mean are you as solid as they were? Can I touch you? Can I make love to you?"

"You made love to them?"

"You know what I mean!" he cried and reached for her.

She knelt down in front of him and stretched out her hand as well. And when they met, it was just as it had always been. He felt the softness of her skin, the warmth of it. He saw the wind ruffle the hair on her head and the smaller dark hairs on her arm.

It was too much for him. He could feel his inner fortitude unraveling. All the bands of sinew and metal he'd wrapped tightly around his heart to hold it together after her death, began to crack and fray. He feared if they broke completely, his heart would simply pump itself wildly into pieces and he would die.

"You'll be okay," Mattie said. "Stop looking so constipated."

He huffed out in embarrassment. "Make love to me."

"In front of our daughter? Out in the open like this?"

"Yes!" Emery said, carefully shifting Violet off his chest so she lay on one of the flattest stretches of concrete. He rolled up to his knees, wincing at the pain of the rocky surface, and took both of Mattie's hands in his. Then put a hand to her face and ran it down the cheek gently. "I remember everything about you," he said.

He leaned forward and she met his lips gently, warm and wet, offering him her tongue, letting him pull her body up against his so he could feel her breasts press into him, his arms slide down her back to her bottom.

He broke the kiss. "Make love to me!"

She pressed her head down to his chest and shook it. "No."

"Because you can't," he said, his voice almost breaking. "Because you're not really here."

She looked up at him and he could see her own eyes were wet too. "I'm as real as you need me to be, my darling."

"I need you to be a hundred percent real!"

She smiled sadly. "No, you don't. You might have once. You learned your way past it."

"How?" he cried out and shook his head. "By giving up a bunch of painters who *couldn't* have been real?"

"As real as me."

"I didn't ask for them! I only wanted you!"

"But they were the ones you needed. So they were the ones you got. Besides," she smiled and touched his sweaty, oily hair with her fingertips, "I was there the whole time too. I was your cheering section."

"'Find it.' Yeah. Over and over. A bit of a pest, in fact. You never said *what* I was supposed to find."

She laughed and pulled his head down to kiss him again. "Everybody told you. You were supposed to find yourself, of course. Whatever it was that would give you purpose again in your life, to help you move on and reengage with the world."

"So you sent me painters..."

Another laugh. "You still don't get it, do you. *You* sent you painters, Emery. You knew all along what it was you needed and your brain supplied it. It's just that your brain is so creatively rich and powerful that it kind of dragged more than just yourself into it."

"Violet."

"And...?"

"Charlotte."

Mattie was playing with his chest hairs at the base of his neck now in that possessive way she'd always had when she'd felt threatened by the many women who'd thrown themselves at "Emery Lake the Famous Artist" over the years. "She's very attractive."

"She's not you."

Mattie smiled up at him. "Even *I* am not me, dear."

Emery pulled her close to him again so he could feel her softness and her heat. He even felt her heartbeat and her breath on his chest just like he used to do lying in bed with her in the middle of the night sometimes. When he needed to remind himself he had her. That he hadn't lost her through some stupidity. That she was still there with him.

He took a deep breath and murmured without releasing her, "You realize you're telling me I'm crazy."

"Maybe," she murmured back. "Or maybe I'm telling you that your artistic gift, like the gifts of the painters you chose as your guides, is so strong and rich that it experiences the world in a way that most of the world can never understand."

He snorted. "So for me, it's real."

She pulled back, found his eyes, and nodded. "For you and those caught in your dream, it's real. But Emery, I hope you see that it's only the first step."

A cold shiver went through him. "What do you mean?"

"I mean that I have an oath to extract from you, Emery John Lake."

THE OATH

The chill went deeper into him as Mattie held his eyes. "What kind of oath?" Emery said.

She shook her head. "Don't look at me like that. It's a good oath. It comes out of you recognizing the full extent of this power that you have."

"The power to summon up dead people and talk and fight with them?"

"The power, big man, to look at reality in ways that others can't see and then *teach* them to see it that way."

"Like I did with Charlotte and Violet. Yeah, that worked well."

"You didn't like that?"

He frowned at her. "What do you think?"

"Then choose a better reality!"

"Just like that."

"Yes, just like that. You're an *artist*, Emery. You always have been. It's in your bones. It's in your skin. It's in the way you move, the way you see things, feel things, hear things. All of it. When you've been at your best—and oh, I was so happy to be able to see you at your best, my love!—you've taken things from the world around you and put them together in ways that quite frankly made everyone gasp. You talked about them clutching their hearts with wonder, but what I saw was their minds bursting with whole new worlds of perception. *That* is what you can do. *That* is what you have a duty to do, for yourself, for Violet and me, and for the world."

He drew back from her then, pushing up from his sore knees to walk to the steel railing they'd stuck along the edge that plunged what looked like thousands of feet. His knees felt rubbery as he looked from that to the sun breaching the eastern horizon – a challenge, a promise, and a demand.

Emery felt Mattie step up behind him. He reached back for her hand.

"I'm not sure I can do any of this without you, Mattie. I'm not sure I want to."

She wrapped an arm around his belly and pulled him back a step from the railing as she pressed herself into his back. "You can. You will. You would not be here, you wouldn't have climbed all the way up this mountain with our daughter on your back, if you were not ready to move on. You know that, don't you."

It was like what he'd challenged Charlotte with – accepting what she deep down knew to be true. And Emery, deep down, knew that what Mattie told him now was true. He would go on. He had to. He owed it to every famous painter before him who had shown the way.

"And the oath?" he asked.

"It's simple," she said, snuggling against his back. "Be a good father to Violet and...try to be happy."

She was releasing her grip around his waist. In a sudden panic, he said, "Wait!" and spun around to hold her around hers.

"One more kiss first," he said and lowered his head.

She met his lips and it was all the tenderness their love had been, the faith, the trust, the love. He closed his eyes to savor it and store it firmly in his memory where it belonged. And with his eyes still closed, as she pulled away, he said, "I promise."

* * *

He opened his eyes to see only Violet on the mountain top with him. But she was sitting up, using both hands to hold in what had to be a massive headache. Her face looked rather green around the edges, her eyes bloodshot.

But there was a kind of wonder in them as well.

"Did I just see...Mom?" she croaked.

"As clearly as you saw Picasso-the-asshole."

She squinted up at him as he walked over and tried to squat beside her. His legs gave out and let himself collapse onto his rear, his back to the base of the giant cross. Holding up a hand to shield her eyes from the sunlight, Violet looked around the entire mountaintop. It was devoid of other people. Just them, the sunshine, the morning wind, and patches of grass and trees lower down. Beyond, an entire world was just waking up. She swiveled her head around to look at it then brought her head straight again as if it had just been lanced with pain.

"Neither of them," Violet said, articulating carefully, "is ever coming back. Right?"

"Only in here"—he poked her softly on her forehead—"and in here." He poked her just above her left breast.

"God, Daddy, you're corny," she said, but she ducked her head as she did and he saw tears dripping from her cheeks. He patted his pockets for some kind of tissue but had nothing. Then she was waving her hand and swiping her face with the back of her arm.

"It's okay," she said, her voice quavering. "It's okay. I know I'll never... I knew... I just needed *some*body. Daddy, I miss her so much."

He reached out for her and she shuffled over to sit beside him, letting him wrap his arms around her and stroke her hair back from her face.

They sat like that, watching the sunrise, crying and talking, for a very long time.

Until it was time to hike down the mountain together.

A NEW PAINTING

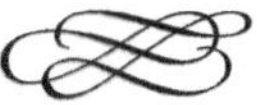

The buzz in the Hebbler Gallery climbed a noticeable amount just as Max finished his tale. He glanced at his watch and saw there were barely minutes until the uncrating. His assistants were already circulating through the crowd and ushering people to this side of the gallery. Max and his street-girl audience of one were standing much where they had been these last forty-five minutes, nearly hidden in the dark corner but with a good view of the crate and crowds now gathering.

Emery was nowhere to be seen.

"Where did they go?" said Amy as she polished off yet another beef crostini that she'd stepped out to snag from a passing platter.

Max smiled, happy she was finally eating, happy that she'd actually stayed for his whole telling. Best of all, the look of intense fear that had been in her eyes when she'd come in had been replaced by one of hunger. And not just hunger for food, Max believed.

"Emery and Violet went back to the Avrochet farm and finished out their time there."

"But he didn't…"

"No. He saw no more dead painters. He said. But he did resume painting, apparently. And kept traveling after Violet returned home. Four months. Then six. Then ten."

"Wait. He kept painting? So you have more of his works? His new works?"

Max shook his head, recalling his irritation at everything about the furtive, middle-of-the-night surprise visit Emery had finally made at Max's Gramercy Park residence, waking up his wife who had never liked Emery anyway, scaring the neighbors. He'd had Max accompany him to the rear loading dock of the gallery so he could direct the oafish moving men unloading a crate he'd had shipped back from France. At twenty by twenty-five feet, it had been far too large to store anywhere else, he'd said.

And Max had blown up at him, harangued him for not calling him for almost a year. How *dare* he then expect that Max would simply roll over, panting, for his latest work.

Then Emery had told Max his story. The rest, he promised, he'd tell in time. And he'd vanished again.

"I think," Max said carefully, "that he wants to re-introduce himself to the artistic world gradually. To give us all time to absorb what he's doing."

"Like Picasso-the-asshole did?" said Amy with an evil grin and licked the last chicken sauce from her fingers.

"Shh! You see that man standing right there? The one with the purple ascot? He *owns* a Picasso that he paid very good money for. And that lady over there with the alligator pumps? She owns not one but *two* sketches by one of Picasso's daughters."

He couldn't restrain his own smirk as he said it and Amy herself almost choked as she smothered a giggle.

"Hey!" she whispered. "Shouldn't you be out there making a speech or something?"

Max glanced at his watch again, nodded, and walked forward until he stood in front of this enormous crate Emery had left him. His assistants automatically switched the subdued colored lighting on the area to indirect white light that was nonetheless clear and bright. With his peripheral vision, Max saw Amy sliding sideways into the crowd. Not to escape, thank goodness, but to get a better view.

Heaven help her if Max's confidence in Emery and his crazy tale were misplaced.

"Good evening, everyone!" he said, and the hubbub of murmurs died away. "For those of you whom I haven't talked with personally this evening, my name is Maxwell Hebbler and this is my gallery."

There was a polite smattering of applause.

"And while some of you, I know, are fine patrons of the arts who regularly attend shows and have in fact passed through these very doors numerous times in the past, there are others who are only here tonight because of the works of one very special artist. He is perhaps *the* most significant American artist living and working today."

There was a slight murmur over his emphasis on the *working*, and another smattering of applause.

"Let me tell you why he is significant..."

Max launched then into a shortened lecture on Emery's career. The entire time he was conscious of Amy and her reaction, using it as a gauge for whether he had gone on too long or was telling them too little.

It was much like he'd done with Lyssa, he realized, back when he was still delivering art history lectures at NYU and had made her sit in on one or two as his "audience spy." It had taken him many years after her death to recognize he was doing mostly just so she would listen to *something* he said.

And this time with Amy?

The comparisons tripped over themselves in his head and he lost his train of thought. He couldn't even remember, in fact, exactly what he'd been talking about.

Amy smiled at him from the crowd and he nodded with a sudden flush of heat prickling his scalp.

"But enough with all of this!" he cried. "To the main event!"

He turned to his four assistants, two on either side of the crate. They lifted their cordless screwdrivers and began removing the screws that held together the front and back pieces of the crate. The wooden protection had been so designed, Emery had explained to him, that suspension wires for the painting itself came up from four holes in the top of the crate, allowing the painting to be suspended from the ceiling while still covered. Max had gotten his staff to attach the wires the very next day.

The rest of the crate pieces were designed much like a stripper's clothes. Undo the sides and two clips at the top and the entire thing could be pulled away in one smooth motion.

As the last two screws came out, Max held up his hand to make his assistants pause. He reached into his suit coat pocket and drew out an envelope. He held it up before the hushed patrons.

"When Emery Lake came to my home three weeks ago, in the middle of the night, with no warning, and presented me with this crated work, he would not let me see it. He would not tell me its name or its subject matter. Only that it was done in his usual mix of oils and acrylics. If it is monstrous, I therefore ask your forgiveness in advance.

"If, as I expect, it is something merely astonishing and new, I ask you to respond as you will and analyze at your leisure. But whatever it is, I can guarantee you it will be something you will never forget.

"So without further ado..." He tore open the envelope addressed to him in Emery's writing, pulled out the single sheet of white paper from inside, and read the four words handwritten there. "I give you...*Morning at Saint Victory*."

With that, he gave a showman's flourish and stepped to the side. Two of his assistants ran the front of the crate off to the side while the other two removed the back.

And a massive swoop of colors from the canvas seemed to sweep through the room.

It was an Emery Lake, Max saw, but it wasn't. It was more. It was the steep southern face of the Mont Sainte-Victoire from up high, in purples and blues, golds and greens. The almost-cloudless Provençal sky and patchwork countryside spilled around it with a striking feeling of depth, as if the entire world was flowing out from the rock.

Becoming.

And spread out across the multicolored face of the Sainte-Victoire, in preternatural sharpness that belied true perspective, men and women, boys and girls, old and young, fat and thin, seemed to be either climbing or descending.

Here, one was terrified and being encouraged by their partner. There, one looked manic to the point of recklessness. Hanging by their hands off the bottom of a photorealistic railing at the very top, a couple of young lovers were kissing in an apparent suicide pact, but you somehow felt like cheering them on.

Max's eyes darted about from figure to figure, getting lost over and over, he realized, in the colors of the rock face itself, certainly part of Emery's intention.

Yet the people! They glowed somehow. Not with light as he used to do to identify his figures transcendent, but from the joy or terror of sheer *life* that he'd managed to capture in each character.

"Expressionist-impressionism," he heard a woman say, only to be cut off by another who argued for hyper-realism, and a man putting forth what he considered a new phase of "pop-abstract emotionalism."

"It's just him, isn't it?" said an awed voice beside him and Max turned to see Amy. Her skinny arms were wrapped around herself and she was swinging her head back and forth as she tried to get the best angle on the painting. "It's everything he went through over there."

"You know, maybe you're—"

"But it's incomplete."

"Pardon?"

"There's something missing," she said. "Something...not sad. Just not finished."

Max felt a tall presence join them and turned to see Emery's daughter standing there, a glass of red punch in her hand. "Violet!"

"Max." She inclined her head.

And though he'd seen her a few times since she'd come back, he was struck again by how very *present* she looked. As if she owned the room, or at least her small part of it. This is how Lyssa should have turned out. Earning her way, proud of her life.

"Did you bring a date?" Max said.

Violet smiled. "You mean like Emery? No. I did bring a guy I'm playing piano with. I'll introduce you later."

"You're Emery Lake's daughter!" squeaked Amy, drawing attention back to her.

Violet turned to her. "And you're very perceptive. I heard your comment about the painting and I agree. I think it's because my father's trying to paint his moments now, more than make statements. Give freer rein to his unconscious."

"Like his wife said," Amy whispered. "'Choose a better reality.'"

Violet shot a pointed look at Max. "You told her."

Max shrugged, embarrassed, but then saw Violet studying Amy. A look of understanding rolled over her face and she turned back to Max. "Lyssa."

Again Max shrugged.

Violet said to Amy, "Go over to the painting and find the

climber with tied-back blonde hair. You figure out what she means, then come back to talk with me."

When she'd left, Violet grabbed Max's arm. "Is it her?"

"Who?"

"You know who. Lyssa. Did you somehow conjure up your dead daughter, Max Hebbler? Because you know—"

"Her name is Amy," Max snapped. "And whatever happened with you and Emery in France, whatever you *believe* happened, that is not the way the world works with me. We make our own magic, yes. I want to help this girl to...I don't know...to make up for my failings with Lyssa. Maybe. But I did not conjure her here. I am merely responding to a fortunate coincidence."

"Sure, Max." Violet leaned forward and gave him a kiss by his left cheek, then by his right, then by his left again, before she pulled back with a smile. "Mm. You smell good. But you know what my dad says? He says that for people who can truly see, the mind finds what it needs."

"He says that, does he? And what does your dear father need right now?"

Violet laughed and took another sip of her punch. She nodded her chin towards the painting and Amy, who stood with the other gawkers, carefully searching the canvas for...

"The blonde woman. His missing piece."

THE DOOR of Unit C inside the fourplex that lay on the southeast side of Les Milles looked exactly as Emery remembered it – blank and undistinguished. It was a dull olive green that should have conjured up unpleasant associations, he supposed, but his heart was beating too fast to register them.

He wasn't sure why, exactly, because Charlotte had already buzzed him in from the front door. She hadn't even sounded particularly surprised to hear from him, even though they hadn't spoken since that night in the Château de Vauvenargues.

Which maybe accounted for his nerves. *He* hadn't known he'd come back to her, but somehow she had. Maybe she'd known from the start and so had spent the last eight months figuring out exactly how to tell him she never wanted to see him again.

Grow a pair, Lake, he told himself and knocked on the door.

When it opened, Charlotte stood there looking as lovely as he remembered from the first night she'd come for dinner. Her hair was still lightened and her tan seemed even deeper. Her eyes were bluer than he remembered. Her figure, dressed now in a simple tight cotton tee, was slimmer and her cheeks hollower. Her feet were bare. She held her flute in her left hand as if she'd been playing when he'd buzzed.

"Hello, Emery."

"Charlotte, there is so so much I need to apologize for that I don't know where to—"

She pressed a finger quickly to his lips. "Both of us, yes? We both did stupid things."

"But—"

"And if you feel you must apologize for all of them, then I will apologize for all of mine too and we can spend much of the night doing so. But I will only do this if you first answer me a simple question."

He swallowed. "Ask it."

"Why did you come back to me?"

"Because... Because I..." Damn, he thought he'd worked this one out. This had been a part of the whole apology thing. Now everything he had thought of sounded trite.

"Well?"

It was so much like something that Mattie would have said that the corner of Emery's mouth quirked up and his heart felt suddenly lighter. "Because, in my life now, you are simply better than anything I can imagine."

Charlotte gave him a considering smile and nodded slowly. "All right, you can come in. But first greet me properly. A French kiss, I think."

"American or French-style French kiss?"

"Cheeky boy." She pulled him close. "But you're learning."

WHY WE REMEMBER

"As long as some painters continue to be interested in our ideas or our works, we will not be dead....That does not prevent each new artist from being entirely different, but he or she must also entertain a dialogue with the dead and keep them alive within himself or herself."

-Henri Mattisse, as related by Francoise Gilot
in *Matisse and Picasso*, Doubleday, 1990

Every work of fiction that uses historical characters, locations, or events inevitably blends research and imagination for any number of ends. The author may wish to pontificate, to explain, to laugh at how things were, to add perspective to the present by contrasting it with elements of the past, or simply to add a bit of dash or amusement to an otherwise quotidian tale.

Often, though, it's done out of an intense love of the time, place, and people, what they represented, what they inspired. That's the case here. I'm not a history buff who believes things were better in some past time period, but I am a great student of the recurring preoccupations of humanity. Physical circumstances and conditions change; human nature, not so much.

And there are people from the past I've just always wanted to hang out with, share some heart-to-hearts with. A month in France, viewing the paintings of Morisot, Manet, Monet, Pissaro, Degas, Renoir, Cezanne, Van Gogh and Picasso, living and walking through the places they lived and painted, walking the fields and olive groves around the *Mont Sainte-Victoire,* then writing my fantasy about it all in *Chasing the Minotaur,* gave me the opportunity to do some of that.

For those of you who wonder just how closely my representations of the late great painters depicted here follow true history, I invite you to go explore their works and lives on your own. See some of their paintings up close if possible. Let them speak to you.

Two of the books I relied on heavily for the day-to-day details of the painter's lives were *The Private Lives of the Impressionists,* Sue Roe, Harper Perennial, 2006, and *Picasso, Creator and Destroyer,* Arianna Huffington, Avon Books, 1989.

I hope you enjoyed *Chasing the Minotaur.* You can find out about more of my work and subscribe to my newsletter at *www. terryhayman.com/* or drop me a line at *terry@terryhayman.com*

ALSO BY TERRY HAYMAN

Chasing the Minotaur

Jessica Falls

Raised by a Vampire

Collections

Being Human

Off World

Dark Paths

Life Knots

Used by Magic

Shorties

Vamp

ABOUT THE AUTHOR

Terry Hayman is a former lawyer and actor who now writes full time in the wilds of North Vancouver, British Columbia, where he lives with his wife and children. His stories have appeared in numerous anthologies and in magazines ranging from *Boys' Life* and *Woman's World* to *Grain* and *Dreams of Decadence*. You can what he's currently working on and sign up for his mailing list at *www.terryhayman.com* or e-mail him at *terry@terryhayman.com*.

TO LEARN MORE...

Hi,

I hope you enjoyed the read. If you'd like to find out about more of my work and what I have in the pipeline, subscribe to my mailing list at www.terryhayman.com.

You'll also get access to goodies like fiction exclusive to members of my mailing list, previews of new cover designs, maybe the disclosure of some of my pen names, and the chance to share your thoughts and feedback on any number of creative things I'm doing.

As members of my list, you get heard because I value your voice and readership.

Subscribe today and get a FREE PDF of THE FIRST STORY I EVER SOLD!

www.ingramcontent.com/pod-product-compliance
Lightning Source LLC
Chambersburg PA
CBHW050818190726
48286CB00007B/1910